"We're the product of our ancestors, Mr. Tonji, and those ancestors knew terrors we cannot comprehend. The Quarn have worked on a first-class horror for us, and this convoy is to be the carrier."

"A carrier for a mental disease?" Tonji said contemptuously.

"Yes. But a disorder we've never seen before. An amalgam of the fundamental terrors of man. Stop the Jump, Mr. Tonji. And the transmission."

I noticed that my hand was tightening convulsively on the console at my side. Tonji stood unmoving.

THE STARS IN SHROUD

Look for this other TOR book by Gregory Benford

JUPITER PROJECT

GREGORY BENFORD

THE STARS IN SHROUD

TOR

A TOM DOHERTY ASSOCIATES BOOK

THE STARS IN SHROUD

Copyright © 1978 by Gregory Benford

A TOR Book

Published by Tom Doherty Associates,
8-10 West 36 Street,
New York, N.Y. 10018

Cover art by Angus McKie

First TOR printing: December 1984

ISBN: 0-812-53181-7
CAN. ED.: 0-812-53182-5

Printed in the United States of America

For my father,
James Alton Benford

"Know thyself?" If I knew myself, I'd run away.
—GOETHE

Don't follow leaders; watch the parking meters.
—BOB DYLAN
"SUBTERRANEAN HOMESICK BLUES"

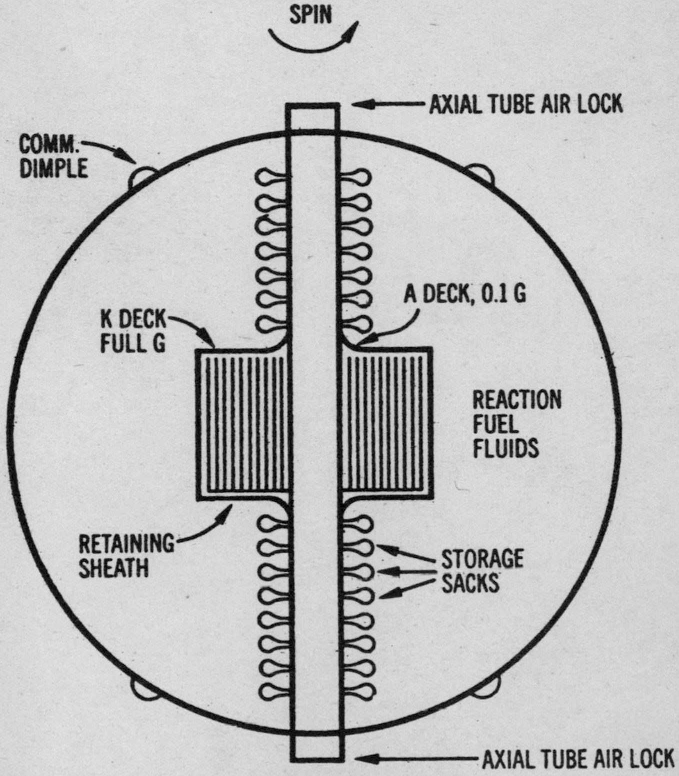

SPIN

AXIAL TUBE AIR LOCK

COMM. DIMPLE

K DECK FULL G

A DECK, 0.1 G

REACTION FUEL FLUIDS

RETAINING SHEATH

STORAGE SACKS

AXIAL TUBE AIR LOCK

LIFE SYSTEMS
SCHEMATIC CROSS SECTION FOR
SPHERICAL JUMP CLASS VESSEL
"FARRIKEN"

(PROPULSION SYSTEMS OMITTED)

Part I

1

THE PLACE TO begin is at the bottom of the trough. How long I had gone through the motions, living days as alike as beads on a *konchu* wire, I don't know. We had been in the apartment—such as it was—a long time.

Something happened, about an hour into the morning shift.

Unlike many, I still worked. In the dark corridors no one would notice the red-rimmed crater like an eye at each shoulder and elbow. And who would care? They were too wound up in themselves, by that year, to raise an eyebrow at what had once been a crime.

I drew the line at my waist: no socketing at hips, knees, ankles. Too many and your body won't restore the tissue, even under sproc treatments. So I labored at our sim board, hooked into distant machines, visions of far-off places tapped through to my opticals. I was immersed in the jerky thrust of an assembly network, swinging raw and fragrant dirt to the side with my right arm, while the left chunked organiform slabs down into quick-molding foundation fluids. My glance rippled over the grid layout. Every jointed nerve nexus commanded a linkage in the assembly net, processing raw ores into impersonal, blank-walled housing. My sockets linked to machines. I was a neural computer, hired by the hour. The buildings were going up halfway around Earth. I bossed the work through satellite comm.

I'm sure it spooked the kids. There was Dad pinned like a zombie to the board, quivering and jerking and muttering for most of the morning. Then I'd collapse and sit, numb and staring, blank-eyed, enough work done for the day to buy us extras.

Their mother would coax them into watching the screen, and they'd leave me be. But this morning—

"*Dad*-dy, why do we have to watch this old stuff?" Romana said, jerking her head up with a regal look.

"Um?" (Still dazed.)

"None of the other cubes in this block even *carry* Schoolchannel any more."

"Um."

"And it's *boring*," put in Chark, his thin voice piping. "Everybody knows you can't learn fast without tapping."

Romana: "We're going to turn out to be *rennies*."

"Rennies?"

"Renegades, Ling," Angela said from the kitchen cloister. "It's the new slang."

"Schoolchannel makes you a renegade?"

"Well, it really means, you know, out of fashion."

"Um."

Angela came into the living room, wiping her hands on a towel, and looked at me with her mouth tightening. I knew what was going to happen.

"Don't you think they have a point, Ling? Finally?"

"No."

I looked away from her. Chark dialed the volume down on the screen, and everybody very carefully sat still. I wasn't going to get away with a quick victory.

"*Dad*-dy . . ."

"If you'd seen that counselor at the Center, Ling. Tapping is necessary. You were out there yourself. You—"

"*Yes*. I was out there. And none of you were."

Romana, who is nine, began reasonably, "The Assembly says tapping is for the common defense . . ."

"It's useless. Pointless. Harmful. There's—"

I stopped. It wasn't going to do any good. Their faces were closing up, going blank. I couldn't tell them the guts of what happened out there. That was buried away in datafile somewhere, sealed against all but high-priority access. Some remnant of Fleet training kept me from talking. That, and a curious inability to focus on that past, a desire to skitter away from it.

Angela broke her silence. I could tell from the brittle edge in her voice that the words had been dammed up for a long time.

"*Why* do you tell them such things? They—they'll respect you even less if you try to pretend there's some big mystery about what you did out there. You were just a shuttle Captain. A pickup convoy, to get the survivors off Regeln after the Quarn hit it."

"Uh huh."

"And you didn't even get many off, either."

"Something happened. Something really happened."

I got up dumbly and moved toward a cabinet, thinking to get a drink, and when I reached out for balance my hand came down on something on the cabinet. It was the Firetongue Stet. The fifty-centimeter block felt cool and reassuring. Having it here was an outright violation of Fleet regs. Even though it was out of date now, I could conceivably be executed for keeping my Commander's Stet after I was court-martialed. But I'd substituted a dud, a blank Stet, when the time had came in the official decommissioning ceremonies. To cling to some last bauble of the Fleet officer I had been?

The children were dead silent, not even swinging a foot with nervous energy, the way they get when they sense that the adults have forgotten they're around and maybe a fight is about to start. Angela and I both noticed it at the same time; the children were our lines of communication now.

"All right. We'll talk about it later," I said.

The kids grumbled a bit and went back to their screen lecture. Angela walked into the bedroom. *Probably to pout,* I thought sourly. One more nick in an eroding marriage.

We would talk. Oh yes, there would be a plentitude of talk. I had been a man who acted. Now I was a mumbler, a parody. I had lost momentum, and Angela's coming accusations and complaints would sting. But I couldn't deflect them. Maybe I didn't care to.

I sat down. I hadn't really thought about Regeln for a long time. That seemed all buried now, a subtle and somehow faceless past. I had tried to ride the events as they came to me, to swim between the smashing waves, but in the end I had washed up on this barren shore.

To wait.

And while waiting, to be reborn among the dead.

2

IT WAS SUPPOSED to be a quick, daring run: Loop my ship into the Regeln system, drop planetward, scoop up whatever was left before the Quarn returned.

The crew didn't take it well. Fleet had already lost many ships. A month before they had taken us off a routine run and outfitted our ships with enough extras—blister pods for defense, mostly—to put the convoy on the lowest rung of warship class.

But men take longer to adjust. Most of them were still nervous and edgy about the changes. They were suddenly *oraku*, warrior status. They didn't like it—neither did I—but there was nothing to be done. This was an emergency.

I had us roar out of orbital port at full bore, giving the ships that hot crisp gunmetal smell. That perked them up. But maintenance is only maintenance, the hours stretched long, and soon they found the time to think, to wring out self-doubts, to fidget. In a few days the results began to come up through the confessional rings: anxieties, exclusion feelings, loss of phase.

"I told Fleet we'd have this," I said to Tonji, my Exec. "These are traditional men. They can't take a sudden change of role." I let go of the clipboard that held the daily report Stet. I watched it tumble slowly in the weak gravity.

Tonji blinked languidly. "I think they are over-reacting to the danger involved. None of us signed for something like this. They aren't men who hired on to win a medal—a bronzer, as ship's slang puts it. Give them time."

"Time? Where am I going to get it? We're only weeks out from Regeln now. This is a large group, spread over a convoy. We'll have to reach them quickly."

He unconsciously stiffened his lips, a gesture he probably associated with being tough-minded. "It will take effort, true. But I suppose you realize there isn't any choice."

Was that a hint of defiance in his voice, mingled with his habitual condescending? I paused, let it go. "More Sabal, then. Require all senior officers to attend as well."

"You're sure that's enough, sir?"

"Of course I'm not sure! I haven't got all the answers in my pocket. This convoy hasn't had anything but shuttle jobs for years."

"But we've been reassigned . . ."

"Slapping a sticker on a ship doesn't change the men inside. The crews don't know what to do. There isn't any confidence in the group, because everyone can sense the uncertainty. Nobody knows what's waiting for us on Regeln. A crewman wouldn't be human if he didn't worry about it."

I looked across the small cabin at my kensdai

altar. I knew I was losing control of myself too often and not directing the conversation the way I wanted. I focused on the solid, dark finish of the wood that framed the altar, feeling myself merge with the familiarity of it. Focus down, let the center flow outward.

Tonji flicked an appraising glance at me. "The Quarn were stopped on Regeln. That's why we're going."

"They'll be back. The colony there beat them off but took a lot of losses. It's now been twenty-four days since the Quarn left. You heard the signals from the surface—they're the only ones we got after their satellite link was destroyed. The correct code grouping was there, but the signal strength was down. Then transmission faded. Whoever sent them was working in bad conditions, or didn't understand the gear, or both."

"Fleet doesn't think it's a trap?" Tonji's features. Mongol-yellow in the diffused light of my cabin, took on a cool, distant look.

"They don't know. I don't, either. But we need information on Quarn tactics and equipment. They're a race of hermits, individuals, some say— but somehow they cooperate against us. We want to get an idea how."

"The earlier incidents . . ."

"They were just that—incidents. Raids. Fleet never got enough coherent information out of the surviving tapes, and what there was they can't unravel. There were no survivors."

"But this time the colonists stood off a concentrated attack."

"Yes. Perhaps there are good records on Regeln."

Tonji nodded, smiling, and left after proper ceremonies. I was sure he knew most of what I'd told him, through his own sources, but he'd seemed to want to draw the details out of me, to savor them. Why? I could guess: the better the mission, the gaudier the reports, then all the faster would rise the fortunes of Mr. Tonji. A war—the first in three centuries, and the first in deepspace—has the effect of opening the staircases to the top. It relieves a young officer of the necessity for worming his way through the belly of the hierarchy.

I reached out, dialed a starchart of Regeln's neighbors, studied.

The Quarn had been an insect buzzing just beyond the range of our senses for decades now. Occasional glancing contacts, rumors, stories. Then war.

How? Security didn't bother to tell lowly convoy Captains—probably only a few hundred men anywhere knew. But there had been a cautiously worded bulletin about negotiations in the Quarn home worlds, just before the War. But no one had ever seen one face to face. The Council had tried to establish communal rapport with some segment of Quarn society. It had worked before, with the Phalanx and Angras.

Among the intellectual circles I knew—such as they were—it was holy dogma. Sense of community was the glue that held a culture together. Given time and correct Phase, it could bind even alien societies. In two cases it already had.

And it wove a universe for us. A world of soft dissonances muting into harmonies, tranquil hues of waterprints fading together.

To it the Quarn were a violet slash of strangeness. Hermitlike, they offered little and accepted less. Privacy extended to everything for them; we still had no clear idea of their physical appearances.

Their meetings with us had been conducted with only a few individual negotiators.

Into this the Council had moved. Perhaps a taboo was ignored, a trifle overlooked. Perhaps. It seemed the mistake was too great for the Quarn to pass; they came jabbing into the edge of the human community. Regeln was one of their first targets.

"First Sabal call," Tonji's voice came over the inboard. "You asked me to remind you, sir."

It was ironic that Tonji, with all his ancestors citizens of Old Nippon, should be calling a Sabal game to be led by me, a half-breed Caucasian—and I was sure it wasn't totally lost on him. My mother was a Polynesian and my father a truly rare specimen: one of the last pure Americans, born of the descendants of the few who had survived the Riot War. That placed me far down in the caste lots, even below Australians.

When I was a teenager it was still socially permissible to call us *ofkaipan,* a term roughly analogous to *nigger* in the early days of the American Republic. But since then had come the Edicts of Harmony. I imagine the Edicts are still ignored in the Offislands, but with my professional status it would be a grave breach of protocol if the word ever reached my ears. I'd *seen* it often enough, mouthed wordlessly by an orderlyman who'd just received punishment, or an officer who couldn't forget the color of my skin. But never aloud.

I sighed and got up, almost wishing there was another of us aboard so I wouldn't have moments of complete loneliness like this. But we were rare in Fleet, and almost extinct on Earth itself.

I uncased my formal Sabal robes and admired their delicate sheen a moment before putting them

on. The subtle reds and violets caught the eye and
played tricks with vision. They were the usual
lint-free polyester that shed no fine particles into
the ship's air, but everything possible had been
done to give them texture and depth beyond the
ordinary uniform. They were part of the show, just
like the bals and chants.

During the dressing I made the ritual passes as
my hands chanced to pass diagonally across my
body, to induce emotions of wholeness, peace. The
vague fears I had let slip into my thoughts would
be in the minds of the crew as well.

The murmur in our assemblyroom slackened as
I appeared. I greeted them, took my place in the
hexagon of men, and began the abdominal exercises,
sitting erect. I breathed deeply, slowly, and made
hand passes. At the top of the last arc the power
was with me and, breathing out, I came *down* into
focus, outward-feeling, *kodakani*.

I slowed the juggling of the gamebals, sensing
the mood of the hexagon. The bals and beads caught
the light in their counter-cadences, glancing tones
of red and blue off the walls as they tumbled. The
familiar dance calmed us and we moved our legs
to counter-position, for meditation.

My sing-chant faded slowly in the softened acous-
tics of the room. I began the Game.

First draw was across the figure, a crewman
fidgeting with his Sabal leafs. He chose a passage
from the Quest and presented it as overture. It was
a complex beginning—the Courier was endowed
with subtleties of character and mission. Play
moved on. The outline of our problem was inked
in by the others as they read their own quotations
from the eaves into the Game structure.

*   *   *

For the Royal Courier rode down from the hills, and being he of thirst, hunger, and weariness, he sought aid in the town. Such was his Mission that the opinion he gained here of the inhabitants of the village, their customs, honesty, and justice (not only to the courier, but to themselves), would be relayed to the Royal Preseme as well. And then, it is said, to Heaven. Having such items to barter, he went from house to house . . .

After most entries were made, the problem maze established had dark undertones of fear and dread. And rippling them slowly through my fingers, began the second portion of Sabal: proposing of solution. Again the draw danced among the players.

It comes to this:

You are one of two players. There are only two choices for you to make—say, red and black. The other player is hidden, and only his decisions are reported to you.

If both of you pick red, you gain a measure each. If both are black, a measure is lost. But if you choose red and your opponent (fellow; mate; planet-sharer) votes black, he wins *two* measures, and you lose two.

He who cooperates in spirit, he who senses the Total, wins.

Sabel is infinitely more complex than this description, but contains the same elements. The problems set by the men ran dark with subtle streams of anguish, insecurity.

But now the play returned to me. I watched the solution as it formed around the hexagon. Rejoiced in harmony of spirit. Indicated slight displeasure when divergent modes were attempted.

Rebuked personal gain. And drew closer to my men.

"Free yourself from all bonds," I chanted, "and bring to rest the ten thousand things. The way is near, but we seek it afar."

The mood caught slowly at first, and uncertainty was dominant, but with the rhythm of repetition a compromise was struck. Anxiety began to submerge. Conflicting images in the Game weakened.

I caught the uprush of spirit at its peak, chanting joyfully of completion as I brought the play to rest. I imposed the dreamlike flicker of gamebal and bead, gradually toning the opticals until we were clothed in darkness. Then stillness.

The fire burning, the iron kettle singing on the hearth, a pine bough brushing the roof, water dripping.

The hexagon broke and we left, moving in concert.

3

THE GAME ON our flagship was among the best, but it was not enough for the entire mission. I ordered Sabal as often as possible on all ships, and hoped it would keep us in correct Phase. I didn't have time to attend all Games, because we were getting closer to drop and all details weren't worked out.

In the hour preceding the Jump I made certain that I was seen in every portion of the ship, moving confidently among the men. The number of ships lost in the Jump is small but rising dangerously, and everyone knew it.

I stood on the center bridge to watch the process, even though it was virtually automatic. The specialists and crewmen moved quickly in the dull red light that simulated nightfall—Jump came at 2200 and we kept to the daily cycle. Fifteen minutes before the computers were set to drop us through, I gave the traditional order to proceed. It was purely a formalism. In theory the synchronization could be halted even at the last instant. But if it was, the requirements of calculating time alone would delay the jump for weeks. The machines were the key.

And justly so. Converting a ship into tachyons in a nanosecond is an inconceivably complex process. Men invented it, but they could never control it without the impersonal, faultless coordination of microelectronics.

In theory it was simple. The earnest, careful men who moved around me on the center bridge were preparing the convoy to flip over into *faster* than light. In the same way that a fundamental symmetry provided that the proton had a twin particle with opposite charge, helicity, and so on— the antiproton—there was a possible state for each particle, called the tachyon.

Just as the speed of light, c, is an upper limit to all velocities in our universe, in the tachyon universe c is a lower limit. To us a particle with zero kinetic energy sits still; it has no velocity. A tachyon with no energy is a mirror image—it moves with infinite velocity. As its energy increases, it slows, relative to us, until at infinite energy it travels with velocity c.

As long as man remained in his half of the universe, he could not exceed c. This was a fundamental limitation, as irrevocable as the special principle of relativity.

Thus he learned to leave it. By converting a particle into its tachyon state, allowing it to move with a nearly infinite velocity, and then shifting it back to real space, one effectively produces faster than light travel. The study of the famous tachyon cross section problem—*how* do you make it convert, and then get it back—occupied the best minds of humanity for more than fifty years. It also birthed the incredible complexity of microelectronics, because only with components that operated literally on the scale of atomic dimensions could you produce the coherent, complexly modulated electronmagnetic waves that could regulate the tachyon's Jump cross section.

I smiled to myself in the red glow. *That* had been a triumph. It occurred some decades after the establishment of Old Nippon's hegemony, and made possible almost instant communication with the first Alpha Centauri colony. Particles can be used to produce electromagnetic waves, and waves carry signals.

But not men. It was one thing to greatly enlarge the Jump cross section of a single particle, and quite another to do it for the unimaginable number of atoms that make up a man or a ship.

It was Okawa who found the answer, and I had always wondered why the jump drive did not bear his name. Perhaps he was an unfavored one, though passing clever. Okawa reasoned by analogy, and the analogy he used was the laser.

In the laser the problem is simply to produce a coherent state—to make all the excited atoms in the solid emit a photon at the same time. The same problem appeared in the faster than light drive. If *all* the particles in the ship did not flip into their tachyon state at the same time, they would all have vastly varying velocities, and the ship would tear itself apart. Okawa's achievement was finding a technique for placing all a ship's atoms in "excited real tachyon states." In the excited state their tachyon cross sections were large. But as well, they could be triggered at the same time, so that all jumped together, coherently.

I looked at the fixed, competent faces around me

in the bridge. It was a little more than one minute
to Jump. The strain showed, even though some
tried to hide it. The process wasn't perfect, and
they knew it.

Nothing was said about it at the Fleet level, but
microelectronic equipment had been deteriorating
slowly for years. The techniques were gradually
being lost. Craftsmanship grew rare. Half-measures
were used. It was part of the slow nibbling decline
our society had suffered for the last half-century.
It was almost expected.

But these men bet their lives on the Jump rig,
and they knew it might fail.

The silvery chimes rang down thin, padded
corridors, sounding the approach of Jump. I could
feel the men in the decks around me, lying in near
darkness on tatami mats, waiting.

There was a slightly audible count, a tense
moment. I closed my eyes at the last instant.

A bright arc flashed beyond my eyelids, showing
the blood vessels, and I heard the dark, whispering
sound of the void. A pit opened beneath me. The
falling sensation—

Then the fluorescents hummed again and everything was normal, tension relieved, men smiling.
We were through.

Ahead, a new star beckoned.

I looked out the forward screen and saw the
shimmering halo of gas that shrouded the star of
Regeln. At our present velocity we would be through
it in a day, falling down the potential well directly
toward the sun. There wasn't much time.

We had to come in fast, cutting the rim of plasma
around Regeln's star to mask our approach. If we
dropped in with that white-hot disk at our backs,

we would have a good margin over any detection system that was looking for us.

Regeln is like any life-supporting world: by turns endlessly varied, monotonously dull, spiced with contrast wherever you look, indescribable. It harbors belts of jungle, crinkling grey swaths of mountains, convoluted snake-rivers, and frigid blue wastes. The hazy air carries the hum of insects, the pad of ambling vegetarians, the smooth click of teeth meeting. And winds that deafen, oceans that laugh, tranquility beside violence. It is like any world that is worth the time of man.

But its crust contains fewer heavy elements than are necessary for the easy construction of a Jump station or a docking base. So it fell under the control of the colonization-only faction of Fleet. They had moved in quickly with xenobiologists to perform the routine miracles that made the atmosphere breathable.

Drop time caught us with only the rudiments of a defense network. There simply wasn't time to train the men, and we were constantly missing relevant equipment. I wished for better point-surveillance gear a hundred separate times as we slipped into the Regeln system.

But no Quarn ships appeared, no missiles rose to meet us. Tonji wanted to get out of the sky as soon as physically possible, even though it would've been expensive in reaction mass. I vetoed it and threw us into a monocycle "orange slice" orbit for a look before we went down, but there turned out to be nothing to see after all.

Our base was buttoned up. No vehicles moved on the roads, not even expendable drones for surveillance. I had prints of the base defenses, even the periscope holes, but when we checked, there was no sign that they were open. Scattered bluish clouds slid over the farmhouses and fields of grain, but nothing moved on the surface.

There wasn't time to think, send down probes, play a game of cat and mouse. I had a drone massing out to the system perimeter, where radiation from the star wouldn't mask the torch of an incoming Quarn ship, but I couldn't rely on it completely.

"Skimmers ready, sir," Tonji said.

I rang Matsuda on inboard and placed him in temporary command of the convoy in orbit. "Tonji is coming with me. If the Quarn show—"

"Yes sir, I'll deploy to intersect—"

"You will *not*. Give us an hour to boost."

"But sir—"

"If we don't make it, mass out. Don't hang around. These ships are worth more than we are."

Tonji smiled, and I cut off Matsuda. The shuttle down was slow and gentle; it was built for cradling flatlanders. I carried the Firetongue Stet. Regeln's sky flitted past, a creamy blend of pinks and blues like a lunatic tropical drink, and then we were down.

The shock troops had cracked the outer defenses, inactivated them, and stalled at the Firetongue perimeter. I carried the Stet in its case, by regulation the only officer who could handle it. The Stet unkeyed the Fleet-wide Firetongue pattern, so that a crew could pass through the man-charring mines seeded around each Fleet base.

My hovercraft pilot was jumpy; we bounced on landing. I was out of the hatch before they got chocks under the wheels, and a Lieutenant came toward me at double time. We rigged the Stet into electromag detectors, purged errant traces, and started the men out in single file.

Crystal wafers winked in the air. My ears picked up a soft percussion as sensors probed us. I followed the 3D gridded display, using lifters to bound over null points.

Firelanced air crackled around us.

The men murmured, frightened. Orange sparks played in open air.

I kept on, defusing the nodes of the Firetongue array, widening the corridor.

Behind me something hissed.

A man screamed.

I didn't stop. The Firetongues, alerted, were even touchier.

One, two—the last nodes trembled and evaporated, each a point in space that rippled blue green red and was gone.

Each Firetongue perimeter is the same, so each Fleet Captain has access to all bases. But a flaw in the ferrimemory will cancel the code, kill the bearer. I slipped the Firetongue into its jacket with relief.

"Who was that?"

"A Corporal," Tonji murmured. "Lost his nerve."

"You—?"

"A Tongue burned away his leg."

"Oh." Tonji could legally have executed the man for breaking ranks in a Firetongue field. I was quite sure he would've, had not the Tongues done it for him. Even a healant unit can't patch a missing leg.

A man came running up. "Had to drill and tap, sir," he said quickly, saluting.

"Blow it," I said. We ducked behind a gentle rise a hundred meters from the portal. I hugged the dirt. The smell was odd, sweet-sour. For the first time I sensed this place as alien, a fresh planet.

The concussion came, sharp as a bone snapping. Debris showered us. I moved up with some men into a hanging pall of dust. The portal yawned only partway open, a testament to the shelter's designer.

Three runners went in with lights. They were back in minutes.

"Deserted for the first few corridor levels," one of them said. "We need more men inside to keep a communications link."

Tonji led the next party. Most of the crewmen were inside before word came back that they'd found somebody. I went in then with three guards and some large phoslamps. None of the lighting in the corridors of the shelter was working—the phosphor leads were cut.

Men clustered at one end of the corridor on the second level, their voices echoing nervously off the glazed concrete.

"You've got something, Mr. Tonji?" I said. He turned away from the open door, where he had been talking to a man whose uniform was covered with dirt. He looked uncertain.

"I think so, sir. According to the maps we have of the base, this door leads to a large auditorium. But a few meters inside—well, look."

I stepped through the door and halted. A number of steps beyond, the cushioned walkway ended and a block of *something*—dirt, mostly, with fragments of furniture, wall partitions, unidentifiable rubble—rose to the ceiling.

I looked at Tonji, questioning.

"A ramp downward starts about there. The whole auditorium is filled with this—we checked the lower floors, but the doors off adjacent corridors won't open."

"How did it get here?"

"The levels around the auditorium have been stripped bare and most of the wall structure torn out, straight down to the bedrock and clay the base was built on. Somebody carted a lot of dirt away and dumped it in here." He glanced at me out of the corner of his eyes.

"What's that?" I pointed at a black oval depression sunk back into the grey mass of dirt, about two meters off the floor.

"A hole. Evidently a tunnel. It was covered with an office rug until Nahran noticed it." He gestured back at the man in the dirty uniform.

"So he went inside. What's there?"

Tonji pinched his lip with a well-manicured thumb and forefinger. "A man. He's pretty far back, Nahran says. That's all I can get out of Nahran, though—he's dazed. The man inside is hysterical. I don't think we can drag him out through that hole, it's too narrow."

"That's all? One man?"

"There might be a lot of people inside there. We've heard noises out of several of these holes. I think this thing that fills the auditorium is honeycombed with tunnels. We've seen the entrance of several more from the balcony above."

I checked the time. "Let's go?"

Tonji turned and started back through the door.

"No, Mr. Tonji. This way."

For a second he didn't believe it, and then the glassy impersonal look fell over his face. "We're both going to crawl in there, sir?"

"That's right. It's the only way I can find out enough to make a decision."

He nodded slowly. We spent a few minutes arranging details, setting timetables. I tried to talk with Nahran while I changed into a tight pullover suit. He couldn't tell me very much. He seemed reticent and slightly dazed. Something had shocked him.

"Follow immediately after me, Mr. Tonji." We both carefully emptied out pockets; the passage was obviously too narrow to admit anything jutting out. Tonji carried the light. I climbed up onto the slight ledge in front of the dark oval. I looked across the slate grey face of the thing. It was huge.

I waved with false heartiness and began working my legs into the hole.

I went straight down, into nightmare.

4

MY THIGHS AND shoulders rubbed as gravity slowly tugged me down the shaft. I held my arms above my head, close together. There wasn't room to keep them at my sides.

Cracks slid by. Glistening mud. Pebbles.

After a moment my feet touched, scraped, then settled on something solid. I felt around with my boots and for a moment thought it was a dead end. But there was another hole in the side, off at an angle. I slowly twisted until I could sink into it up to my knees. Hands rasped on broken stone.

I looked up. It wasn't more than five meters to the top of the shaft, but I seemed to have taken a long time to get this far. I could see Tonji slowly settling down behind me, towing a light above his head.

I wriggled into the narrow side channel, grunting and already beginning to hate the smell of packed dirt and garbage. In a moment I was stretched flat on my back, working my way forward by digging in my heels and pushing with my palms against the walls.

The ceiling of the tunnel brushed against my face in utter blackness. I felt the oppressive weight of the packed dirt crushing down on me. My own breath was trapped in front of my face and I could hear only my own gasps, amplified.

"Tonji?" I heard a muffled shout in reply. Light licked the tunnel in front of me. I noticed a large rock embedded in the side. The auditorium was filled with a skeleton of stone that supported the packed soil.

I came to a larger space and was able to turn around to enter the next hole head first. The entrance was wide but quickly narrowed. I felt ooze squeeze between my fingers. The walls pressed down. Some of the clay had turned to mud.

A chill seeped up my legs and arms as I inched forward. I twisted my shoulder blades and pulled with my fingers. The going was easier because the passage tilted slightly downward, but the ooze sucked at me.

I wondered how a man could have gotten in here. Or out.

We know why you're here, though, don't we, Ling? Your lust to prove yourself? To be at the center of action? Captains stay in the rear, Ling . . .

With every lunge forward my chest scraped against the sides, rubbing the skin raw and squeezing my breath out. It seemed just possible that I could get through.

Tonji shouted. I answered. The reply was muffled against the wall. I wondered if he had heard. I could feel the irregular bumps in the wall with my hands. I used them to mark how far I had come.

Progress was measured in centimeters, then even

less. My forearms began to go stiff and numb. I should never have come down here. Foolish, foolish. But I wanted to know—

A finger touched the wall, found nothing. I felt cautiously and discovered a sudden widening in the tunnel. At the same instant there came a scraping sound in the night ahead of me, the sound of something being dragged across a floor. It was moving away.

I got a good grip on the opening, pushed—and was through. I rolled to the side, hugged the wall. Flickers of light from Tonji showed a small, rectangular room.

No one in it. A row of darkened holes sank into the opposite face.

Tonji wriggled through the passage, breath steaming in the cold air. His lamp poked yellow in my eyes, though it was on low beam.

I found I could get to my knees without bumping my head. I stretched out my cramped legs. Rubbed them to start circulation. Looked around, wary.

"Nothing here," he said in a hoarse whisper.

"Maybe. Throw the beam on those holes."

He played it across the opposite wall.

A shrill scream.

A head of filthy hair wrenched further back into the uppermost hole.

I started toward him on hands and knees and stopped almost immediately. The floor below the holes was strewn with excrement and trash. Tonji swallowed and looked sick.

After a moment I moved forward. My boot rattled an empty food tin. I could barely see the man far back in his hole.

"Come out. What's wrong?"

The man pressed himself further in. I picked my way toward him. He whimpered, cried, hid his face from the light.

"He won't answer," Tonji said.

"I suppose not." I stopped and looked at some of the other holes. The sour reek on this side of the room was intolerable. I hadn't noticed it in the tunnel because there was a cool draft blowing from one of the holes in the wall. It kept the air in the room circulating away from the tunnel we'd used.

"Flash the light up there," I said.

A human hand hung out of one of the holes.

Cloth and sticks had been stuffed into the opening to try to keep in the smell.

There were other holes like it. Some others were packed with food, most of it partially eaten.

"Can . . . we go back?" Tonji asked.

I ignored him. I scrabbled closer to one of the openings with a larger mouth. Dank, clammy air. In the empty silence I could hear the faint echoes of wailing and sobbing from farther inside. They mingled together in a hollow wail of despair.

"Bring the light."

"I think it's getting colder in here, sir." He hesitated a moment and then duck-walked closer.

The man was still moaning to himself in his hole. I clenched my jaw muscles in involuntary revulsion and with an effort of will reached out and touched him. He cringed away, burrowing down, sobbing with fear.

There was part of a sleeve left on his arm—the light blue cloth of the Fleet. I looked back at the tunnel we'd just used and estimated the difficulty of pulling a struggling man through it. The phos-lamp struck a rainbow from an oily rivulet.

"We're not going to get any more out of this," I said.

The cold clung to my limbs again, but Tonji was sweating. His eyes darted as if expecting attack. The silence was oppressive. I seemed to hear more clearly now the convulsive sobbing from farther inside the mound.

I motioned quickly to Tonji. We pressed ourselves back into the tunnel. I made as rapid progress as I could, with him scrambling close at my heels.

The dead weight squeezed us with rigid jaws. I tried to notice markings on the sides that would measure how far we had come, but I began to get confused. Fingers scraped on crumbling rock.

It took me a moment to realize the air was definitely worse. It clung in my throat, and I couldn't get enough. My chest was caught in the tunnel's vise, and my lungs would never fill.

Between wrigglings to squirm up the slight grade I stopped to listen for sounds from the men at the entrance. Nothing. The long tunnel pressed at me. I gave myself over to an endless series of pushing and turning, rhythmically moving forward against the steady hand of gravity and the scraping of the walls.

Tonji's lamp sent dim traces of light along the walls. I noticed how smooth they were. How many people had worn them down? How many were in here?

And, God, *why*?

The tunnel began to narrow. I got through one opening by expelling all my breath and pushing hard with my heels. Coming in hadn't seemed this hard.

Gravel bit my thigh.

Boots slipped on slime.

An open space temporarily eased the pressure, and then ahead I saw walls narrowing again. I pushed and turned, scrabbling on the slick dirt with all my strength. A flicker of light reflected over my shoulder. I could see the passage closing even further.

Impossible. A massive hand was squeezing the life out of me and my mind clutched frantically at an escape. The air was positively foul. I felt ahead and grunted with the effort. The walls closed even more. I knew I couldn't get through.

My hand touched something, but I was too numbed with the cold to tell what it was.

"Light," I managed to whisper. I heard Tonji turning, breathing rapidly, and in a moment the beam got brighter.

It was a man's foot.

I recoiled. For a moment I couldn't think and my mind was a flood of horror.

"Back," I gasped. "We can't go this way."

"This . . . way . . . we came in."

"No." Suddenly the air was too thick to take it any longer.

I started to slide backward.

"Go on!" He hit my boots with a free hand.

"Back up, Mr. Tonji."

I waited, and the dirt pressed at me, closing in everywhere. It was only mud. What if it collapsed?

Tonji was silent.

After a moment I felt him move back.

I had been holding my breath ever since my hand felt that human foot. I let it out as I scrambled back down the tunnel. The man hadn't been there long, but it was enough. The air was thick with it.

I noticed I was sweating now, despite the chill. Had we taken the right hole when we left the man back there? We could be working our way further into the mound, not out of it.

How long could I take the air? I could tell Tonji was on the edge already. Did we miss a turn coming out and go down the wrong way? It was hard to imagine, in the closeness of the tunnel.

My ribs were rubbed raw. They stung whenever I moved. Weight closed on me from every direction. I pulled backward slowly, trying to collect my thoughts. I moved automatically.

After a few moments my left hand reached out and touched nothing. I stopped, but Tonji went on, as if in a stupor. I listened to his moving away, blinking uncomprehendingly at the hole to my left and trying to think.

"Wait! This is it!"

We had both missed the turn, somehow. The air had dulled our minds until we noticed nothing without conscious effort.

I turned and worked myself into the opening. Tonji was returning. The lamp's yellow bite was almost painful. He moaned something, but I couldn't understand.

The passage gradually widened, and I caught glimmerings of light ahead.

Out.

Safe. Yes.

In a moment I was standing in the vertical shaft. A man dropped a line down to me. My hands slipped on it several times as they pulled me up.

For a few minutes I sat by the entrance, blinking, puffing, numb with fatigue. The men crowded around us, and I looked at them as if they were strangers. After a while I picked out a lieutenant.

"Get . . . Jobstranikan down here." Jobstranikan had psychotherapy training. This was clearly his job.

Orders were given. Men scattered. After a moment I got up and changed back into full uniform. A runner was waiting outside the door, his nose wrinkling at the stench I had ceased to notice.

"Sir, reports from lower levels say there are more like this. There appear to be people in them, too. The coordination center was untouched, and it's five levels down. I think they've got some of the tapes ready to run."

I turned to Tonji. "Try to get that man out of there. Do it any way you can, but don't waste time. I'll be in the center."

The walk through the next two levels was like a trip through hell. The stink of human waste was overpowering, even with the ventilation system sighing at full capacity. Arc lights we had brought down threw distorted crescents of faint blue and white along walls smeared with blood, food, excrement.

Echoes of a high, gibbering wail haunted the lower floors, coming from their hiding places. They had burrowed far back into the walls in spots but most of the tunnel mouths were sunk into monstrous, huge mounds like the one above. They weren't hiding from us alone; their warrens were surrounded by piles of refuse. They had been in there for weeks.

Jobstranikan caught up with us just before we worked our way to the center.

"It is difficult, sir," he said. "It is like the legends—the country of madness, possessed by devils and monsters."

Legends of the Riot War, I remembered. A foul time.

"What's happened to them?"

"Everything. At first I thought they had a complete fear of anything that they could sense—light, movement, noise. But that is misleading. They screech at each other incoherently. They won't let us touch them. They cry, scream, and fight if we try."

"Has Tonji been able to get any of them out?"

"Only by knocking them unconscious. One of his men was bitten badly when they tried to drag that man out. Getting anyone out of this mess is going to be a major job."

There was a guard outside the center. Broken bits of furniture and electronics gear were strewn down the corridor, but inside the center itself everything was in order.

"The hatch was sealed electronically and coded, sir," the officer inside explained. "We brought down the tracers and opened it. Somebody must have seen what was happening and made certain no one could get in here before we arrived."

I walked over to the main display board. Technicians were taping the readouts we would need from the center's computer bank, working with feverish haste. I motioned Danker back to duty and turned to the officer.

"Have you got any preliminary results? Is there an oral log that covers the Quarn attack?"

"No oral yet. We do have a radar scan." He fitted a roll into the projector attachment of the display board. "I've cut it to begin with the first incursion into this system."

Phosphors dimmed. The green background grid of a sensor scan leaped into focus. The relative locations of the other planets in the Regeln system winked purple—lumps of cold rock, mostly—and a small Quarn dot moved on the perimeter of the screen, glowing a soft red.

"They took their time getting here, apparently." The projection rate increased. More dots joined the first to form a wedge-shaped pattern. A blue line detached itself from the center of the screen and shot outward, shrinking to a point: a defensive move from Regeln.

"All available missiles seem to have been fired. The Quarn took a few hits, but could outmaneuver most of them. I'm afraid we launched too soon, and by the time our seekers were within range, their fuel reserves weren't up to a long string of dodges."

The red dots moved quickly, erratically, in a pantomime dance with the blue defenders. The distance between them was never short enough to permit a probable kill with a nuclear charge, and eventually the blue dots fell behind and were lost. They winked out when their reaction mass exhausted.

"Except for the atmospheric ships, that finished their defenses. This colony wasn't built to carry on a war. But something strange happened."

The Quarn ships drifted toward center screen at an almost leisurely pace. A small missile flared out, went into orbit around Regeln and disappeared.

"That was the satellite link. They got that and then ..."

"And then left," I finished. The red dots were backing off. They gradually picked up velocity, regrouped, and in a few minutes slipped off the grid. The screen went black.

"That is all we have. This clipping covered about

eight days. We can't be sure anybody was watching the last part of it, because the recording mechanism was automatic. It stopped when it ran out of film. This room may have been sealed any time after they launched their missiles.

"None of this explains what happened here. The Quarn didn't touch Regeln, but this shelter is full of lunatics. Something made the Quarn stop their attack and leave." I looked around at the banks and consoles. I could feel a tightness forming somewhere. That old feeling of rightness, certainly of position, was slipping away.

"Get every record you can, in duplicate tapes if possible," I ordered, trying to shrug off the mood. The officer saluted, and I went back into the corridors with a guard detail. I made a note to get respiration packs down here as soon as possible, and meanwhile held my breath as long as I could between gasps.

The route we took back was different, but no less horrible. Here there were bodies lying among the wreckage, most of them in advanced stages of decay. Two of my guards gagged in the close, putrid air of the corridors. We kept moving as quickly as we could, avoiding the half-open doors from which came the faint shrill gibbering of madmen. Most of the bodies we saw had been stabbed or clubbed and left to die. A large proportion were women. In any contest of strength they wouldn't last long, and they hadn't received any special consideration.

When we reached the perimeter Tonji had established, the air improved. Men were moving along the corridors in teams, spraying the walls with a soapy solution.

"The water and drainage systems are still working,

so I decided to use them," Tonji said. He seemed to have recovered from the tunnel. "Wherever we can, we're sealing off the places where they lived. We can keep the halls clean."

Jobstranikan came around a nearby corner portal we'd blasted through only a short while before. "Any new ideas?" I asked.

"Not as yet, I fear." He shook his head, and the long Mongolian locks tangled together on the back of his neck. He wore it in traditional semi-tribal fashion, like most of my officers. It was dull black, in the manner of the soldiers of the Kahu and the Patriarch, and braided at the tail with bright leather thongs. The style was as old as the great central plains of Asia.

"I can make no sense of it. They fought among themselves at first, I think, for the bodies we've found are at least weeks old. Since then they've stayed back in those holes they made for themselves, eating the food supplies they'd gotten earlier. But they don't want to leave. Every one I've seen wants to burrow into the smallest volume possible and stay there. We've found them in cupboards, jammed into ventilation shafts, even . . ."

"Signal, sir." We were passing a temporary communication link. He handed me a receiver, and I pulled the hushpiece over my head. If this was what I thought it was, I didn't want anyone to know before I told them.

It was Matsuda. "Our drone is registering approaching extra-solar ships. Preliminary trajectory puts them into the Regeln orbit."

I let out a long breath. In a way I'd almost been expecting it.

"What's their Doppler?"

There was a pause, then: "It is not enough for

them to be braking from a star jump. The specscope says they are on full torch, however. They couldn't have been accelerating very long."

"In other words, this is the same group that hit—or didn't hit—Regeln the first time. How long can we have on the surface?"

"Sir, readout says you can stay down there about five hours and not incur more than five percent risk to the convoy. Can you get them out?"

"We'll see," I said, and went back to Tonji.

5

IT WAS IMPOSSIBLE. Using all shuttles and skimmers, we saved a little over three thousand, only a fraction of the colony's population. Most of the interior of the shelter was never reached.

As it was, we boosted late, and a Quarn interceptor almost caught us. A yellow fusion burst licked at us as we pulled away. We never saw what the rest of the Quarn did to Regeln.

After a few unsuccessful attempts I decided to stop trying to communicate with the lunatics we had scattered among the ships. Jobstranikan wanted to try treatment on some of them, but the medics were having a hell of a time just patching up their injuries and infections and treating malnutrition.

The Quarn didn't try to follow us out of the system. I thought this strange, and so did Tonji.

"It does not make sense," he said. "We don't know a lot about their drive systems, but they might have a good chance of catching us. It would certainly be worth a try. If you've set a trap, why spring it halfheartedly?''

"Maybe it's not that kind of trap," I said.

Tonji frowned. "Do you mean they might be waiting for us further along trajectory? We're already out of detection range of any Quarn ships, and Jump is coming up. They'll never trace us through that.''

"No, nothing. It was just a thought," Not a well-defined one, at that. Still, something was bothering me. It wasn't lessened any when Tonji reported the results from intelligence.

"The computer analysis of the colony's radar scan is finished," he began. "Regardless of what happened to the colony itself, the machines have a low opinion of Quarn tactics. Regard.''

He flicked on a screen above my desk and the pattern of red and blue points in a green three-grid began to repeat itself. "Notice this stage, shortly after initial contact.''

The blue dots danced and played as they moved in, performing an intricate pattern of opposing and coalescing steps. The red Quarn ships back-pedaled and moved uncertainly.

"The Quarn had ballistic superiority and more maneuverability. But notice how they avoided the Regeln missiles.''

The red points dodged back, moving in crescents that narrowly avoided the feints and slashes of blue. The crescent formed, fell back. Again. And again. The Quarn were using the same tactic, relying on their superior power to carry them beyond Regeln attack at the cusp-point. I'm not a tactician, but I could see it was wasteful of energy and time.

"They continued this until the interceptors ran out of reaction mass. If they'd been pitted against equals, the engagement would not have lasted two minutes."

I clicked off the screen. "What does it mean?"

Tonji poked the air with a finger. "It means we have got them. Over the last year they've had the luck to hit border planets that weren't first-line military emplacements. We haven't had a look at their techniques because they didn't let anyone get away. But these tactics are schoolbook examples! If this is the best they can do, we'll wipe them out when our fleets move in."

He was overenthusiastic, but he was right. Our defenses were solidly based on the Fleet principle, with interlocking layers of tactical directorates, hundred-ship armadas, and echelons of command. It was very much like the surface aquatic navies of Earth history. On these terms the Quarn were disastrously inferior.

The news should have quieted the unease I felt. Instead, it grew. I began to notice outbreaks of rudeness among the crew, signs of worry on the faces of the officers, disruption of spirit. The tedium of caring for the colonists could certainly account for some of it—they refused to be calmed and had to be restrained from destroying their room furniture. They were using it to construct the same sort of ratholes we'd found them in.

But that wasn't all. Crewmen began missing meals, staying in their cabins, and not talking to anyone else. The ship took on a quiet, tense mood. I ordered resumption of the Games at once.

6

WE ALMOST GOT THROUGH IT.

There was devisive talking and nervousness instead of the steady calm of self-contemplation before the Sabal began, but the opening rituals damped and smoothed it. I thought I detected a relaxation running like a wave through the hexagon. Muscles unstiffened, consciousness cleared, and we drew together.

It is usual in the Game to choose a theme which begins with a statement of the virtue of community, tests it, and then returns to initial configuration, the position of rest. I anticipated trouble, but not enough to make a change of game plot necessary. The plot ran smoothly at first, until we came to first resolution point.

One of the lower deckmen, who had been in the shelter caverns from the first entry, was called by the chance of the game to report the decision. He hesitated, looked guiltily at his cards and beads, and then spoke. He displayed a sum of choices which profited a few at the expense of the many.

Something stretched thin in the layered air of the room.

I could feel the group teetering on edge. The men were straining for sense of harmony and trying to decide how to play when their turn came. A bad play isn't unknown to Sabal, but now it could be dangerous.

I repeated the confirmation ritual, hoping it would calm them—and myself—but the next play was a choice of withdrawal. No gain for the individual, but the group did not profit, and the net effect was bad. Fear began to slip from member to member down the hexagon.

The plays came rapidly now. Some tried to reinforce the message, and cast configurations that benefited the group. They were swamped, one by one, and the Game began to fall apart.

I used the chant. Tranquility, detachment. The words rose and fell. Interpenetrating. Interconverting. The mosquito bit the bar of iron.

My own cast held them for a while out of respect for my position, but in a quick string of plays its advantage was nibbled away.

Then the flood came. A dozen casts went by, all having loss of Phase. The theme was not gain, but a pulling away from the group, and that was what made the failure so serious. Withdrawal strikes at the social structure itself.

I seized control of the Game, breaking off a subplot that was dragging us deeper. I drew a moral, one I'd learned years before and hoped to never use. It slurred over the resolution of the Game and emphasized the quality of the testing, without questioning whether the test had been met. It was an obvious loss, but that was all I could do.

The hexagon broke and the men burst into conversation, nearly panic-stricken. They moved out of the room, jostling and shoving, and broke up as they reached the halls. A few glanced quickly at me and then looked away. In a moment the only sound was the hissing of the air system and the distant quick tapping of boots on deck.

Tonji remained. He looked puzzled.

"What do you think it means?" I said.

"Probably just that the mission was too much for us. We'll be all right after landfall."

"I don't think so. Our Games before worked well, but this one shattered before it was half-finished. That's too much of a change."

"What, then?"

"It's something to do with this mission. Something . . . What percentage of the crew have regular contact with the Regeln survivors?"

"With the way the nursemaid shifts are set up now, about sixty percent. Every man who's replaceable for more than an hour on his job has to help feed and clean them or assist the psych teams who are working on the problems."

"So even though we're off Regeln, most of the men continue to see them."

"Yes, but it's unavoidable. Our orders were to bring back as many as we could, and we are."

"Of course." I waved my hand irritably. "But the Game failed tonight because of those survivors, I'm sure of that. The strain of putting this set of crews into war-status duty isn't small, but we've allowed for it in our planning. It doesn't explain this."

Tonji gave me a stiff look. "Then what does?"

"I don't know." I was irritated at the question, because I *did* know—in a vague, foreboding sense— and his question uncovered my own fear.

"The Sabal Game has something to do with it. That and the way our ships—hell, our whole society—has to be run. We emphasize cooperation and Phase. We teach that a man's happiness depends on the well-being of the group, and the two are inseparable. Even in our contacts with alien races, until the Quarn, we spread that philosophy. We try to draw closer to beings who are fundamentally different from us."

"That is the way any advanced society must be structured. Anything else is suicide on the racial scale."

"Sure, sure. But the Quarn apparently don't fit that mold. They've got something different. They work almost completely alone and live in cities only, I suppose, because of economic reasons. Most of what we know about them is guesswork, because they don't like contact with others, even members of their own race. We've had to dig out our own data bit by bit."

Tonji spread his hands. "That is the reason for this mission. The Regeln survivors may be able to tell us something about the Quarn. We need an idea of how they think."

"I don't think these madmen will be any help. Already they threaten the convoy."

"Threaten? With what?"

"Disruption, mutiny—something. All I can say is that when this Sabal started, the crew was in bad condition, but they could be reached. They still communicated."

"Yes, but—"

"During the Game, though, the tension *increased*. We didn't witness here the exposure of what the men were thinking. Their fears were augmented, piled on top of each other. I could feel it running through the subplots they made a part of the Game. There's something we do—and the Game is just a way of concentrating it—that increases the imbalance we picked up from the Regeln survivors."

"But in the Game we duplicate our society, our way of living. If *that* amplifies the unbalance . . ."

"Exactly," I said despairingly. "Exactly."

7

I SLEPT ON IT that night, hoping something would unravel the knot of worry while I slept. Over a lonely breakfast in my cabin I reviewed the conversation and tried to see where my logic was leading.

A sense of dread caught my stomach and twisted it, turning to lead the meal of rice and sea culture broth.

How can a man step outside himself and guess the reactions of aliens utterly unlike him? I was trying to find the key to the riddle of Regeln with all the elements in full view, and yet . . .

Something formed. I let my senses seep out into the ship, feeling the delicate rhythms of life, reaching for the . . . other. An alien element was there. I knew, with a new certainty, what it was.

I picked up my teacup and focused on my kensdai altar. The deep mahogany gave me confidence. Power and resolution flowed outward from my body center. I balanced the cup lightly in my hand.

And slammed it down.

Jump was coming. I had to stop it.

I had forgotten that Tonji was to be bridge officer during the Jump. He was making routine checks in the somber green light of morning watch. Men moved expertly around him, with a quiet murmur.

"Great greetings of morn, sir," he said. "We have come to the point for your permission to Jump."

Then it was already late, far later than I'd thought. I looked at him steadily.

"Permission denied, Mr. Tonji. Ready a subspace transmission."

I could feel a hush fall on the bridge.

"May I ask what the transmission will say, sir?"

"It's a request to divert this convoy. I want the expedition put into decontamination status until this is understood."

Tonji didn't move. "Jump approaches quickly, sir."

"It's an order, Mr. Tonji."

"Perhaps if you would explain the reasoning, sir?"

I glanced at the morning board. It showed a huge sick report, most of the names accompanied by requests to remain in quarters. All divisions were undermanned.

It fitted. In a few days we wouldn't be able to operate at all.

"*Look,*" I said impatiently. "The Quarn did something to our people. Perhaps something smuggled in by an agent. I don't know exactly how, but those colonists have been given the worst trauma anybody has ever seen."

"An agent? One of our people?"

"It's been done before, by idealists and thugs alike. But the important point is that when we picked up Quarn ships on our screens they weren't trying any maneuvers to throw off detectors or give false images. It was a classic ballistic problem they presented to us, and all we had to do was leave Regeln early enough to outmass them. They *wanted* us to escape."

"But look at their maneuvers on that first run against Regeln, the one that ran our people underground. That's all the evidence we need. They're *children* when it comes to military tactics. The second approach was simple, yes, but it was probably all they could do."

"I don't think so. Not if the Quarn are half as intelligent as the rest of our data tell us. So their first attack *did* drive the colonists under—fine. It got all the Regeln population in one place, inside the shelter, where whatever techniques the Quarn knew could go to work. What looked like an error was a feint."

"I do not—"

"*Think.* A knowledge of sophisticated tactics is a rather specialized cultural adaptation. For all we know, it may not be very useful in the kind of interstellar war we've just gotten into. The fact that the Quarn don't have it doesn't mean they're inferior. Quite the opposite, probably. Regeln was a trap."

"If it was, we escaped," Tonji said sharply. The Mongol mask descended.

"No, Mr. Tonji, we didn't. We're just serving as a convenient transport for what the Quarn want to get into the home worlds—the Regeln survivors."

"But *why?*"

"You know the analogy we use in the Game.

Mankind is now, at last, an organism. Interdependent. We're forced to rely on each other because of the complexities of civilization." My own voice sounded strange to me. It was tired, and a note of despair had crept in.

"Of course," Tonji said impatiently. "Go on."

"Has it ever occurred to you that once you admit society is like an organism, you admit the possibility of contagious diseases?"

"You toy with words."

I grimaced and went on.

"The survivors. They're enough of a test sample to set it off, apparently. An average crew member spends several hours a day with them, and the continual exposure is enough."

"Why aren't you affected, then? And me. And the men who aren't on the sick list—why don't they have it?"

"Minor variations in personality. And there's something else. I checked. Some of them are from the Offislands, like me. We're different. We didn't grow up with the Game. We learned it later on the mainlands. Maybe that weakens its effect."

He shook his head. "Yes, this thing the colonists have is different, but . . ."

"It claws at the mind. It's irrational. We're the product of our ancestors, Mr. Tonji, and these ancestors knew terrors we cannot comprehend. Remember, this is a new psychosis we've found on Regeln, a combination. Fear of light, heat, heights, open spaces. That last one, agoraphobia, seems strongest. The Quarn have worked on a first-class horror for us, and this convoy is to be the carrier."

"A carrier for a mental disease?" Tonji said contemptuously.

"Yes. But a disorder we've never seen before. An amalgam of the fundamental terrors of man. A collective society has the strength of a rope, because each strand pulls the same way. But it has weaknesses, too, *for the same reason.*"

The men were watching us, keeping very still. I could hear the thin beeping of monitoring units. Tonji's skin had a slight greenish cast, and his eyes looked back at me impersonally, cool and black.

"We're carrying it with us, Tonji. The survivors are striking the same resonant mode with us that the Quarn found in them. The Quarn hit at us through our weaknesses. They're hermits, and they see us more clearly then we see ourselves. Our interdependence, the Game and all of it, communicates the disease."

I noticed that my hand was tightening convulsively on the console at my side. Tonji stood unmoving.

"Stop the Jump, Mr. Tonji. And the transmission."

He motioned to an assistant. Jump count ceased. He stood for a moment, eyes wary. Then he took a quick backward step, came to attention, and saluted. When he spoke the words were measured.

"Sir, it is my duty to inform you that I must file Duty Officer's Report when your dispatch is transmitted. I invoke Article Twenty-seven."

I froze.

Article Twenty-seven provides that the duty officer may send a counterargument to the Commander's dispatch when it is transmitted. When he feels the Commander is no longer able to conduct his duties.

"You're wrong, Mr. Tonji," I said slowly. "Taking these survivors—and by now, most of the crew—

into a major port will cause more damage than you or I can imagine."

"I have been observing you, sir. I don't think you're capable of making a rational decision about this thing."

"Man, think! What other explanation can there be for what's happening to this ship? You've seen those tapes. Do you think the scraps of information on them are worth the risk of delivery? Do you think *anyone* can get even a coherent sentence out of those lunatics we're carrying?"

He shook his head mutely.

I looked across the dark void between us. He was a man of the East, and I represented the dead and dying. In the histories they wrote, the ideals my ancestors held were termed a temporary abnormality, a passing alternative to the communal, the group-centered culture.

Perhaps they were right. But we had met something out here, and I knew they wouldn't understand it. Perhaps the Americans would have, or the Europeans. But they were gone.

I should have anticipated that the lost Phase we all felt would take different forms. Tonji chose ambition above duty, above the ship.

If Fleet upheld him there would be a fat promotion for him. And I stood here, bound by rules and precedents. If I made a move to silence Tonji, it would count against my case with Fleet. We were on a rigid schedule of procedures now that the Article was used. Nothing I could do would stop it.

"Mr. Tonji! You realize, don't you, that one of us will be finished when this is over?"

He turned and looked at me, and for a moment a

flash of anticipation crossed his face. He must have hated me for a long time.

"Yes, I have thought of that. And I think I know which one of us it will be . . ."

He didn't finish the sentence aloud. He mouthed it, so only I could see his lips move.

". . . *ofkaipan.*"

8

HE WAS RIGHT. Fleet wanted to study the survivors in depth. They weren't interested in a convoy commander with suspicions and a theory. And Tonji, a Mongol, had ample political contacts.

We lingered in real space for a week, waiting for the decision, and then Jumped.

My trial was short.

even though our guts are twisted up inside? Until we're transferred to some rat warren, when our guts jam up completely, where we'll live in slimy rooms like closets, just like—" I stopped myself from saying, *like Regeln*.

Her hand tightened convulsively in mine. She wept. "You know that can't be helped! We, we are in a . . . stage of evolution. Evolution of society. Withdrawal is necessary. No one says we are doomed, Ling. You're imagining that. We can achieve greater Phase later. Everyone says—"

"And meanwhile the Quarn take one system after another. They've cut us off from many bases already. We can't muster the men to stop them." I snorted contemptuously. "Maybe if we're lucky they'll cut us off from our own lies before all this is over."

"Now *that* is completely unreasonable," she said icily, her tears gone. "There are signs of improvement, the news says so. Progress of the . . . the sickness, is slowing."

"For cases removed at third or fourth hand from the Regeln survivors, yes. They got a weaker initial exposure."

"That's just a theory. You don't *know* that."

"Um." I grimaced in the inky closeness of the hallway.

"It's like all your other ideas, like not letting Chark and Romana have tapping."

"Letting Fleet and the government alter their minds, you mean, with one of their stopgap schemes for increasing the war effort. Let Chark have a frontal tap so all he cares about is torch chamber design, say?—and will never be happy when he's not doing it? 'A permanent career,' they call it. That's right, I won't assent to that. Our children

need every bit of mental balance they have to stay
alive, to live as a defeated race. I don't intend to
rob them of it."

She trembled in frustration. We passed by wan
yellow phosphors of the lower-level apartments,
the narrow Slots hastily thrown up by a harassed
government for more severe cases. Whimpering
came from the little holes where things that had
been human beings were curled up into tight balls,
desperately trying to shut out the light, the sounds,
all of the awful yawning enormity of sheer open
space. The terror of openness. Of horizons.

Beside me Angela stopped trembling. She descended into her glacial silence, keeping only a
fingertip touch with my hand to retain her orien-
tation. The walks didn't seem to do her any good
any longer. I supposed there was a limit to their
therapeutic value. I had insisted from the first that
we all walk outside our apartment as much as
possible. And in truth we were not as ill as many
others who had contracted the sickness later than
we. Perhaps we could achieve a kind of plateau.
There was something in me that fought against
the clutching fears. The sharp words between Angela and myself sometimes even seemed to help, to
calm us both. I could not believe Angela believed
completely what she parroted. She had been in-
fected by me with more than the Plague. By an
unspoken mutual consent we clung to the spaces
of our apartment, forced Chark and Romana to
live there. At times the children would move suddenly from one room to the next, and a frozen
terror would slide into their faces, a mask of fear—
but we made them stay. Small victories. Stale-
mates became triumphs.

Even so, the world was not real to me. It was

filled with a thousand devious horrors—the accidentally thrown phosphor switch, an unsuspected window in an unfamiliar wall.

Out on the edge of our pitifully shrinking Empire, Fleet played at war with the only toys it knew—ships, missiles, beams—while its enemy (and what was he like, to be so wise?) fought with the only ultimate weapons between races: their weaknesses.

Men who had climbed to the stars now cowered in Slots, driven by horrors inherited from the first amphibians. I did not feel at home on Earth any longer. It had been long since I had peered out to see the stars like tinsel on sky's smooth cloak.

My life lay now in halls pooled in darkness, in places packed with people whose faces I hated, because they were mine as well.

Waiting . . . waiting . . . The days pressed in.

I would welcome the Quarn when they came.

Part II

Part II

1

ENERGY RESOURCES RAN LOW, so the streets around our Slot cube were unlit. The Philippines are forever cloud-shrouded, so a dark as thick as anger cloaks the streets.

My first excursion outside our cube was at night. I walked a block, no more. I went without telling Angela. The idea alone would have made her face whiten, her arms hug herself.

But now—

The moment came when the fact slipped free and hung in the brimming air before me, unavoidable now—

That moment when I poked my head through the forgotten grime-caked window and, sniffing day's warm musk, did not flinch from the yellow haze outside.

I had been out before at night, yes, telling myself it was not, after all, that odd an event. But now I had gone on a walk from the apartment, down inky halls, and found the window again . . .

and day lay outside. And I did not turn back.

I opened the window. I stretched into the stinging sun.

No fear. No tremor of anxiety.

The street lay bare, trash clumped in the gutters like brown snowdrifts. Buildings shimmered in the golden light.

Beckoning.

A draft drew out the scent of the corridors behind me, air reeking of piss and foul food and lives gone stale. Even our own apartment smelled faintly of that, when I returned to it from my nightly explorations . . .

I twisted out of the unguarded window, hung by the ledge, dropped.

Now . . . what? I started walking, savoring the warm brush of air heavy with moisture. I had lived near here as a boy. I had played through the infinite buzzing tropical afternoons outside Naga. The nearness of Fleet Central had made my candidacy for Fleet Academy a virtual reflex; to the adolescent I was then the Academy hovered in the space between myself and a looming future, an inevitable bridge, with invisible tinkling waters below. I'd rejected the thought of being anything else. So the man is victim of the boy.

Nothing moved on this street. There was a blurred hum of traffic from the center of Naga, but here all was silence. Storefronts were boarded up. Warehouses yawned empty. I walked idly, mind floating and feet free.

"Hold!"

A man stepped from a doorway. A Fleet officer, Lieutenant Grade Two. He kept a right hand casually resting on the butt of his sidearm. "You are . . . ?"

"Captain Ling Sanjen. Console operator."

"Yes." He fished a note from his breast pocket, checked it. Nodded. "We thought it would be you."

"What? Why?"

"Our night sensors picked you up."

"So?"

"There is a small percentage of recoveries. Fleet wants to talk to you."

"I don't know why. Who says I've recovered, anyway?"

He raised an eyebrow. "Any Slot mole who can stand this sunlight—" he gestured, squinting—"is on his way."

"Well, no, it *is* bothering me." I stepped casually away. "I only came out to get some help. My wife—"

He shook his head. His hand returned to his sidearm.

"Look, I'm just a—"

"I know who you are. You're on the list."

"What list?"

"People we're watching for if they come out of the Slots."

"I'm not feeling very well, I . . ." I wobbled a bit and tried to look dazed.

He smiled. "Nice try, but no bronzer. You're too valuable to let go."

I started to walk away.

This time the sidearm came out.

Fleet Central was the same: jutting architecture simulating flight, gleaming hallways, padded lobbies, the steady click and bustle of efficient mystery; a steel cathedral.

They kept me for two days before I knew anything more than the patrol officer had let slip. They tested, poked, attached sensors, interviewed me, left me waiting for hours—in a word, treated me like a package of meat in their factory. I learned nothing. I was getting bored and fidgety by the end of the second day, while I waited in a large office, until the door opened and a Fleet officer came in.

It was Tonji, his Mongol mask in place.

He held out his hand. "I am happy you recovered."

I didn't stand. I didn't shake the hand.

"From the reports I gather you have done remarkably well."

"You son of a bitch."

"Quite remarkable, considering that you had no help. No therapy whatever—unless you are lying about that. Some have, you know."

"How did you come by those double stars? Have all bastards become generals, or is it the other way around?"

"I see things have not changed as much as I would have wished."

"They never will."

He gave a small laugh. "You must get over this."

"Why? I was right."

"This is unproductive."

"For whom?"

"For you. Surely *I* don't care."

"The past between us isn't dead."

"It is for me."

I stood up suddenly. "We'll see—"

"How many times you can hit me before a trooper comes through that door?"

I clenched my fists, judging the distance.

"The answer is, not many. Perhaps three." He looked at me steadily. "Perhaps even fewer."

We stood there for a long moment, and something seeped out of me. This was Tonji's game. He couldn't lose it—otherwise he wouldn't be here, exposing himself this way. So the next move would have to wait. How long a wait it would be I didn't know, but one thing was sure—neither of us would forget. Tonji's smile made that quite clear.

I sat down. Tonji nodded. We began to talk.

It was a simple proposition. Fleet officers were a bit less vulnerable to the Quarn sickness, whatever it was, but not very much. The ranks were thinning. Worse, because of the unpredictable nature of the disease, sensitive points had to be overstaffed, in case of loss of several high officers at once.

The trade lanes of the Empire were in a shambles. Quarn attacks on bases had abated somewhat, but fear laced every communique. It was becoming increasingly difficult to hold together the several hundred worlds of the Empire by occasional visits by a full-status Jump carrier. And there were fewer Jump ships all the time.

"So that's why I'm valuable," I said.

"Yes," Tonji murmured. "Quite to the point. You are reliable."

I laughed bitterly. "You've testified just the opposite."

"You understand my reasons at the time."

I waved at his double stars. "Of course."

"The point is that you are now . . . immune . . . to the disease. We can trust you to not fall victim again"

"So you're going to give me a ship?"

"No. Oh no."

He looked at me calmly. "We would not go that far."

"Why not?"

"You are inexperienced. You managed convoys before."

"So did you."

"Do not ask for the impossible."

"Don't ask me to read your mind."

"An attitude of—"

"Screw that."

"I doubt that you realize your true position."

"I believe I do."

"Each officer is in fact a supplicant before the Fleet."

"Again: screw that."

"You have changed, Sanjen."

"Just 'Sanjen'? No title?"

"You *have* no title if I, if Fleet does not choose to reinstate you."

"A point. Very well, what then?"

"A Base Commandant position."

"With attendant neighboring ship command?"

"Yes, but that will be trivial. It is the Veden system."

I paused. Veden was an eccentric case among the worlds—a gigantic storage house for the Empire's trade goods, a way station that served the full 200-parsec span of the Empire.

"Why me?"

"The past Commandant died—natural causes, nothing unusual."

"And you don't wish to replace him with a sorely needed full line officer."

Tonji made a thin, cynical laugh. "You do occasionally read matters well."

I thought a moment. "My family . . ."

"They cannot go, certainly."

"They're ill, yes, but—"

"There is no sign of the Quarn sickness on Veden.

Perhaps the Hindics of Veden are immune—" he shrugged—"who knows? But Fleet will not introduce cases into Veden."

"That is an unusual hardship for a Commandant."

"Who do you imagine you *are*, Sanjen?" Tonji rasped with surprising ferocity. I suddenly saw that beneath the mask he was a man under pressures that abraded him.

"I should take what Fleet lets dribble from its fingers, then."

"Poorly stated," Tonji said, clipping off the words sharply.

"But true."

Tonji said nothing. He stood rigidly, hands clasped behind him, the traditional waiting-warrior stance.

I stood up. "I'll think about it."

Tonji blinked, showing a slight flicker of surprise. These last few moments were the first in the conversation when he did not seem fully confident.

"A Jump vessel leaves soon which can easily make a pass by Veden. We need a replacement now. I believe—"

"I'll think about it," I said, and left.

2

AT FIRST ANGELA was restrained, simmering, saying nothing until I asked her a direct question—*You do understand what I'm talking about, don't you?* —and then as she warmed up, as the reality of my two days' absence became full-bodied in my telling of it (she had thought I was dead somewhere, or scrabbling like a demented animal in a Slot, or simply drifting, shambling, through endless shadowed corridors), the fear settled into her, her eyes seemed to bulge more with each detail I brought out, and the rage steamed up through her and she said, "*No.* You're saying, you mean you'll just, just *leave* me?

"It will enable you, the children, to have a better chance for recovery. Better care. Fleet will—"

"With everything outside collapsing? What use is *that*?" She rose up from her chair, balled both fists.

"And there is duty. Mine. I need to go."

"Do you *care?*"

I stood silent, because in fact I didn't know. Did she?

"No. No," she shook her head.

"Perhaps it's not that simple—"

"After they took everything away from you?"

"The past can't be corrected—" I began, and felt a sudden flash of rage at myself. Tonji had made a similar, scuttling excuse. "You owe them *nothing*."

"You're right. I'm not talking about doing anything for them."

"Then what—"

"The Empire . . . no, it's not even that. Humanity. I. I think something can still be done for some worlds. Veden, maybe. Then—"

"Ling, even if you *believe* that, how can you abandon us here?"

"I think Earth is safe. For a while, anyway."

"You don't *know*. No one does."

"Right. But I have to follow my instincts."

"Your instincts." She stood there, puffing slightly, her billowy housedress sighing as it moved. "Saving Veden, whatever or wherever that is." She stopped again, just staring at me. Her upper lip was damp with perspiration. I didn't look at her eyes. "Ling, you're not going to do this."

"No. I am."

"You're not."

"I'm . . . I'm cured now, Angela," I said, trying to get some warmth back into my voice, which had become dry and brittle.

"Cured."

"That makes a big difference. In what I can do. In what my duty is."

"Is that it?"

"What?" I wiped my brow, dazed. Even here in our apartment stench layered the air.

"Is that why you're going?" A pause. "Ling?"

"I . . . we'll talk again, later. I need time to . . ."

"To what?"

"To *think*, damn it!" I turned on her. "To *think*!"

So I slammed out of the apartment, banging the door hard enough to wake Chark and Romana, to go for a walk, yes a walk outside in the warming sun, to *think*, and though I did a lot of that in the days to come, I really never did understand why I was going, or what this meant to Angela and me, but one fact I never questioned: I was going, yes, of course, I was going.

3

TAKE A REAM of paper, heavy fiber, its threads of rag content webbing the slicked surface—take it in the right hand and riff through, a sheet at a time, listening to the *snick* as each edge scrapes across your thumbprint, and then go faster, so the *snick-snicksnick* blurs into a high cry like birds unseen above the clouds. There, that's it—the way the hours went by as I began to prepare for Veden, to make myself once more into a dim glimmering of the Fleet officer I had once been. The hours *snickered* by me:

Exercising. Running in the Fleet park, the Philippine forest hugging close to the pacing trails, animal calls punctuating my puffing silences. The Slots had thickened my waist, softened my arms, blurred my physical awareness.

Updating. I was behind on Fleet policy, Fleet strategy, even tactical modifications. The Fleetwide Firetongue Stet had been changed, because of fears that the Quarn had captured one. So the Stet in my apartment was useless now. I resolved to keep it, though.

Maneuvering. Tonji was surprised when I called in to accept—"I wondered if I would see you again, Sanjen," he said. I had to talk my way out of the usual attendance at Fleet ceremonials, the rewelcoming ritual, a reception. I had no desire to be pressed to the Fleet bosom.

Husbanding. I took walks with them in the dim corridors of the Slots where we still lived. Linger. Listen. Wander. Wait. I could feel them struggling against the fears, the gripping anxieties that I was free of now. Angela and the children balked at the new apartment I found them. She hung back, was unable to leave the bedroom for two days. Even when she mustered the strength, her mouth sagged awry like a gate off its hinges. Chark and Romana spent endless slack hours in front of the 3D.

Fathering, yes. If there was guilt here it was in the fathering. The world defines a brace of years for childhood; of parenthood there is no riddance. If I seemed to chafe under these scratching facts, it arose from my own impatience, once my unconscious had allowed my decision to float up into reality: to be off, gone, to stride the skies once more. Call it callous—I did, repeatedly, and was as helpless to quell the guilt as a sunjammer is to slip free of the solar wind.

I had, of course, the refuge of duty; a comfortable harbor. I settled there, finally, reasonably untroubled. For what, really, could I do for them unless they recovered? I grew up in the leafy abodes of the rural Philippines, learned from a portable slate. Chark and Romana, denizens of apartment and hallway, had been learning that their future would be a succession of riveting sixty-minute episodes, loaded with healthful educational snippets, all of which would make them appear heroic, compassionate, dutiful to the greater aims of humanity, and attractive to the opposite sex. Perhaps, in the end, it would be better for them to believe that than to stare into the abyss I knew.

Then living with Angela became easier. She had seen me cast off into high vacuum before as a convoy Captain; once convinced I was going, she rehearsed the litany she knew.

Oddly, matters improved.

We had had the sickness together for nearly a year; it invaded everything. In those times, at night she would lie, as often as not, in a valley of damp sheets we made for ourselves by our own labors, her legs slack and obliging, a well to pump if anyone should wish. And I still did desire her, although I was well versed in this territory, a commuter where once I had been explorer.

Somehow, the balance shifted when I resolved to go. After that, we no longer went to bed like dutiful laborers in a factory, bound to go and sweat. Instead we spent long hours, arguing first with diminishing fervor and, later, discovering a last saving grace note on the now dim chord of marriage. I rediscovered old rhythms in her. Her surface was once again an intimate sweaty field of calluses, pores, a geography of wife with aged favorite hollows and valleys and moles, all places worn smooth by my eyes. There, and *ah*: her thin black eyebrows would arch high and hang there, skin slick and electric.

At times in our arguments she would simply

repeat my name, head hanging in a soft despair, a mutual funk, *Ling, Ling, Ling,* and afterward, during our all-encompassing battering, a pocket of my mind would trip out a play on the name, chimes in the night, Ling equals lingam. Though there was some verve to it, these times were still only spaces in a continuum, a zest for the known; Angela was still wife. (The word, the word—Anglo-Saxon, *wif,* "woman." I wondered how different the Mongol culture would be had not English already become the effective world language before the Riot War. Thoughts of Old Nippon and the Mainland were couched in terms familiar to Shakespeare. The word. A known language, a known wife. Comforting. But comfort alone wasn't enough.)

I saw Tonji once more. He had been chosen to deal with my re-entry, since—in the logic of Fleet—he'd known my "difficulties" in the past and would be able to assess my recovery. Even granted that, I saw no reason why he should formally hand me my Commandant materials and the new Firetongue Stet and deliver the customary lecture.

"I have little time," I said, cutting him off. "You can freeze-dry that pretty little speech."

Tonji grimaced. An underling handed him the fleet outbound file on Veden and he gave it to me. "Ah . . . one last point."

"Yes?" I turned to go.

"Your primary task is to stabilize Veden. Socially, I mean. We must keep the Flinger system intact and functioning."

"Of course."

"And . . . the Veden system is singular. The orbital dynamics, I mean. There may be some difficulty on planetary approach."

"I accept risk."

"Yes." Tonji smiled broadly and saluted. I thought nothing of it.

4

I DIDN'T GET along well with the ship's officers on the long voyage out. The *Sasenbo* was a Prime Class vessel, and I was dismayed to find it crewed by political appointees, leftovers, officers long on desk savvy and short on discipline; or so they seemed to me. Most appeared motivated by a shrewd but stupid ambition; their primary concern seemed to be whether their socks matched.

And there was no Sabal game. None. Not any more.

After a few rude exchanges in the officers' mess I took to having meals in my room—as a passenger, I could by rights. So I studied dispatches, read research summaries on the Quarn, exercised, thought of Angela—an odd sensation despite our kernel of differences; abstinence makes the heart grow fonder—and often walked the vast ship, studying it. I had seldom been on a Prime vessel.

They all look like beach balls from the outside, threaded by one thick axis. The skin is dimpled by comm pods, weapons ports, sensors, and, at each end of the protruding axis, skimmer ports. None of this is visible from inside, of course. The axis *is* the ship. People and other delicate items live at the center of the beach ball, inside the axial tube. The beach ball is filled with colloidal fluid—fuel—which shields out Jump radiation and other undesirables. The beach ball skin is flexible organiform, to adjust for varying fuel loads, and ordinary cargo hangs at regular intervals from the axis, wrapped in sacks to separate it from the colloids.

You can see all this if you go to the full-G deck— the outside deck of the axial tube. The view is murky because of the reaction fluid. You're standing on a transparent floor, peering down—"out," really—at a swampy universe. Blades of light from the axis cut shafts through it. Bags of cargo hang down into the colloids, kept aligned by the centrifugal tug of rotation. You can't see the organiform skin. It's too far away—over two hundred meters. Anything you could see through would be pretty poor radiation shielding; you'd fry while playing tourist.

That's all the scenery there is. Life evolves—as far as we know—on the surfaces of conveniently spherical planets, so if you look up, you look out. But in deep space "gravity" has to come from rotation, so the canonical geometry is the cylinder. Life creeps on at its petty pace inside the spinning cylinder, and overhead lies not infinity and/or salvation, but the null-g point, the axis. *Sasenbo*'s axis was eye, ear, nose, throat, alimentary canal and—most important—spine. The decks, A through K, were concentric cylinders rotating about the spine: bridge at A, excess storage at K. My cabin was on C. I exercised often in the axial gym, rebounding off rubbery walls in elaborate bank shots. I was there when the *Sasenbo* Captain summoned me.

He was in his couch on the bridge deck, conferring with a dutiful crescent of Lieutenants. One of them gave me a sour look as I approached, and they dispersed. The Captain said, "Oh yes," distracted, and thumbed a fresh readout. "We were programming your drop."

"I assume you can put me into a planetary ellipse?"

He looked up, blinked with surprise. "No. Oh no. You know that."

"Why not?"

"Why, we aren't planning an intersection with Veden's orbit at all. You have to go through the Flinger."

"*What?*"

"Fleet informed you of this difficulty."

"They sure as hell did not."

"It's here—in your briefing manifest." He waved at the readout. "General Tonji himself, I see."

"He didn't mention it."

The Captain frowned. "Odd. Well—" he shrugged— "it's not my affair."

"It's impossible for a one-man craft to go through the Flinger."

"No it isn't. Merely difficult. A precise maneuver."

"Why can't you drop me near Veden?"

"The gravitational potentials are too extreme, too variable. Probability of Jump failure—not just for you, for *us*, the parent ship—is unacceptable."

"What's the uncertainty in my injection velocity?"

He consulted his readout. "Thirteen kilometers per second."

"Impossible!"

He smiled mirthlessly. "Unavoidable. The potentials—"

"If I miss, the neutron star gets me."

He nodded judiciously. "I would say. Certainly that's the most probable outcome."

"Such a maneuver is *not* Fleet policy."

"Correction: *was* not."

"*Is* not. I—"

"Our error rate is high." He waved a hand at the long tube that was the bridge. "Fleet adopted new measures several months ago."

"I could get killed." At the ceremony Tonji had smiled broadly.

"So could we all, if we tried for Veden itself. I imagine that's why so many officers turned down this particular assignment."

"Others?"

"Before you, I mean. Quite a few."

I stood, breathing deeply for a long moment. "All line officers, I imagine."

"Ummm. Yes." He was already pondering another display. "Too dangerous for them, I take it. Veden's the special case, you see—nothing else in the Empire to match it for navigation mishaps. Before, with reliable Jump scanners, it wasn't so hard. But now—"

"Uh huh," I said.

5

W*altz of the billiard balls*, I thought muzzily. The stars were big ones and I was a dwarf. *Sasenbo* was the cue, tapping me gently away. A classy ricochet off Jagen, using gravity's soft brush. A bank shot. Once free, I'd surge out from the two stars, back to the life of straight lines and cozy causalities. *Snick*—we're racing for the Veden pocket. It yawns. I drop *pock* into Newton's well.

A good dream, yes.

I floated up out of it.

Three days now since I climbed in my pod and drifted up through *Sasenbo*'s hollow axis. Past pale white skimmer craft in their berths, past storages and capped ports, past the storage sacks that hung outward from the axis, teardrop shaped, head down into the vast sphere of fuel fluid. Out, through the gaping jaws of the aft lock. Clamshell doors opened. Magnetic fingers plucked me forth, unhusking me, cupped a pocket of fields around me. *Ting*—and the Jump flux rippled, expelling. Stars leaped into being. I took sightings, weighed vectors and momenta, nudged the pod this way and that.

And dreamed. There was nothing else to do. By meditation I dropped my oxy consumption to allow some reserve at the other end of my carom. But sleep stretched thin. I came drifting up, sandy-eyed, thirsty, lifting thumb-fingered my suit helmet shield—

Violet cut my eyes. I squeezed them shut. Polarizers buzzed.

After a time I found it. Not through the port— that I togged shut—but on my screens. Lekki blotted out half of space, dark whirlpools churning her. Streamers gouged into naked blackness. Say *F2 star* and it means nothing; stare at Lekki and tremble. Jagen made her more fierce, but the deep violet of her light still jabbed at my eyes, even over the screens.

I felt a tug now. A fleck of dust slowly coasted forward, past my hand, and pinned itself to a console key. Tides. Jagen.

There: a dot appeared at Lekki's rim and crawled across. The image warped. Detail of a vortex behind it flickered and faded as the dot moved.

Jagen, the Black Dwarf. Neutron Being. Key to the Flinger. Nine klicks in diameter, massing a scratch below Sol, old and cold now. A supernova birthed it, probably, sending Lekki off the main sequence for a bit, but somehow not erasing the biosphere of Veden. Now Jagen whirled about Lekki, fast, incredibly fast—a thousandth of light speed, my Doppler stuttered. A vast source of momentum.

Fuzzy light haloed Jagen as it vanished around Lekki. Of course—the gravitational potential at the neutron star's surface refracted light from Lekki, scrambling detail. A lens made from gravity.

Refracting light, yes; soon, refracting me. I fell.

It was a simple process, really. Mr. Newton wouldn't have furrowed a brow over the Flinger; he spent only an evening, over port and snuff, on Leibniz's mathematical challenges to the learned of Europe, and solved those without recourse to his methods of fluxions. An evening's entertainment, mere warming of the frontal lobes after a day at the Royal Mint.

Ah, Newton, be with me now: my pod fell obliquely toward the Lekki-Jagen system, intersecting the Jagen orbit smack-on, diving at the neutron star as it rushed toward me.

I was to pass close to Jagen, on the face away from Lekki, dipping deep into Jagen's steep gravity well. With a nimble balancing of velocities, I'd weave through the Neutron Being's brutal pull, coyly allowing myself to be nearly captured, looping around Jagen, then breaking free. Escaping, I'd be on the side of Jagen facing Lekki. A turnabout.

But by then Jagen would've stolen my speed, braking me from the *Sasenbo*'s relative velocity down to a pedestrian planetary clip. In a sense, my aim was to undergo an elastic collision with the neutron star's gravitational field. It was like bouncing a ball off the rear fender to an express train. The ball came off with less velocity than it had before. The train—ergo, Jagen—gained a little.

So went the arm-waving, the theory. But *Sasenbo* had spat me out with 3.64 km/sec error in insertion velocity. I fought. I trimmed, vectored, scrabbled sidewise, deformed my smooth hyperbolas into squiggly new curves.

My fuel burned away to nothing.

Falling. Checking. Falling. And here it came—

Jagen, a dark fleck. Its fields stretched my pod,

sucked at my feet. Blood rushed from my head. I
felt floaty, thick-tongued, magical. The Black Dwarf
reflected precious little light and shone a naked
red, ancient, long shorn of its megaGauss magnetic fields. My own fields surged and built, batting away the sleeting protons which tried to riddle
me.

We wrapped around. *Ping, click* said my cabin.
Something howled in the walls. Lekki loomed large.
Below, huge rippling waves of plasma roiled and
tossed, all at the beck of the little giant. Magnetic
fields fought gravity.

I groaned (—or was it the pod that spoke? flecks
darted at my edge of vision, my ears popped, confusion swam—). Jagen plucked with massive fingers at my sleeve, coaxing me down to her slick
surface, where surely the crunch of electrons over-
coming their own Fermi pressure and collapsing
in onto protons, wedding to birth neutrons—that
crunch must ache, split the head, yea, neutrons
pressing, pressing at a thousand million million
grams per cc, sucking me through to stretch thin
and spatter its skin and fry into gammas and x-rays,
ah—

But no.

The hand eased. Fingers slipped, caught, slipped
again. And were gone. We backed away from the
Black Dwarf. I sucked in cooling air. My hands,
aching from hovering over the consoles, floated
before the wrinkling screens. It was a forgiving
universe. Even my own sweat smelled good. Nice
try, Mr. Tonji, but no bronzer.

Ofkaipan.

On the long swooping ride out to Veden, my
alcohol store squandered in a grand celebration, I

had ample time to mull over the word. It leaped to the frontal lobes, always ready. My parents had taught me what it meant, and then life had ground it in—

Better not go into that restaurant. *You know*— embarrassed nudge of elbow. You quickly walk on.

Shake hands at a reception, feel their slight cold withdrawal. The formal face smiles but the eyes, the eyes, they glitter. Tonji.

Deliveries to your home are slow, poorly packaged.

Insolent servants of your superior officers cast you a look, give you the quick up and down—*does he wear shoes?*—and smile, ever so slightly. They make a face behind your back; you catch it in a mirror.

In a shop: *Perhaps we can find something more suitable in here—* They lead you to a rack of marked-down merchandise, scruffy, out of fashion.

With: I'm sorry, the Commandant is out. We don't know when to expect him back.

And: You realize, of course, there may be a delay in taking care of this matter. This office is very busy.

Stares in crowds. Best not to go down that street.

A look of *Why did he come here? It was a general invitation, of course, but everybody knows—*

It doesn't happen all the time. Just enough to keep you off balance. You never know when it's a natural mistake. That's the worst of it: never knowing for sure.

So I took it out, that old pain, and rubbed it some. The old scabs came off and pus oozed out—so it wasn't healed, after all; were you surprised? —and then blood, and flaky dead skin pulled away so I could see it clearly again. Old pains are the best. They age well, like wine. It looked as though I had a good crop.

Some time passed.

And so I put it back in its corner, and tried to forget for a while. Veden would be different. And enjoyed the long arc up and out.

Part III

1

I FELL TOWARD VEDEN, toward rebirth. It might be possible, a new beginning. My fuel was spent. If the pickup shuttle failed to reach me, I would take a long, smooth ellipse down into her. Flame like a coal, fall a cinder. A sacrifice to her regal orbit, marred only by an animal cry of despair at frequencies to which she never listened.

Who did she listen to, spinning with ancient purpose? To Lekki, Star of India? Or to the dark mote that raced with frantic energy, the Neutron Being?

Gods and planets do not speak. She would not say.

"Have you on visual," my suit spoke to me. "If you can drop a little lower I'll match on my present trajectory."

I thumbed on my binocs, but without a referent I couldn't pick out the shuttle. I stretched my arms and legs as far as the cylinder allowed—it was conveniently casket-sized—and unlocked the jet plates. A slight nudge forward. A tug of acceleration at my back. The shuttle came sliding up from the white rim of Veden as though on an invisible wire, sure and swift and impersonal, a black spot against the muted whites and blues. Veden swept closer, serene as though in meditation, soundless.

"Your course is bracketed," the shuttle pilot's voice came through thinly in the crackle and hiss of my suit radio. "Secure attitude control board."

I never tire of the stately maneuvering of craft in orbit. They move as though some unheard rhythm times them, unperturbed and answerable to no one. The shuttle drifting toward me gave the perfect illusion of freedom. But it was doomed to fall into the sea of air below us and regain its mortality, be weathered and aged even as men are.

The shuttle jetted gas, blurring the crisp outlines of Veden below it like heat waves on a warm afternoon. Heavy shielding around the comm pod identified it as an atmospheric craft. Delicate spines of antennas would be retracted before the atmosphere could sear them away at reentry.

A black rectangle grew in its side. I coasted straight into it. Inside harsh violet lights winked on and I could see the braking pads standing out from the walls of the pickup port.

Why violet? I blinked. The afterimage faded very slowly. My polarizers had compensated almost immediately, but the instant of lag had been enough to blind me in one spot of my vision field for more than a minute.

I watched the port grow, using my peripheral vision. The shuttle was outfitted for a variety of tasks. Grapples tucked under the belly, waldo arms recessed beneath the pilot's slot, and a long thin cut ran down its side—from there would come the thin delta wings for skipping along the top of the atmosphere.

"I'm coming in nicely," I said. The violet rectangle grew, filled the port. We hit the pads gently. I heard a faint clank as something wrapped around the outside.

"Contacts register correctly," the pilot said. "Are you familiar with the mechanism for securing—?"

"I'll mention it if I have any trouble," I said. "But why the colored light? It's rather difficult to see in here." I popped the release on the capsule hatch, and the violet came flooding in. It would have been unbearable without polarizers. I pushed off gently with my elbows, drifted out of the capsule and up to the ceiling.

"Oh, I'm sorry, sir. I've got the illumination set for Veden surface levels. Switching over to Earth standard."

The violet phosphors died and white ones flared into brilliance above them. Everything was silent, except for the small *pings* of my suit contracting as I moved. Gently, gently. I remembered my deep space work of decades past and kept my knees bent, moving slowly and thinking through every action.

The elastic cables were fitted into slots near the capsule. I reeled them out and used a suit jet to swing around the capsule in a circle, the line trailing after me. The third cable grip refused to close for a moment when I tried to lock it, and I was afraid it had cold-welded in the open position, but after some tapping it shut. The lines restrained any motion of the capsule perpendicular to its axis and two axial rods kept it from sliding out of the cocoon of cables. I checked the job twice. If the capsule with all my luggage in it broke loose when we hit the atmosphere, it could go straight through the shuttle's skin.

"All done," I spoke into my suit mike. The blinker over the exit winked twice in confirmation and a panel slid back into place, shutting out the stars. I slipped through the circular exit tube and found it easy going because of the rungs inside. A few twists and turns following the blinkers, and I dropped into a flight seat.

"I routed you through to the copilot's spot, sir," the voice said. I turned to my left and saw a small man looking at me across an imposing bulge of hardware. "It's a more comfortable seat than the passenger compartment. The view is better here, too."

His skin was jet black. A Negro? But I'd thought none survived the Riot War. Something about the virus blight that swept down out of Europe.

Then I realized the cabin was illuminated in violet and my polarizers had cut in the moment I entered. The pilot's skin must be the muddy tan of the Indians, but my polarizers deepened it to black.

"Lance Officer Shandul, sir." He gave an abbreviated salute. I nodded back.

"This is what the sunlight is like on Veden, Mr. Shandul?" I waved an arm at the phosphors ringing us. "I knew it was weighted in the ultraviolet, but I'm not prepared to take much of this."

"Yes sir, perhaps I can lower it somewhat. I fear we are not modified to permit Earth illumination levels here in the cockpit, for which I am sorry. Upon re-entry we will not need interior lights at all. I can extinguish them in a few moments. I hope it will not be uncomfortable for you."

"No, no. Just take us down." I looked out the

transparent nose of the shuttle for the first time. The horizon was a sharp brittle line dividing the milky swirls of Veden's oceans and clouds from the obsidian depths of nothingness. My polarizers smothered the stars so that the curve of the planet gave way not to the glimmering sparks of distant life but to zero, blankness, the fatal cold entropy death. Shandul touched a control, and the ship spun slightly. Lekki slid into a corner of my vision, screaming to be seen. I glanced at it, and it turned white. Careless. I would have a blind spot there for minutes.

I looked down at Veden. ("Down" by training; the anti-g pills were working, and even peering straight down at the surface I didn't feel the visceral clench of infinite, terrifying fall.) Now that I knew what her light was like, I thought I could see a tinge of reflected violet in the white of the clouds.

"It will require a few moments to complete recalculation of orbits, sir."

"Why? Aren't we on a one-orbit ellipse?"

"No sir. The delay in picking you up came from the time necessary for me to complete satellite maintenance."

I frowned. I had thought the wait was a little long. "What kind of maintenance?"

"Micro-meteorite repair for damage to weather observation devices, sir. Also replacement of some failed components. We do not have many opportunities to get this shuttle into orbit of late, so I was ordered to finish all the backlog of work up here."

"Ordered by whom?"

Shandul glanced at me hesitantly. Even through the helmet I could read from his expression that he sensed the possibility of getting into the middle

of a dispute between officers, and that was the last
thing he wanted.

"First Officer Majumbdahr, sir. We are very
poorly supplied with chemical fuels here on Veden
and . . ."

I froze an interested expression on my face and
stopped listening. A technician will ramble on for
hours about his speciality, and it can be fascinating,
but for the moment I wanted to enjoy the view.

Still, he'd told me something I hadn't expected.
It was natural for a way station world like Veden
to be low on chemical fuels—with a population of
seventy-odd million and low crustal abundances
(a scrap of a world, really), it couldn't support a
major industrial base to manufacture them, and at
transport rates on the Jump. Earth certainly wasn't
going to ship fuels out here. But somehow I'd expected Veden to be better off than *this*. Imagine
delaying weather satellite repair to save fuel!

It was another reminder of how unimportant
Veden, as a world, was in the eyes of Fleet. Veden
had been a convenient reservation to give the
Hindics. Slowly, as the ramships gathered here
and the Flinger grew in importance, this strange
double-star system became important. But the real
treasure was the Dwarf, not Veden. One should
not mistake the caretaker for the king.

Clouds like frozen custard slid by below. A witch's
wail chorused; turbulence as our craft fell. Through
some scattered holes I could make out topography.
The dots of ivory ice caps at the poles, smothered
in snow clouds, already lay over the curved rim of
Veden at this altitude. Below, large lazy oceans
gave me nothing to see. We fell toward the single
continent now—three thousand klicks long, a great

rectangular splotch, almost the only dry land on the planet. I craned to see it.

We fell faster; rockets snarled to slow us. Below, fat bunched clouds like cushions clung to the sharply cut coastline of Baslin, mother continent of New India.

It was raw. The battered coast gave way to mountains that lanced into the interior. A giant had stamped down the edges of Baslin and plucked up the middle, for now a plateau rose in the center. Winding fingers of rivers carved and slashed at its edges, cutting narrow valleys. It was a work uncompleted, a stone forgotten when the sculptor walked away and threw his tools into the empty seas.

Indian reservation, I thought, grimacing at the pun. Beholden, like most of the Cooperative Empire worlds—dependent on Earth's advanced technology that held off alien biospheres, the high-quality microelectronics that Earth controlled, the bioengineering that prevented subtle genetic damage from abnormal radiation levels. It was this last, Earth's cellular consummation devoutly to be wished, that held most worlds.

"Parachute deployed," Shandul called. The sharp crack of the ejection snapped me forward against my restraining belts. Parachute? Dissipating velocity with a chute was efficient, but most prosperous areas didn't take the trouble.

We banked above the great mesa. Every human on Veden lived there, drank from its rivers, peered over the edge—if he dared—into the boiling hot chaos of the windswept lowlands. The jungle was a riot of intense magentas and yellows between slate-grey peaks that jutted up and tore the clouds. Below the river writhed, and I suddenly recognized it: Tankjor, the torrent that bled Baslin's major lake, The Lapis. And on the shores of those quiet waters was Kalic, our destination, capital of Baslin and thus Veden.

We hit an air pocket with no bottom, and I felt a sudden wave of nausea snatch at me. Guiding rockets fired in synchronization with dull slapping thumps that rattled my teeth. We banked slowly.

Ahead fractured purple and green winked from The Lapis, and the lattice of Kalic's streets fanned out to greet me. We dropped into a low comfortable glide. Lekki broke from behind a virginal white cloud as we cleared the stony margin of the last peak.

A great grey expanse loomed ahead. Shandul corrected. The ship dropped like a sack of sand again, and colors tumbled off to my side as we turned for final approach.

A glimpse of tranquil sky framed by mountains. A quiet drifting feeling. The shuttle jarred, rumbled, and we were rolling on our landing gear, land animals again, slaves of gravity.

The shuttle coasted up to wing of a long low building at the edge of a grey field. I could make out a mass of men standing in formation. As we drew nearer, they stepped off into three squares with a delegation out front, all casting long shadows in the late afternoon.

"Thank you, sir. If you'll exit through the side—" Shandul gestured to a port that slid open. I stepped out onto a platform. I opened my suit to external pressure, and a wave of magic burst over me. It was a long, solemn dirge of some complexity, but it grated. More appropriate to a wake, perhaps. Or it might be a subtle indication of how the staff felt about their new *ofkaipan* Director.

"Greetings, sir!" an officer called at my elbow, and the troops in formation snapped into a salute. I tried to make my replying salute as clipped and neat as possible, but the suit was a hindrance.

"Mr. Majumbdahr," I said, "your men look very well turned out." It was easy to recognize his long jawline and elaborately curled hair from the personnel records I'd studied on the *Sasenbo*. I turned to the next man, shorter and obviously a purebred Hindic.

"My compliments to you as well, Mr. Gharma. I believe Mr. Shandul is under your command—he handled his ship nicely on the trip down."

All through this my polarizers clicked madly off and on as I turned at angles to the direct violet glare of Lekki, which was setting on the horizon.

"If I can get this off, I can review the troops," I said, reaching for my helmet.

Majumbdahr gestured to stop me. "Sir, this light is harmful to your eyes. We've shortened the ceremony to allow for this. A few more minutes and we can escort you inside, where it will be more comfortable."

I frowned but said nothing. The band broke into a slightly brisker tune, heavy on cymbals and drums. Probably the Veden anthem. I stood still until it was over, returned a last salute, and followed Gharma and Majumbdahr down the ramp to the field. We walked along a roped-off path in front of the troops with an appropriately regal silence and entered the Fleet Control building. Inside there was a medical party waiting for me.

"I should think, Mr. Majumbdahr, that a review of the troops is standard for the introduction of a new Fleet Control Director." My voice carried an edge.

An officer with surgeon's insignia raised his hand. "I believe Mr. Majumbdahr was acting on a request by me, sir. We received word that you had not been acclimatized to Veden, due to the shortness of time. I feared exposure to Lekki without your polarizers would damage your retinal tissue." As he spoke, our party walked along a dimly lit corridor. I felt awkward and irritated, dragging along my suit like a slow-witted bear.

He turned to the rest of them outside a doorway— I noticed his name plate read Imirinichin—and said, "I believe we can fit contact filters for you, sir, without the rest of the Control staff following us around. If you please?"

"Yes, surely." I waved a hand and they broke up. Imirinichin, a lean man with the slow smile and wrinkled eyes of one who jests well, putting on goggles.

"The light in here is adjusted to be comfortable for you, and tolerable for me if I wear these. If you'll sit in that chair—"

A nurse came in wearing the same goggles and helped me lower my bulk into place. She expertly unfastened my helmet. In a moment I was free of the suit and no longer feeling like a turtle caught in a sand pit. She lowered a cantilevered mask over my face, fitted twin cylinders to my eyes with care, and flipped a switch.

The room went dark, and a competent hum came from the apparatus around me. In a moment the computer had measured my cornea, made inquiries with my retinal cells, mused over the patterns of red blood vessels, and switched itself off. The mask came away. "The first thing a newcomer notices is the high ultraviolet content of Lekki. Exposure to it will burn out a man's retinal tissue

in a few days. There's infrared in intensities suffi-
cient to keep the planet's ecological processes
going—photosynthesis and so forth—but the atmosphere can't filter out enough of the violet to make
it comfortable for eyes that were developed in the
green jungles of Earth."

"So what do I do?" I should have expected something of the sort as soon as I popped out of Jump
space and saw Lekki.

"Well, it's no problem—your contacts are being
made up now."

I blinked and popped my two lenses into my
hand. "Store these, then." Like ninety-nine point
something of the human race, I wore ordinary
contacts. (Interesting: Humanitarian though uni-
versal medical care may be, Darwin was right.
We've had nine centuries to prove him out. Bad
genes linger; we've insured that, from defective
eyesight alone, not one human in ten could survive
a day in the droughted Africa where the race was
born.)

A chime rang. A tiny box popped from a chute
transport slot. In a moment tears ran down my
face as I tried to fit in contacts that nearly covered
my entire cornea. I wrinkled my face.

"They must be that large, sir, to protect the
entire eye," Imirinichin said. "These make the best
of a bad situation. The original colonists developed them."

I looked up into a room bathed in dusky twilight.
The contacts filtered out most of Sol-normal light.
Imirinichin was nearly blind in this room.

"No, even worse," he said when I asked. "I'm
adapted. Permanent colonists—and that's nearly
everyone on Veden; we are—" he glanced downward—"somewhat isolated . . . well, they have their

retinal patterns altered, cell grafts, tincturing, all to accommodate Lekki's spectrum. The alteration is much more comfortable than the contacts you're wearing."

"Permanent, though."

"Yes. I gather you are here on rotating assignment?"

I nodded. I couldn't hope to be kept in service after what the Council called the "current crisis" was over. If it was ever over.

"No skin treatments, then, for you."

"Or else I'd have to live near an F-sequence star thereafter?"

"Yes. Veden would never have been colonized but for the Flinger. Adaptation is irreversible."

"What about bioadapts?"

"I'll send the injections around in the morning. Also the formal Fleet uniform for Veden. It covers you nearly completely, sir."

"From the ultraviolet." I shook my head. "But . . . when do I see normal colors again?"

Imirinichin looked chagrined. "We can't get compensation over the entire spectrum. Colors will be shifted and changed for you. I hope it will not be of great inconvenience . . ."

2

SCIENCE IS SPECTRUM ANALYSIS; art came into the world with photosynthesis. That's the way I like to think of it: not knowing, but using.

Inconvenient? The greatest favor a friend can do for you is, every so often, to tilt the world at five degrees.

Colors dance, fresh-scrubbed. The universe becomes a fuller place because you must notice it.

So for the rest of that day I went around in a distracted daze. Light appeared latticed, shifting abruptly through three shades as I watched. Hues blended. Veden became a chromatic chorus.

Gharma came toward me, his smile flashing brilliantly against chestnut brown skin pocked with the large pores of the Hindic. He was a heavyset man with dark hair and eyes that expanded a fraction just before he spoke, as though the words were going to explode out of him. We exchanged pleasantries while, outside, fractured spatterings of yellow beckoned. He curled his words lazily, laying them out precisely for the inspection of the listener.

Majumbdahr followed him, taller and with the slightly slanted eyes and lighter complexion that spoke of his mixed ancestry. "It's after normal working hours," he said. "I don't think a tour of the Fleet Authority offices would be particularly useful for you today, sir."

"I presume you've gathered the usual summary for my review?"

He smiled. "Certainly. But do you want to read them on your first evening on Veden? I imagined perhaps you would care to meet a few under-officers . . ."

"No. It was a tiring trip. I will probably want to sleep. Now, my offices?"

We shot up seven floors and emerged in an ornately styled warren of carpeted rooms walled with imposing bookshelves in something like leather and wood, but with a raw orange cast that signified their native origin. My suite: chartrooms crammed with orbital simulation displays and read-out screens, space for secretaries and aides, conference chambers (more leather, more wood), a private communications link that could override the Control facilities in an emergency, tape files, and lastly my office, hushed in soft textures and tones, space for pacing or thought or meditation, an enormous desk—wood again—with every conceivable aid built into it. It overlooked the field. A forest beyond underlined the wavering wink of Kalic's city lights in the distance. Dusk was ending and blue shadow fingers cloaked the field.

"The summary, sir," Majumbdahr said. I took the case with a large red "PRIORITY" seal on it and tucked it under my arm as we went out.

"Your quarters are some distance," Gharma said. "I believe Mr. Majumbdahr has taken care of preparations there."

"Fine," I said, my voice echoing in the elevator as we went down. "I would like to see both of you gentlemen tomorrow morning, nine hundred hours. We'll have quite a bit to talk over."

Gharma said good night, and Majumbdahr led me out the front entrance. It was a rather impressively delicate structure, curved lattices supported by columns and cantilevered beams of rakish tilts that would have been impossible in heavier gravities. Everywhere curves; no angles, no sharpness or sudden contrast to jar the eye. A man's voice reflecting back from the building carried a tinkling note of hidden laughter.

Majumbdahr pushed the car's throttle forward, and we pulled out silently. Steam cars fueled by low-grade hydrocarbons are common in the colonies; on Earth they are rare, owing to the depletion of our final reserves.

Kalic: spires, cubes, towers, ovoids, hummocks of subsurface dwellings, an air of quiet and tranquility impossible on Earth for centuries past. Our sedan turned onto country roads, into the velvet shadow of a hill. I knew the local flora, from a Stet I'd read on the loop out from the Flinger. As we passed three snakeblossoms jerked up at the roadside, hissed—they were that loud—and puffed out their petals. Poison motes danced. Through the low, flowery brush, I could see beyond the blue winking of water.

"A well-formed world," I murmured. Veden's equator and the plane of the ecliptic are aligned, giving mild climes here on the mesa. Just compensation, I thought, for the perpetual storms that raked the lowlands, where the air grew thick and acrid.

"Your home has The Lapis at its doorstep," Majumbdahr said. "Lekki rises directly across the lake most of the year."

Fleet had found it good policy to house their prime officers in the best residential districts of the Member Worlds. That established their social class and made for easy relations with civilians who ran local matters.

I ordered Majumbdahr to stop the car where we could overlook The Lapis. It was a solemn flat blue. A holy place, I knew, used for ritual bathings. I pointed to something gliding in far across the lake, catching the last ruby glint of Lekkilight. I knew a slight change in gravity opened up new possibilities, but—"A bird?" I inquired, pointing.

Majumbdahr squinted. "Not likely. In the lowlands, perhaps, such huge beasts would live. No, it must be a man with a featherwing."

The house was a faint blur high up the hill, its pale light filtered through slender ferns. Mist gathered. We purred up the driveway and stopped at the base of the ramp. Something fluttered low over our heads, busying the air, and lit in a fern. It warbled a high singsong call. Friends answered down by the lake, a sad note that drifted up through the gathering wetness of night. I breathed deeply, relaxing. So this was to be home.

The house had a look of softspun aluminum, of tile, of blackened enamel. Its roof floated high above visible support. Chunks of warm yellow light reached out to gather the forest around it like a blanket.

We got out of the sedan, and I strolled up the ramp, hands in pockets. More warbling calls. Then something came gliding, silent as a wisp of fog.

A bark. A roar.

Orange flame forked out of the sky.

I turned.

A dark winged form behind the stuttering flame.

Something stung my face. I skittered to the side.

A hail of fractured concrete nipped at my heels, spattering into my eyes.

The orange forking leaped near. I darted left, then right. Majumbdahr shouted something. I dove to the side. The ground split behind me. A flash—

Then nothing.

Silence again, but no bird calls. Moments went by on tiptoe, fingers to their lips. The winged man was gone. An instant later I heard the mutter of his assist engine cutting in. In a few moments he would be klicks away, could go down anywhere in the forest and hide.

My obedient glands shot a brew of adrenalin and sundry hormones through me as Majumbdahr and I prowled the grounds. Nothing moved. The pocked rampway testified to his firepower: twenty-four energy bolts, including the last blistering shot.

"Somebody," I said to Majumbdahr, my muscles singing with the adrenalin, "somebody here doesn't like me."

"Sir, I have no explanation . . ."

"I don't expect you to."

"It is most unusual."

"Maybe somebody's prejudiced against Fleet Commandants these days."

"But Veden is a peaceful community."

I stood, hands on hips, craning my neck at the sky that had so recently spat at me. "Think you can trace that flyer?"

"No. There are many." Majumbdahr sighed, exasperated. "The weapon, perhaps."

He got on the car comm, sent out a bulletin. "Don't let Security send a team out here!" I called out.

"Why not, sir?"

"I'll take care of myself. They can patch up the ramp tomorrow."

"Sir, I think—"

"I repeat, I'll look after my own safety." If a staff gets the idea that their Commandant hides behind a phalanx of guards whenever matters get touchy, he will command their actions but not their respect.

Majumbdahr nodded thoughtfully, mouth tightening.

"Meanwhile, let's go inside. Apparently the house is well insulated; whoever is inside seems to have heard nothing. Don't mention this."

The fog was rolling in over it now, bringing body and flavor to the air. Creatures trilled airsongs again.

The thick door was opened by a small brown man with a touch of gravity in his manner. Patil, the houseboy, I learned, an honored domestic of many years' service. He was quiet and efficient and had us seated within a moment by an open fire (burning wood!), sweating drinks in our hands. He introduced Jamilla, a woman of indeterminate age and smooth skin with a look of playfulness about her: my second-rank domestic, cook, and bedchamber girl. Majumbdahr explained that although Veden was infrequently visited, the normal formalities and liberties common to the Empire were the custom here, too, and I should not have difficulty in adjusting.

We walked onto a stone platform that jutted out

from the house to clip the tops of trees that grew from below. I was still wearing my Spartan coverall that was standard gear with space suits.

"Patil will dress you in the Fleet uniform appropriate to Veden on the morrow," Majumbdahr said. He looked at me curiously, as if trying to understand this strange new Director who demanded the official Summary in his first hour on the planet, showed no interest in meeting other officers his first evening, and ordered that an attempt on his life be officially ignored. Fine; let him.

A small creature, something like a mouse with bat wings and furry topknot, coasted in through layers of fog and landed on my shoulders. I picked him up on a finger and saw his wings were translucent and covered with fine pearly drops of moisture.

"An air squirrel," Majumbdahr said. "Scavengers, if you let them be. They're really too friendly for their own good."

"There seems to be much flying life here." I listened to the beat of wings above us and the faint high cries of pursuit.

"Low gravity. We have not been harmful to most of the forms, so they do not resettle on other parts of Baslin."

"Why couldn't they migrate to the lowlands and leave the plateau to men?"

He smiled. "The same reason we do not live there. With both Lekki and the Black Dwarf nearby, Veden is subject to large tidal forces. The winds and heat of the lowlands are too variable and totally unpredictable. Up here on the plateau we know the prevailing winds—always inward, from the sea. The flying animals do, too. They couldn't survive in two-hundred-kilometer gales any better than we."

He took the air squirrel from my finger, coaxed it with a crumb from his pocket, and threw the bread up into the air. The animal leaped, caught it with a snap, and coasted away on an updraft. I looked at Majumbdahr and decided I liked him. Which was well, for if I followed my plan, he would be one of the few Vedens I would know.

We said our ritual farewells. I finished my inspection of my home, Patil and Jamilla following at a discreet distance and seeming pleased when I approved. I exchanged pleasantries with them, saw that my belongings from the shuttle were stored properly, and had Patil lay out my bedclothes.

A warm bath braced me. Shortly afterward I sprawled on my bed and cracked the seal on my case.

I studied the Situation Report from fleet Headquarters first. This was what I'd been waiting weeks and months to see. As a passenger on the *Sasenbo*, I'd heard rumors and gossip but no reliable hard information about the war, but now as a Director and Commandant, no matter how low, I was entitled to know.

Siganex IV had fallen. The same pattern as on Regeln: a tactical feint by the Quarn, the Plague descending, death and chaos. A 3D starchart showed the new boundaries of the Empire and probable points for the next Quarn attack. It was a shock. The last such display I had seen was shortly after Regeln, and the pitful collapsed ball I saw now was a fraction of the Empire then. Several isolated outposts had fallen in the last few weeks, I noted, and the pinpoints of light which indicated Fleet's dispersal of ships were asymmetric, obviously unable to coherently defend the contracting boundaries.

I thumbed for a closeup on my flatpad display device and the region around Lekki and the Black Dwarf leaped into focus. There were few neighbors. Fourteen lights out the red star Elaren blazed down on a small radio-ferrite extracting mission. Beyond that were a few other temporary expeditions on inhospitable worlds, there for limited economic purposes. The nearest full-status colony, larger even than Veden, was Calning, in orbit around a massive gas giant of a planet that in turn circled a G3 star. None of these had detected Quarn. The nearest contact was seventy-eight lights out, a very recent sighting only seven lights from the massive colony and base at Beta Hydri. The Quarn appeared to be trying to pinch the Empire's sphere into two irregular volumes of human-occupied space. But if past experience was any help, this pattern was as much the product of the Quarn's irregular tactics and seemingly random strikes as anything else.

That was the point: the fact that Veden was buried deep in the remaining Empire volume was no insurance that Quarn would not appear here tomorrow. This was an arbitrary war, not played according to the traditional game psychology of Fleet's computers. As yet no one knew how or even why the Quarn took a planet. Or what could stop them.

So Veden wasn't safe. I would have to oversee the steady rain of transferring ships dropping out of Jump space, looping around the Dwarf and off to some new destination with only a brief burst of news as greetings—oversee it all, keep the Jump ships and ancient ramscoops moving, while watching over my shoulder to see if the Quarn had suddenly winked into existence behind me. And Leibniz had once proposed that this was the best of all possible worlds.

I picked up the Local Situation Report, then tossed it aside. Gharma and Majumbdahr could brief me on that tomorrow. I was hungry for more details about the Quarn, but the terse Fleet dispatch wasn't giving anything away that it didn't have to.

A persistent fact cropped up in the reports: When outmaneuvered, Quarn ships burst into a rosy fusion death pyre. No Quarn had ever been captured. Curious—suicide, rather than contact with men? No, it was more than merely curious.

Next came the Local Personnel file. I checked the names and positions that interested me and the small piezoelectric monitor beamed a request back to the computer sitting under my offices. It squealed as the required information logged into its ferrite memory. I cradled the flatpad on my knees, flexed my back, which was becoming accustomed to significant gravities again, and started to read.

Mahesh Majumbdahr, age forty-seven Earth years, height two meters (same as myself), hair black, eyes black, born Earth (I raised my eyebrows at that) to Mainland parents of low stock; parents emigrated when he was five, settled on Veden. Attended usual series: primary, technical, sensitivity, and arts, showed proficiency in athletics and played *odeynsn* professionally for four years, enjoyed some fame as writer of haiku, joined Fleet at age twenty-five. Security cleared maximum for Lekki system. Married on long-term contract, terminated two years ago with mutual consent.

There was much more relating to his professional career, and I absorbed it automatically. But what I was after was more than the raw facts of the man: I needed to know what bias he had, how well he could work on a closely personal basis. Most of that can only be judged by intuition.

Lapanthul Gharma, age fifty-two Earth years, one ninety centimeters, hair brown, eyes green, descendant of three generations native to Veden, considered high caste (this last a recent entry; perhaps caste was only lately added as relevant data?) and of high standing in local sect (unnamed). Parents both of notable rank; father recently retired from political circles to devote his time to meditation and enlightenment (insert note: rumored he was forced out in power play by agricultural interests). Entered Fleet service at age twenty-one and declared for commission two years later. No known other interest. Same security clearance. Married permanently. (Interesting. Quite rare.)

I went down the list of other staff members, some of them unusual, others dull as dirt. Strange what personnel will think relevant and stick in a man's file. I read several accounts of illicit affairs and resultant difficulties, none of them bearing even slightly on Fleet business or security reliability but quite juicy, then chucked it aside. No time for gossip. (Not much, anyway.)

With surprise I felt a touch of hunger. I sounded a chime over my bed, and Jamilla came in with lowered eyes, took my request for fruit, and padded quietly out.

I leaned back and thought about my two executive officers . . . Gharma seemed more steady, but less fond of the spark of a new idea. Majumbdahr might make a better friend, if that was what I was after.

And maybe I was. I had decided on the *Sasenbo* to save my time on Veden, not become tangled in the thousand loose ends of a military command. There was only one way to do that: find a core of men you can trust and let them make a lot of the decisions. Gharma and Majumbdahr were going to be the core. It had to be more than the usual delegation of authority—every officer knows to release some of his hold or he'll end up ordering his own paper clips—and I would have to play it by ear.

I needed time. Let Fleet agonize; not for me the plugging of holes in a crumbling dike. There was no joy left for me in the warm knit of Sabal. The Quarn had cut those cords.

Veden had never used the Sabal game. It was the spiritual center of the Hindic minority, a small fragment of the Empire brave enough to colonize this planet when it was the most dangerous of all the known worlds. That was before the Flinger was conceived, before anyone knew this system could be so vastly useful. Once the Flinger was begun, Veden still successfully resisted the Mongol culture. Perhaps, all told, this was the best place for me now.

I was a Commander again, but without the spiritual matrix Sabal had given me. Adrift. Maybe there was something on Veden for me. In the guttering ruin of the Empire, Veden might flicker as the only remaining light. Here, at least, I could savor life again, and ponder. Earth had gone stale for me long ago.

The Hindic and the Quarn. Unknowns, all. Veden

was at least human. The Quarn held all the mystery of the unknown.

Jamilla entered with a bowl of cylindrical fruit and a snifter of red liquid. The fruit was tough at first but after a moment's chewing released juices with the flavor of warm almonds. The drink was a clashing—a tang of oranges, with a smooth background like apricot nectar. Somehow they resolved each other and quenched my thirst.

I caught Jamilla studying me with interest. No more than a fraction of the people here were Mongol in descent, and certainly she had seen few Polynesians such as me. I supposed my lighter hair and thin beard (a gene of the Caucasoids, that) were unusual, but . . .

Normal formalities and liberties, Majumbdahr had said. I raised an eyebrow in speculation. It had been a long time.

I finished eating, put the tray aside, and made a formal sign understood throughout the Empire.

Jamilla smiled and unfastened the brass buckle at her side. Her sansari was a wisp of cloth wound into expert folds over her slim body. Watching her gracefully remove it was an entertainment. She came into bed with the good taste not to extinguish the lights as she entered. She was a scent as sweet as the wind.

In the night I rose, heart tripping, the winged man filling mind's eyes and the thought raced: *who was he?* A Fleethater? Religious fanatic? A man hoping that a better universe could come out of the muzzle of a gun? What a sad old idea.

I opened *click* the garden portal and sucked in frosted night breeze. I felt like calling out into the muted darkness. *You wouldn't have killed Fleet, you know. It goes on.*

It goes on. On and on, until disorder eats even the Empire. The Quarn were on the side of entropy, the final winner in all this mad scramble.

Entropy. The amber dimming of all suns, the blunting of all momentum.

And neither you nor I, my enemy, can do anything about that.

3

IN THE MORNING Patil aided me in fitting my Fleet Kochu robes. They shielded the wearer from Lekki's ultraviolet and were robes only by convention, for they retained pants and vest. The only addition was a cowl that rode on the back of my neck and could be slipped over to shade my face.

My contact filters flushed the morning with an orange tinge even though Lekki's violet dot threw shattered dancing light up to me from The Lapis. The water traced a pencil line of horizon across two-thirds of the view. I could see the current ripples as the triple tides of Lekki, the Dwarf, and Pincter, Veden's moon, pulled at the lake. The beach a hundred meters below was a broad white plain worn smooth by the hissing waves.

All this I saw while blinking the contacts into place and walking down the cratered ramp to my staff car. The driver saluted and with a slight piping of steam we went down into the world of men.

I wasted an hour in the unavoidable preliminaries in my new offices: nodding at secretaries, exchanging ritual salutes with second- and third-rank administrators, accepting a traditional welcoming gift of burnished rice and layered spices (take one mouthful, then offer it to the troops). Then to the main conference room, filled with twenty staff workers. Their eyes widened slightly as I ignored convention and sent them all on detailed, eminently defensible tailchasing jobs that would take days or weeks to complete. Correlate fluctuations in rice crop and number of ships passing through the Flinger; compile composite history of all minority economic alternatives used on Veden which had applicability to Empire economy; detail origin of more recent sects (this I could actually use); each division prepare reports, sharpen up training schedule, stipulate defense capability, justify all current supply levels. The orders were a compendium of jargon and catchphrases, but it accomplished the result: keep them busy, get them out of the room. Only Majumbdahr and Gharma remained.

"Now tell me about Veden. What are the people thinking?"

"Not very much thinking is being done," said Majumbdahr slowly. "There's a great deal of reacting, though."

"How do you mean?"

'They're confused. The reports from the colonies further out haven't been precisely encouraging."

"Are you sure this isn't simply what you've been hearing from the population of Kalic alone? On Earth the city populations are breaking down much faster than the rural areas."

"Even on Veden, sir," Gharma broke in, "there

are not substantial numbers living among the
jungles. They are not a significant group."

"Why aren't they spread out?"

"You haven't seen Kalic yet," Majumbdahr said.
"Veden isn't like the other colony worlds—the
Mongol cluster-home isn't popular here."

Gharma gestured with his hands as if a flower
were unfolding. "Our cities are as pods on a
quasimakas plant, spaced to insure adequate sunlight and full growth. The openness of the growth-
lands is always with us. To live otherwise is . . .'
He stopped awkwardly, realizing that he had almost implied a criticism of the Mongol aesthetics,
to which presumably I subscribed.

I gave him a smile. "I quite understand. The
same principles once held even on Earth. Necessi-
ties of population change these things." I turned to
Majumbdahr. "I take it you feel even the citizens
of Kalic and the other outlying cities are not truly
in what the Empire would regard as an urban
environment?"

"Yes, as far as I understand Fleet's analysis."

"I think it is certainly true, sir," Gharma said.
"Veden is much more stable because of it."

Majumbdahr looked at him a little sourly. "I
wonder about that."

I glanced a question.

"Well, sir," he said quickly, bringing his hands
together on the opaque grey of the conference table,
"I don't like the feeling that's running through
Kalic. I wasn't born here, but I think I have a good
grasp of the gestalt. People are seething inside. It
hasn't come out yet, but it will."

Gharma shook his head. "As you may see, sir,
we have talked of this before."

"Natural enough. In the absence of a Director

you were responsible for knowledge of the political side. It's an open secret that Fleet is now relying more on its reports from Directors than the official opinion given by the Embassies."

Gharma blinked rapidly. "Oh no, I'm afraid you do not understand. This is not a political matter at all. We are speaking here of the tranquility and enlightenment of the people."

I nodded, silently pleased. They were both showing a sensitivity that might easily have been drilled out of them by now, in Fleet. I couldn't use men who thought like political hacks, glutted with detail and trivia, afflicted with a hack's smug myopia.

"Of course," Majumbdahr waved the comment away with rough hands too large for the rest of his body. "But sit in the temples, Lapanthul"—side glance to me—"Mr. Gharma. The stirring. Their meditation is not enough."

"Is that true, Lapanthul?" I said.

"I do not *feel* that it is—and that is the final test. But I am not quite as, ah, basic as Mahesh. I do not move in quite the same spheres as he."

Majumbdahr settled back in his formed plastic chair. "What he means is that his sect is very high in caste, and mine lies somewhere in the middle." He grinned. "It gives one a different slant, I'd imagine."

"Caste? I'd thought . . ."

Gharma cleared his throat. "Yes, it does exist on Veden. We all know the Empire has no such thing, but I have heard that we are not alone—other colonies, and not Hindic in origin, have caste, or something like it." He said this with the somewhat stiff and defiant air of a man confessing a minor but habitual vice.

"But *caste*. The term . . ."

"Historically it was an evil thing," Majumbdahr said. "The choice of word is unfortunate. I've always held it should be something like 'station.' With this he glanced up at Gharma. "But the social conventions favored the traditional term. It does not have the same connotation as in Old India."

Gharma smiled brilliantly. "He means to say, *not yet*. Mahesh thinks we're headed that way, nonetheless."

I realized that they were good friends, despite their differences. There was a warmth in their argument, as though it were an old shoe they felt comfortable wearing.

"All right, so there's caste," I said, sighing slightly. There was something about this conversation, a sort of agonizing slowness to converge on the point that may have been just the Hindic way of doing things. I was going to have to get used to a more indirect approach. "It would seem that by traditional sociological principles that would make Vedens more secure, happier with their place. But that's no help. People throughout the Empire were contented, they hadn't lost phase. But I've seen all of them struck down by the Plague. They had no defense."

Gharma looked suddenly sadder. "We know that. I don't understand how it could happen, when—"

"Have you had any cases here yet?"

Both of them looked slightly startled, as though the thought hadn't occurred to them that Veden was vulnerable. "Nothing has been reported—" Gharma started.

"Do you know how to recognize the symptoms? Has Fleet sent through instructional information, case histories?"

"Yes, a little. I have read it myself. It is difficult to believe." Gharma shook his head slowly, as if realizing for the first time that the Plague was real and not just the abstract subject of a series of dispatches.

"Break out all the material you have on the Plague," I said. "Form up classes from personnel not on essential duty. Get space in the civilian press for full coverage: how to spot the symptoms, first signs that you may be getting it yourself, treatment, history, the works. You've delayed on this too long. We've *got* to be prepared." I banged my fist on the table.

Gharma got up and went over to a wall communicator, spoke into it in a whisper, and returned. "Done," he said softly.

How could they have let it go? It was one thing to be bottled up on this outpost, watching the ships flash through the Flinger but seldom having one land—and quite another to forget about defending the planet.

"I take it these measures are of some use against the Plague?" Majumbdahr asked.

"Perhaps, perhaps," I said, distracted. Did they know how much I'd been through? Forget it; no time to worry. "They seem to slow it down, and sometimes keep the people alive. That's all we know, but it's enough."

"I think the people probably know more than you'd think, Lapanthul," Majumbdahr said. "There have been numerous news services' reports, 3D programs. Not much, to be sure"—he glanced at me to show that he knew as well as anyone about Fleet censorship—"but I think they may be prepared for the Plague, when it comes. Giving them the complete facts will make it easier—fear comes from the unknown, not the known. That's why they're in the streets—fear."

"The streets?" I asked.

"Civil disturbances," Gharma said earnestly. "A few, and quickly contained."

"What about?"

"Fleet movements aren't well-kept secrets," Majumbdahr said. "A lot of civilians work in Communications, so they know there isn't a respectable Task Force near this system. If the Quarn come, we'll stand alone, with just a few ships."

Gharma nodded. "I don't think they realize quite that they *are* afraid. The violence is so undirected—"

"Reporting, sir!" It was an official fleet secretary I'd sent on a makework assignment an hour ago. "Fleet vessel *L.S. Caton* has passed formal recognition procedures after emerging from Jump space and requests final orbital check for their Flinger orbit."

A mass of jargon; it meant I had to give my final meaningless approval of an orbit already programmed for the ship. The *L.S. Caton* had been locked into the course several days ago, but the ancient formalities of the Port Master had to be observed.

"Granted." I really didn't give a damn about the empty motions of Fleet business any longer. I wanted to see Veden, to meet the myriad sounds and smells of a new world, where there were still real problems to solve, not sit in this office.

"Mr. Majumbdahr! Do you think you could find a suitable restaurant in Kalic for lunch?"

4

EVERYWHERE THERE WAS COLOR. Magenta fronds, tangled snake vines of a chilled deep green, the impersonal dull tan of the roadway—and all crowned by a clear sky of even blue. The colors reminded me of my contact filters, and I blinked rapidly a few times. They were occasionally uncomfortable.

We crossed the large bustling square in the noonday rush. Clicking of a hundred sandals. Murmur of conversations as knot of friends drifted past. No matter how far humans might fly in their machines, these things held constant.

Cramped shops displayed their wares with abandon, letting robes and bolts of cloth spill in gaudy excess from their boxes. Beads and ancient books shared display cases; fruits and spices competed for the same spot in a window. There was a cheerful easiness about it, and the people were the same: talking, laughing, greeting the price of items with a feigned sharp bark of disbelief.

We cut across the square with Lekki straight overhead, burning a hole in heaven. A few men and women clad in raiments were speaking to the passersby of their mission in life, advising them of the benefits that accrued to anyone of their chosen faith. But not pushing it, not with the intense drive of the cultists I had seen on Earth. There was a relaxed air here. *Fine*, I thought. *But I am beyond that old snake oil now.* Five of the women in a circle chanted,

> I am
> Not great or small
> But only
> Part of All.

We turned into a narrow street, almost an alley, that was the exact opposite of the clean, broad streets I'd seen. Here the even sheet of plastiform street changed into a bumpy track of winding black cobblestone. Some shops huddled together, and others sprawled; all were busy with people buying and selling, bartering in high-pitched tones, inspecting the goods, eyeing the shopkeeper. It was like a page of history. I recognized emblems and signets of Old India, some even dating from before the Riot War.

"This is part of the 'reconstructed' district," Majumbdahr said, "devoted to retaining the atmosphere of the Hindic past. Much of it is honest and true to the original. Those rice bins"—he gestured at an enormous tub with an indecipherable scrawl in red on the side—"contain pure strains a gourmet would have recognized even in Old India. They're kept in controlled environments so the Veden ecology doesn't alter them even slightly."

"All this to retain the old ways?"

"The flavor of the past. These things, these crafts and methods"—he motioned about us—"were part of the Rebirth of the Hindic people after the Riot War. It is well to keep them. They might be useful even again."

I looked at him curiously, wondering if he was thinking of the Quarn.

We passed through streets that seemed to reek of ancient ways and thoughts. I paused occasionally to watch a grinder or a spindrifter at work, saw an elementary syncon computer being used to operate a foundry that produced images of Fanakana, a winged dragon-dog of early (and now dead) mythology, walked among carved erotic statues ten meters high, sniffed the grainy texture of air filled with the sweat of work and the reek of spices.

It was a bit unconventional for Majumbdahr to bring me here. Usually a Fleet under-officer would take his superior to a more formal and military luncheon, to demonstrate his seriousness. But, then, Majumbdahr was an unconventional officer.

I remembered one of the incidents related in his file. Some years ago, in a lesser post, Majumbdahr had dined alone in the Kalic officer's mess. The room was busy and waiters did not notice him, seated in a far corner. He became impatient. But instead of stalking out, Majumbdahr went to a phone booth and called a restaurant that delivered meals. He asked them to bring a spiced dahlma to the officer's mess. When it arrived, he made no great show of eating, but a few officers noticed, and the story spread. The Commandant heard of it and investigated the standards of service in the mess. Soon matters improved. And through it all Majumbdahr had said nothing, never raised his voice in criticism. It was an effective technique.

We reached a small squat restaurant and found our way inside through near-total darkness, sweeping by bead curtains under the guidance of a wrinkled old headwaiter.

"It is very fine," I said after we were seated. "I have seen nothing to equal this district anywhere in the Empire."

Majumbdahr smiled depreciatingly. "Really? But these things are necessary—cultural drifts occur without them. How is it done on Earth?"

"By symbols, mostly," I said, trying to phrase my answer correctly. "We—or, rather, they—focus on the part rather than the whole. Instead of a statue, a stone. A forest becomes a plate of wood. And there is the Sabal Game, of course."

He nodded. "The Game is played here, as well, but only by a few. We do not find it particularly relevant to our needs."

Nor mine, I thought. *What was?*

The waitress brought a steaming plate of rolled breads like pappadums, meat-soaked sauce inside. "What replaces it?" I asked.

"A number of things, perhaps none of them as impressive as the Game. This district, for one. The isolation we have from the rest of the Empire helps, too—few cross-cultural influences manage to get here, and when they do they're sometimes so extraneous as to have no effect. And of course the tradition of the Savant, the Saint, the Guru."

I finished the breads—which had turned out to be a sort of woven rice cake instead—and paused. "This meat? It is—"

"Of course," Majumbdahr shrugged. "Organic products."

"I've heard of colony planets on which—"

"Not here. No lower forms are slaughtered."

I smiled and continued eating a side dish of marinated vegetables placed at my elbow. The alternative to the organic tanks—once it was agreed that animals, being spiritually of the same Order, could not be harmed—was vegetarianism, a singularly difficult and unhealthy path.

"Savants, you said?" I continued. "We had few of those on Earth or the colonies I visited."

"I don't believe the practice is part of the Mongol heritage. In the dead religion of Confucianism it had a place, I'm told, but the Riot War ended that."

"Some hold it died in the First Republic that was formed on the mainland just before the War."

Majumbdahr bit his lip. "Perhaps, but it doesn't matter." He didn't want to get involved in the intricacies of Empire political history, particularly since they might still touch on the present. "The old ways of Zen, when they reached the inlands after the War, fairly well destroyed the appointed station of the Guru. One doesn't need a guide to find what is all around him and yet within himself."

"I would not put it quite that way," I said, laughing gently. I remembered my first instruction, the koan I had wrestled with for seeming ages when I was a boy. It was a classic ambiguity, simple and full of depth for meditation. Its eleventh-century name (Christian reckoning) was the "Three Barriers of Hung-Lun."

Question: Everybody has a place of birth. Where is your place of birth?
Answer: Early this morning I ate white rice gruel. Now I'm hungry again.
Question: How is my hand like the Buddha's hand?

Answer: Playing the lute under the moon.
Question: How is my foot like a donkey's foot?
Answer: When the white heron stands in the snow, it has a different color.

The first answer? It indicates that facts of birth and death are snowflakes in the great wind of time, as trivial as the eternal cycle of hunger and satiety. The second: let loose your constant reasoning, sing to the moon, and be the Buddha. Be *here.* And the third? I do not think I can express it, even now, in words.

That was the first stage, zazen, individual perceptions of the Essential. After that came social awareness, the gestalt, Sabal. But after that, what?

Once I crashed on a frozen world. As a young Fleet officer I'd been delegated to make a short run to a way station there. I blew a wing coming in. I snapped a forearm and quickfroze it, but I couldn't chill down the three crushed ribs. My comm failed high up, so there was no trace on me. I had to walk out. Through ice fields glimmering blue and white, through rock and snow.

There were human renegades there, descendants of criminals who'd washed up in that solar system five hundred years before. They had quaint practices. They thought travelers were stalking horses sent by God, for the virtuous to take out their anger on. First they'd hunt you, then they'd run you for a while in the open, then they'd cut a few tendons and run you some more. It would take you a week or more to die.

I shot three of them but a fourth slashed my side with a bone knife. Five others started running me, letting me get just enough ahead to think maybe I was breaking into the clear. That went on for three days. By that time my rations were gone and my right leg, where a spear had ripped the insulation, was going dead on me.

I worked my way through a narrow pass in the ice. My last personnel charges had timers; I set them and blew quite a few tons of ice into the pass. That gave me time, but by then I couldn't use it. I walked a while. Then I crawled. I passed out.

When I woke up. a product of my delirium was shuffling at my shoulder. It was thirty meters across. Skin like crinkled tar, a huge cone at the top, gnarled legs at the bottom. It put a feeler in my mouth; I couldn't stop it. The feeler turned out to be a tube. Something warm and sticky and maybe sweet came through it. I drank the warm whatever and peered at the cone, which was slowly tilting around toward me, and went to sleep.

When I woke up, it was gone. No tracks in the snow, nothing. I lay there for a day and prepared to die. My lead on the hunters was now a day, maybe two.

In the long night my delirium came again. Perhaps the cone creature visited me, with its shambling, achingly slow walk and sticky brown tube. Perhaps the wind made me hear voices. I went into a place where there was a stilled center. It was a space different from the sureness I knew in the Sabal Game, a territory where I skated, skated over a sheen: the ice that films the universe. I sensed it as Other. The fulcrum of my salvation.

In the morning I woke and walked. I reached a power nexus the next day. A skimmer came for me.

Seven years later on a convoy flight I chanced on a scientific report from that world. They had found a huge lifeform, one that communicated by radio. Its principal sensory organ was an immense radio antenna, evolved for some unimaginable communications. It clearly sensed the stars and some small prey—but what else? Attempts to make contact seemed fruitless.

So the cone creature was not from my delirium. Was the sense of Other also real?

An ancient philosopher once observed that when a man saturates himself with alcohol and sees purple snakes, we laugh. When a man fasts and sees God, we listen. Should I laugh or listen?

We had finished the coriander-laced curry, and the world had taken on a deep, salty tang. I had relaxed in the lazy warmth of the meal, but then Majumbdahr said intently, "You were correct about the preparations, sir."

"How so?" I focused on business again.

"We erred."

"By not briefing staff and important locals, setting plans for Slots, and so on?"

"Yes, that. We had no one of your experience. Here news of Fleet seems so distant."

"My experience?"

"Well, yes."

"What experience?"

"You . . . contracted the illness yourself, sir, I believe?"

"So?"

"Not many recover, it is said."

"So it is said. I wouldn't know."

"Still, sir, it is an unusual accomplishment . . ."

I cracked a wry smile. "My unconscious did all the work."

"We believe in fate here, sir."

"Look," I began, indulging my taste for contradictions, "being superstitious is bad luck in itself. Don't—what's that?"

A low rumbling cry from outside, the sound of many voices.

"It might be some Lancers, sir. They are a new sect. We have been urging local authorities to keep them under control, but—"

Impatient at the growing babble outside, I got up and threaded my way through the topple tables of the restaurant.

Majumbdahr called, "Sir, that man will—" At which point he did. He turned to hurry away from the entrance and slammed into me, almost knocking me over. The man blundered on without a glance.

I went to the entrance. The crowd was backed up flush with the old worn shops, facing toward the narrow street, packed in tightly. I couldn't see a thing. Some faces were tense, others unconcerned. Obviously the running man had sensed something he feared. The chanting came nearer. It was almost covered by the babble of conversation from the pedestrians, obviously expecting a show.

Majumbdahr materialized beside me. "Help me break through," I yelled.

Together we pushed against the wall of backs keeping us from the street, shoving together until something gave. I jostled forward through the bodies, ignoring scowls and snarls. In a moment I was near the front.

The Lancers had just gotten to this point and were streaming by, shouting something about Veden and rights, waving tapestries on bamboo poles, stamping and hooting and jamming the onlookers back from the center of the path. The crowd didn't seem to be worried or afraid; they treated it as a lark, an entertainment. It seemed to me a lot of noise for nothing—it was impossible to tell what they were shouting about.

Then I heard a slight scream from further back in the Lancer column. A sharp cry of pain, a bark of outrage. Then another. People around me stirred. The barrage of sound from the Lancers increased in volumes, but now I could hear the screams clearly over the chant.

Majumbdahr caught my eye and gestured toward the cries, which seemed to be getting closer. I nodded, asked a question with my eyebrows. He shrugged. Evidently this latest touch was new to him, too.

And to the crowd as well. They pushed back toward the shops, trying to get away from the center of the street. In a moment I stood alone. Men and women struggled, pressing into the already crowded shops.

The Lancers came on. The chant faded. Standing there, even in my coverall uniform and cowl, I felt exposed as I waited for whatever was coming around the next corner. But an officer does not run.

The end of the Lancer column broke around the corner of a shop further down the alley. Young men in loincloths, perhaps a dozen, carrying short, stubby clubs. They lashed out at the crowd cowering in doorways.

Majumbdahr stood at my right. One of them laughed, struck a man in the side, hurled an oath at him, and passed on. The Lancers in column were smiling, too. A lark. A holiday afternoon, for them.

They saw us. Three broke out of file and converged on us, rocking the clubs loosely in their hands, casual.

I went back into rest position, left forearm out, right leg cocked back and keeping balance over my body center. Right arm tucked into side. Training school memories. Watch their faces, focus forward, eyes front but seeing everything to the sides.

The first one swung a club down with his right. I blocked with my forearm, dropping further back. He went slightly off balance. I raised my right knee, shot out a chopping foreleg kick. It caught him in the stomach. I dropped back to balance.

The kick wasn't strong enough. *Getting old.* He came forward again, this time favoring his right side where the kick had landed. Side chop with the club, very fast. I stepped back again, watching him move. The man had a sour, panicky smell. No opening worth the chance.

The third man stood aside, watching.

Majumbdahr was moving in the corner of my eye, trying to wrestle his man to the ground. Mine came at me again. This time he rushed matters a bit. His right foot came down too early for the overhead blow he'd planned.

I stepped forward, chopped his arm. I shot my left elbow into his face as he stumbled past me. He smacked hard on the obsidian cobblestones. He shook his head, too dazed to get up.

The third man cursed us and ran, hooting wildly. Majumbdahr had his pinned to the ground. I felt a little silly, a senior officer fighting in the streets. Were the civilians eyeing me curiously?

"Send for the police!" I shouted at one of them. Then I noticed the crumpled form farther down the street.

It was a girl, unconscious. Her black hair fanned out in a crescent around her head, and there was an ugly red patch on her scalp. I cradled her head to see if there were any other wounds. Someone came over and volunteered that the Lancers hadn't struck her; she must have fallen in the rush.

Police whined over in a helicopter and dropped into the street on ladders; evidently ground transport through the reconstructed district was too slow. I held the girl's head and ignored the two Lancers who were led away. She was injured in a stupid, pointless demonstration—if that was the right name—and I felt responsible. If I'd pressed Gharma about civil disturbances, I might've been working on the problem instead of sightseeing in town. And this was just the sort of thing that reeked, disquietingly, of the Quarn.

It had the feel of strangeness, of people going off their precarious balance. The Hindic peoples were always pacifists. We even had trouble recruiting Fleet base personnel on Veden. A group like the Lancers was totally at variance with the traditions here. Yet they *were* here, and the crowds had smiled, perhaps even identified with them. Why? Did the Lancers express something they all wanted to say, but couldn't?

Someone was tapping me on the shoulder. I looked up into Majumbdahr's face and at once realized that I didn't want to let her go.

"Medical is here, sir," he said. "They'll be wanting . . ."

"Tell them . . . tell them to treat her and deliver her to my personal home," I said without thinking. "I want to talk to her." I looked down and saw her for the first time. Black hair, delicate features, She smiled weakly at me.

I watched the ambulance pull away with her and recognized dimly that I was slowly coming out of the slight autohypnosis I'd given myself just before the fight. Training was reasserting itself. Majumbdahr finished talking to the head of the police squad and glanced at me.

"Come," I called waving. "Let's lift."

5

MOMENTUM IS AS momentum does. Thus, Fleet schedules wait for no man, even a puffing Commandant years beyond his martial arts drills. The *L. S. Caton* was passing through the Flinger. I wanted to watch, to sense the flex and flow of my command.

Local police reported to me on the copter journey back: some Lancers detained, but they had no plausible explanation of why their ritual display eroded into brutality. I sent a priority demand for a summary of all such past incidents.

Veden Fleet Control wasn't all that impressive. Most of the Flinger's detection grid was in close orbit around Lekki-Jagen, where things get gaudy. Computers are the same faceless ferrite walls everywhere in the Empire. The large cavern of display screens, verbal input/outputs, primary and backup consoles, low-glare phosphors glowing a sullen red, clacking of tracer prints, mutter of conversations escaping from muffling mikes—the cavern was forgettable. Except for the display screen.

On the screen Lekki blazed eternal, whipped by Jagen's knotted fist of gravity. I watched a tiny glint of light that was the *L.S. Caton* creep across Lekki's blue snarling face, boosting faster than light. It arced around Jagen's black dot in a deformed parabola and raced away, a graceful and intricate dance of the spheres. Destination: Abbe IV, a fertile planet circling a G4 star over a hundred parsecs away.

The stars are fixed and eternal only for times slightly longer than a man's life. In reality those diamond-bright flecks are roaring through the galaxy, a mad swarm of bees. The galaxy itself has spun around twenty times since its birth, scrambling stars like seeds before the wind. Between Abbe IV and Earth—the *L.S. Caton*'s home port— was a 154.6 km/sec velocity difference. It wasn't enough to wink into Jump space and out again— somebody had to fork up the difference in kinetic energies (relative to galactic center) between the two. That means fuel and time. Far cheaper, then, for the *L. S. Caton* to detour quickly through Jump space to Lekki-Jagen, undergo an elastic collision with the neutron star's field, picking up energy— and then Jump to Abbe IV. Spectacular and cheap— a twinning devoutly to be wished.

Aboard the *L.S. Caton*, of course, it was a nudge in the night. They had only minimal sensors outside their magnetic envelope, just enough to pick up navigation data from us—again, because it's cheap that way. Though the *L.S. Caton* was a mass of tachyons, the gravitational deformations of Jagen swung it around precisely like ordinary matter— gravity plays no favorites. There are, some say, stars and planets in Jump space; but no one has ever lingered near them. Some of the deeper physical laws seem asymmetric; tachyon galaxies may well be deadly to us.

Gharma, efficient and proper, showed me the Fleet procedures; I made notes for study later. "You know what we are, Mr. Gharma?" I said after an hour or two of detail work. "Brokers."

"Sir?"

"Look, stow that 'sir,' Lapanthul, leastwise when we're alone."

"Ah, how do you mean, 'brokers'?"

"We're in-between men. Take an item from Mr. A, exact our percentage, and give it to Mr. B."

Gharma smiled. "This seems inglorious?"

I shrugged. "I don't care." And was surprised to find that, in truth, I didn't. Running Veden Control was grub work in the eyes of the likes of Tonji, but so what?

The scoop ships, gulping down interstellar hydrogen with a giant magnetic throat and spewing it out the end for propulsion, were the long-term backbone of the Empire, little publicized.

A planet that sent out, say, a rare alloy plentiful only in their system, couldn't program the ramscoop ship for a definite destination, because by the time the ship spanned a hundred parsecs at sublight speeds, its target world might have changed economic structure entirely. The time lag was too great.

So the volume of space around Lekki-Jagen served as a storage area, a cosmic clearing house of the Empire. Moving large masses through Jump space was beyond the resources of a new colony planet. But ramscoops were cheap and easy to build. When the colony got a product it thought might sell— and so bring in currency and bartered goods in return—it packed a shipment into a ramscoop and programmed the onboard computer for Lekki-Jagen. When the ramscoop arrived a half-century later, it was cataloged and directed into a waiting orbit.

There it sat. If no other colony bid for it, the ramscoop orbited silently forever, costing its owners periodic docking fees to pay for Veden's Fleet Control. Usually it sold rather soon. Then it was reprogrammed for the buyer's system, dropped through the Flinger, and shot out into deep space at a respectable velocity. The Flinger could cut fifty percent off the transit time of a fifty parsec journey, because without it the scoops required long, weary, expensive years to pick up their initial velocity. The Flinger cut down the transport time for interstellar commerce, making possible the economic Empire.

Thus I was—quite literally—master of a million ships. They were all ramscoops forming a great pancake of orbits in the plane of the ecliptic. Virtually every day we received bids for certain ships— lately, I noted, ones packed with a craftsman's lifework in microelectronics—and, if it met the demand of the seller, I ordered it dropped through the Flinger. The key point was that a ramscoop expended great energy if it had to reach one percent of c, but the ride was easy after that. Above this critical velocity, enough hydrogen isotopes crammed into its maw to feed the fusion fires in its belly; it then quickly boosted to $0.8\ c$ or higher. The Flinger slung scoops out at around $0.02\ c$, and saved the Empire a fortune on each launch.

"How long is this going to last, Lapanthul?"

"Pardon, Director?" (Since I'd ruled out 'sir,' he'd found a substitute.)

"Jagen is spiraling into Lekki."

"Yes."

"When do they touch?"

"Several thousand more years, at least."

"It seems odd that we—the human race—would come along at precisely the right moment to make use of this resource."

Gharma laid his head onto a shoulder, the Veden gesture of acceptance. "Director, 'Each fresh day is a special case.' A saying from our rituals."

"Um."

"Man is a fortunate being."

"Uh huh."

When I reached home that evening, the orange luster of dusk was settling across the water. Flittering sounds of things in flight echoed from the lake. Spindly ferns clothed my home in brooding quiet. I remembered the assassin, then dismissed the thought. As I walked up the front ramp, I noticed a mark on the glass wall of the den, and beneath it a white bird lay sprawled in death on the patio. It was larger than a dove and had delicate striations of blue and pink over its neck. Evidently it had failed to see the glass and had flown straight into it, breaking its back.

Patil admitted me and announced that dinner would be ready shortly. He mentioned the girl, and I asked for her.

She came into the den padding softly on the thick rug. She was tall, a trifle thin, and wore a sansari of rough, durable green weave that set off her black hair.

"I thought I would ask you a few questions about the incident this afternoon," I said, my voice curiously stiff. She nodded. "Your name?"

"Rhandra Minadras of the family Talin."

"Why were you in the street? Were you shopping?"

"No, I was searching employment. I was reared in the country, in agricultural arts. But recently I decided to come to Kalic and attempt something new. I thought the traditional shops would want unskilled labor." She spoke quickly but not with a sharp tone, and looked down at her feet occasionally.

"You know the Lancers?"

She hesitated, shy. Then she looked up at me and, seeing that I was not intent on grilling her—as, doubtless, the police had; I should've thought of that—some of the spirit that twinkled behind her dark restless eyes came forth.

"I've heard of them, met a few. They say their 'demonstrations' are just sport, but I think not!"

"Why?"

"They're afraid. Afraid of the Quarn and what might happen if they reach Veden."

"Strange, for the young to fear so much."

"Oh no," Rhandra said, looking up in surprise, unselfconscious now, eyes widened, "they are the least in Phase. They have not yet come to compromise with the strains of adolescence or cultivated the old ways. I wouldn't expect them to be as secure as an older man."

"Perhaps," I said, uncomfortably aware that I was an older man and felt blessed little inner peace of late. "There was never anything like them before, was there?"

She shook her head, liquid hair rippling. "Not that I've heard. But I'm new to Kalic."

Patil entered and announced dinner. I stood and felt a sudden twinge of soreness in my back, a reminder of the scuffle. "New? You have no lodging, then? Stay in my guest room until you find something suitable."

She made the usual gestures of refusal, but eventually accepted. It was clear she had few plans. My reasons for making the offer were equally vague; I was attracted to her by some elusive chemistry not merely sexual.

Rhandra excused herself for a moment to change into more formal dress. She appeared a moment later in something clinging and walked over to the glass wall overlooking the patio. She stood looking at the mist drift in from the lake.

Suddenly a large bird dropped down from the ferns on wide, powerful wings and glided by parallel to the house, peering in at us with electric yellow eyes. She jumped back, startled, and thumped against a wooden column. She gasped and abruptly began crying uncontrollably. I hesitated, awkward. Then I held her, comforted her. The sound she made, butting into the massive unyielding wood, had hit an odd resonance within me. It reminded me of a bird smashing into a glass wall.

6

IT DID NOT happen that evening, or the one thereafter, but there was a glacial momentum to the event that gradually made the expectation of it fill the air between us, like a thin fog through which we spoke. Once we recognized it, there was an odd tingling moment when we mutually agreed to burn away the mist and then it was done, we could say the things we'd both been thinking and our false uniforms—mine particularly bulky—fell away. It was amazing, a revelation, to act without thinking, to find that my old body, with its calluses, wrinkles, bony knobs, and suet softenings, aging now—the first signs were obvious—could be fun again. In this there lay a betrayal of the spirit I felt the last nights on Earth, a dismissal of the smooth and solemn couplings Angela and I shared. There is a moment in each life, I suppose, when you have passed your catechism and are free at last to believe or disbelieve—it is only parents or society or God knows who else who Make The Rules—and discover life once more fresh, on your own. So I did. She made my body like a bauble again, a toy, a joy. No one had done that for me since Angela, a very long time ago. Nobody. Perhaps this is merely a confession that there are few great loves in a life (virtually all of us can make that confession, sad to say). Or perhaps it was the way Rhandra would look at me. (Kneeling on my bed in a moist tangle of sheets, arms at her side in the wash of yellow morning light, hands stretching as she awakened.) It was a look that opened up some new perspective for me, a fresh continent hanging in the air. It was the first time these doors had opened for her. (I know, there must've been a farmboy somewhere, and—upon asking her—it turned out there was. Or rather, several. But the difference was one of kind.) She and I explored these lands together, using the traditional tools—a lusty, seemingly accidental liking for the same things, plus workable instincts and the familiar gummy organs, full of their own self-wisdom. It filled me, drained nothing. No life-swallowing obsession, this: I worked, Rhandra found weaving and other crafts she'd always wanted to try, and life went on. A Commandant is allowed some latitude, socially (thus Jamilla, that first night). I used it. So in those first weeks I reworked myself under our mutual alchemy, making a sagging bag of bones and brain and guts into a new instrument.

7

FLEET IS A political organism. It needs support among all client worlds. A traditional function of my position was to solidify such support.

"You may be especially interested in this, sir," Gharma said blandly one morning, laying an engraved card on my bare desk. "It is an invitation from the First Bridge Society."

"First Bridge? Odd name."

"A very exclusive private club, Commandant. The original ramscoop that colonized Veden had a strict discipline system. Highest-ranking officers were from the first level of the flight control bridge. The navigators. The club carries now the same connotation." He lowered his eyes. "The previous Commandant was a member."

Ah. This was the first tentative feeler for the sort of social acquaintances a Director and Commandant was expected to make among the natives.

"Decline it," I said, and cut off his startled reply. "I'm not interested."

"Sir, it is virtually a tradition."

"Here's where it stops being one."

Majumbdahr, standing nearby, permitted himself a hint of a smile. And later implied, with a side comment, that the First Bridge types were dreadful bores.

But I did attend a few handshaking fests, in part because Rhandra was a more outgoing creature than I and wanted to see the mysterious struttings of Kalic society. She even persuaded me to spend half a day at the Temple of the Madi, one of the more revered centers.

The Madi turned out to be a heavy woman, her lips a glaring red gash among swelling hills of cheek caked with lemony powder. Her first salutation, "Director Sanjen, this is quite unexpected"— ignored the simple fact that, were I unexpected, she wouldn't be there in ample robes to greet me. Their temple was imposing, a large dome like a sprouting bulb frozen as it popped from the ground. We entered beneath a sloping parabola of grained obsidian, which in turn served as fulcrum for an arc that spanned the lofty pink.

After much talk of Kundalini, the vital serpent, the Madi took us on a tour of the schools. There were earnest lectures on conservation of the vital fluids; attempts to revive the lost Old India art of levitation; men who could pop steel bands wrapped around their chests; men who, it was advertised, could through willpower and proper body control raise the temperature of a room five degrees—or lower it; people who spoke to hallucinations; men who lived, though buried alive for hours; women who whispered to tumbling copper bals and beads and made them leap and dance; a first-order Yogi who could stop his heart for two minutes; walkers on water. Some feats were startling, others looked like sly amateur magic. The more fantastic were not as advertised—the water walker was getting better at it and had performed for small select groups of believers before, but, uh, found his spiritual essence hampered by the presence of doubters.

More to pass the time than anything else, I asked the Madi, "You believe Yoga can counter loss of phase?"

"Perhaps, in time." She waved a silken handkerchief at the gnarled man, who was now beginning the ritual again. "But that is surely not the point. These things must be *realized* with the heart and spirit, not merely with the mind. It may take you a while to come to such knowledge." She made a pause. "Certainly, Director, we shall be prepared to help you."

"Ah. Quite."

"The Benagathaman is more than you might *assume,*" she said, smiling, "coming as you do from the . . . Mongols. "We are an ageless movement. The original faith of the ancient Asia. Not the deformed faith you have known, Director. The *dif*ficulties I hear you and your comrades are finding with those aliens, the, the—"

"Quarn."

"Yes, Quarn. I think it is simply a matter of the wrong spiritual avenue."

"Um. Perhaps."

Rhandra and I lifted off into a brimming violent Lekki sunset, skipping the evening feast at the Temple and sundry other consolations of public religion.

"You told me this would be a look at the faiths of Veden," I said to her in an accusing tone.

"Uh . . . yes."

"It was terrible."

"Right," she said with a shrug of her shoulders, her wry smile apologizing for her countrymen.

The sects in the dome were fairly recent off-shoots of the traditional Hindic religious line. Their absorption in the cheap tricks of Yogi, in the pseudo-rationalization by which the beautiful parable of Kundalini's passage had been debased into exercises of the stomach muscles, and all the rest—it was a falling back into the dark past, reliance on graven images and Gods, an abandonment of the peace and serenity of the Hindic society.

They didn't know it, but these cults and the Lancers were symptoms. Hindic Veden was decaying.

Because of the Quarn? Possibly. When the disease is unknown, any symptom may be important.

But perhaps Veden was simply going bad at the core, like the Empire itself.

Fleet Control had an efficient rumor-mongering service, and its results were duly logged into remote readout storage for use by the Director. Most of the information was worthless. But some reports spoke of a rise in crimes of violence that were hushed up by the close-knit Hindic family structure; the sudden influx of mentally disturbed cases in medical centers; a pattern of breakdown in the rural areas that caused the young to move into the cities.

I peered out the plastiform bubble over our skimmer and watched lights wink on, bright sentinels against the reddening dusk. In the west of Kalic, the inexpensive homes, families were performing their ritual chants for solidarity before the serving of the evening meal. Properly rendered, it brought contentment and security without the dullness of orthodoxy or the weight of dogma.

Part IV

1

So THE DAYS tumbled down. The worst times were the mornings, when I would rise with a dizzy reeling in my head. Nothing seemed to cure it. Inserting my shielding contacts filmed Veden in shimmering light and invariably lifted my spirits, but often only Rhandra's massaging of my neck muscles would steal the tension from me. When first I arose I sensed a humming in the room, and several times dumbly pawed about the draperies, seeking its source, until logic penetrated and I realized it came from inside my head.

Rhandra would follow my wanderings, dimples riding on the crest of her smile, and coax the first bit of breakfast lycheé or somosha into me. She had a ritual joke: only the devotees of a small sect, the Falaquin, still practiced the ancient imponderable rite of ingesting natural alcohols, of the sort used before mankind knew how to remove the hangover-inducing effect—was I attempting to enter the Falaquin Orders? And I would smile and shake my head and mutter that no, I'd been sipping no ancient mystifiers on the side, this was probably some adjustment to Veden that needed to run its course. Biospheres are never alike; Veden was not Earth. Centuries of terraforming had still left many differences, from a pink pollen that made my ears itch to a hypnotic fernweed that I had to avoid.

One particular day when my morning revival waxed long, Rhandra tugged me out of my routine and down to a sprawling arm of Old Kalic. It had been the navel of the continent, Baslin, in the first century of terraforming and colonization. It reeked of ancient ways, a Babylon, Sumer, and Nineveh crouched along a mudstreaked river. Even at early hours the streets were a jumble of rickshaws, herds of panting water buffalo, camels straining under huge bundles, cows meandering. A gang of cortically augmented elephants shuffled in the dust, doing road work without human supervision. Along the river Brahmins and Sadhus and Hindics on pilgrimage were bathing, wringing water from their oiled hair, praying rhythmically, brushing their teeth, doing yoga exercises. Votaries danced, clacking. Temples lined the narrow twisting streets that smoked with dust.

Rhandra and I took a creaky, shallow-bottomed boat along the river, hired from a brown man who scowled at us and flashed, when he thought we didn't see, angry white teeth. We glided silently. Corpses were being washed and put into the cremation flames, licking thick plumes of smoke rising from the pyres. Dogs and ravens poked at the charred remains.

Effective visions, yes. Yet I knew teams plucked the bodies from the river downstream, cleaned the burning grounds, sprayed the area nightly. The animals were treated, freed of disease. All this, to blend the ancient with the present. There were sound sociometric calculations for each nuance.

I pointed to clotted crowds on the far shore. "Big group."

"A savant," Rhandra murmured.

"Let's go."

She frowned, studying the center of the crowd. "I think not . . ."

"Why? I'm interested." I threw the tiller over and we swerved sidewise in the current.

"No. Really, don't."

"I'll only be a moment."

We ran aground. I stepped off into the brown water. Pulled the boat up. Squished ashore.

"Ling, come back."

"Nonsense. Majumbdahr is always urging me to see more of—" I said, turning, and was staring into the face of a big meaty man, centimeters away.

"I have come to learn," I said.

"You are not allowed."

"Come, fellow." I started to walk around him. He blocked my way.

A Commandant should always have respect for the ways of the world he defends. Still, something in this man's manner irritated me. There was something here I sought.

"I came only to see," I said mildly.

He didn't bother to reply. He simply shoved me.

"Now . . ." I held up a hand. He pushed me again. I began to get angry. But he was a big man, and he seemed fanatically intent, his eyes flinty black darting insects.

I backed away. By all rights I could walk anywhere on Veden, as Fleet Commandant. But while training teaches you the rules, experience teaches the exceptions. I took Rhandra by the arm and waded back to the boat.

The man stood stolidly at the shoreline, watching us pole out of sight. His riveting attention pricked at my intuition; I tried to see who was discoursing at the center of the crowd. The distance was too far.

I could make out a murmuring voice, but no more.

2

IMAGINE A RIVER: flecked with foam, swirling and rushing, collector of oddments of debris, bits of dirt, crumbs of civilization.

The Empire is thus. The random currents deposited their burden on Veden and departed, in each instant changing.

The Jump ships, however much glamor is theirs, were only a fraction of the traffic that passed through the Flinger.

Most of the Jump ships were engines of war. Merchants used the more modest ramscoops, since they aren't supported by taxes from hundreds of worlds.

Fleet Control dropped them through the Flinger at an average rate of one a day. As well, one incoming scoop per day had to be laser-guided through the last stages of deceleration and coaxed into a stable ellipse.

That represents a numbing flux of information. I

had to oversee a lot of it, make decisions about anything out of the ordinary.

Although the scoops and Jump ships slingshoted regularly through the Flinger, very few of them ever sent anything down to Veden. There was no reason. Veden had few rare raw materials, no advanced technology, few cultural objects of interest to the predominantly Mongol Empire. We usually got a squirt of news or correspondence on high-frequency laser, and that was it. Usually.

"What's this?" I asked Gharma one day. "The *Chennung*, Jump Class IV, is dropping a one-man flyer."

"A moment," he said, thumbing a readout. "Yes. A replacement for the astronomical observatory."

"Observatory? Where?"

"On the other side of Veden."

"There're only a few islands there."

"Correct," Gharma murmured pedantically. "They have fewer signal/noise ratio troubles if they are shielded from us here."

"Ah." I approved it and tapped it through to store-and-forward. "What're they watching? Optical work?"

"No. Gravitational radiation."

"Uh? Why?"

"Lekki-Jagen."

Radio waves are generated by electrons jiggling back and forth in a wire. Two masses, waltzing about each other, make gravitational waves, at the frequency of their revolution.

"The signal from Lekki-Jagen is big enough to measure?" I said wonderingly. "Incredible."

"Gravitational radiation is an important energy loss. Eventually they will spiral into each other because of it." Gharma blinked at me owlishly.

"How old was the astronomer who recently retired?"

Gharma checked his readout. "The man died at age one hundred and twenty-four."

"Impressive. I'd heard you live longer here, because of the lighter gravity."

"There are other causes for our good health," Gharma murmured with a slight smile.

I chuckled. "What you really mean is that the helter-skelter of the Empire doesn't penetrate here, eh? And you're right. The social pressure cooker on Earth probably cuts a decade or two from our lifespan. Maybe that accounts also for the higher spiritual state you Vedens have achieved."

Gharma's smile changed a fraction as he saw that my words carried a touch of mocking. "That should be better judged by an outsider," he said judiciously.

"Mere cliché sociology, I'm afraid. On Earth our introduction to the Sabal Game comes only after age twenty-five. Below that age physiology makes meditation and group perception difficult."

"So that longevity assures enlightenment?" he asked somewhat stiffly. "But so many decades of playing a . . . game . . . does not boredom set in?"

"No. No." Sudden sense of loss. I glanced at Gharma. "I don't believe it was boredom that drove me out."

Gharma muttered something, perhaps embarrassed that he had triggered a sadness within me.

"I wonder—is Veden so different? Are there different paths open to me here? I—" I broke it off, voice suddenly thick, and waved Gharma away. I thought for a while, my mind a muddle, and then pulled myself back into the workaday world around me.

I leaned back and regarded the display screens. Again the idea swam up to consciousness—why had we come along at this special time? This singular moment when Lekki-Jagen made an efficient Flinger, but before gravitational radiation bled them of energy and the two smashed together.

There is a rule in astronomy, the Principle of Mediocrity. It says that our position in both space and time is more likely to be average than special—partly because, unless there is evidence to the contrary, more intelligent races will be born in average, mild conditions. There's an escape hatch, of course: the fact that we're here when the universe is about eighteen billion years old is caused by the time necessary to evolve intelligent life—roughly, ten or twenty billion years, and what's a billion between friends? Still, the Principle made me stop and wonder. The Flinger was almost too good to be true, a gold mine for the Empire. What were the chances that we'd blunder onto it and find a planet we could terraform nearby? Or were we like summer hikers in the forest, coming upon a feast picnic lunch all laid out, glasses brimming with sweet lemonade, but no picnickers?

I shrugged. Things happen, that's all.

One morning, amid the buzzing in my head, I found faint memories of a dream. Of Angela, of the children, of the Slots. Were they there now? In the dream I walked down slimy halls with yellow gobbets streaking the walls. People were stacked like so many lumps of organic goo, to be tended and noted and, when they died, disposed of.

When I found them there were three holes together, each barely large enough to crawl in and crouch. I ran away.

*   *   *

It isn't sleep that knits the raveled sleeve of care.
It's work.

I set up regular training classes for the troops in
riot control and internal security. The men responded well, glad to be acting again, but trou-
bled (I suspected) at this first evidence of concern
among Fleet Control.

Jagen, the Black Dwarf, spun in tune. Veden was
subject to a biennial coincidence between Lekki-
Jagen, and its moon; an enormous tide rose and
smashed itself against the lowlands. Winds roared
and Fleet Control buttoned up for three days. We
evacuated a few thousand persons from the mountain peaks in the east of Baslin, where the gusts
battered at 300 klicks per hour.

Over the next few months I received more reports of theft and beatings in the cities. Majumbdahr managed to penetrate some of the natural
Hindic reserve in local officialdom against reporting such incidents, and thereafter we got a reasonably accurate picture of what was happening. The
curve for small, random, purposeless crime had a
steep positive slope.

The rumor-mongering facility picked up more
whispers about Quarn spies, planned Quarn land-
ings, suspected neighbors, sightings of strange ships
in the skies.

Domestic issues came and went. Majumbdahr
and Gharma handled them. I kept myself isolated,
romped with Rhandra, seldom attended official
functions. The Madi called, sent invitations, im-
plored me to visit the Temple of Shiva again, to
follow the lessons they offered, to come to ban-
quets and receptions. I was invited to join social

clubs, attend concerts, clasp the moist palms of a hundred strangers.

"If you don't want to go, ignore them," Rhandra said innocently, batting aside five centuries of Fleet tradition.

So I did.

Instead, we walked the streets of Kalic. I joshed with Krishna priests in yellow dhotis and shaved heads, able to see it all as social cement now, free at last of what the Game had meant to me.

We flew through valleys crystalline with the sparkle of fresh rain, swooped over the leafy roof of jungle. We peered over the raw rock margin at the lowlands. They shimmered as though in mire, three kilometers down from the great mesa of Baslin. There were legendary beasts there, giants who sucked in the thick air and broke men like eggs.

In the jungle we surprised something and, rather than retreat, followed the sounds of its thrashing. It was a scorpion, two meters long with a curled stinger like a deer horn. It could run as fast as a horse. I shot to the side of it three times and then had to put a bolt into the scampering legs. Rhandra took a long time getting to sleep that evening.

And always at my back, like a murmur in the distance you can't resolve into coherent words, were the Quarn.

They were deft. When Fleet computers war-gamed a probable assault on a given star, dozen of ships would mass and wait. The Quarn hit elsewhere.

The solution seemed obvious: the vast computer minds were operating on false premises. They thought in terms of feints and shifts, subtle balances of power and advantage. They assigned points to men and ships, solved endless integral equations to assess the economic implications of a given loss.

Clearly, the Quarn did not think that way, The sickness spread along the most-traveled jump lanes, but it also struck isolated worlds. Could a few Quarn infiltrate such planets and have a determining effect?

They were near now. Four months after the sortie against Calning the same scenario I had seen on Regeln went through its grinding logic again. Communication winked out.

By now Fleet sent no expeditions to rescue survivors. They had learned enough, I suppose. Over the next few months two more colonies fell in much the same manner.

Fleet subspace transmissions mentioned them a few times, at first with alarm and then subtly skirting the issue. Then they were gone. We were advised not to speak of these planets again.

In Fleet engagements two of our Jump ships were lost to unknown causes. They simply vanished, ceased transmission.

Four Quarn ships were observed to self-destruct to avoid capture.

After all this time we still knew next to nothing about the Quarn. Analysis showed that they had a tolerance to acceleration about the same as men— assuming the ships were not automatic. They reacted occasionally to laser signals tuned to infrared frequencies. Their ships bore no distinguishable markings.

Somehow this gradually diffused into the Veden population. The informant network picked it up as rumors, then as commonly accepted knowledge.

There were a few incidents of arson and ridicule of police. Political parties that had been dormant formed again. Vegetarian cults, merchants' parties, groups in favor of breaking free of the Empire; they gained members and published newsfax.

The prominent parties demanded to know what defenses had been readied for use against the Quarn. When I first heard this, I laughed—did they think anything would stop the Quarn?

But gestures were necessary. I sent more sensors out on long orbit to the edge of the Lekki-Jagen solar system. The few thermonuclear warheads I had were readied and encased in shells with high-power ionic boosters. I saturated the volume of space around Veden with close-orbiting scoopships waiting to be purchased; they would provide a good screen for orbiting missiles.

Still, I could hope to stop only a few Quarn ships.

The Regeln pattern, though, called for no formal invasion at all. The colonists on Regeln had been disarmed by the Plague. Their defenses had done them no good at all.

I brooded. Things went on as before, I buried myself in routine. Was it deceptive? The chants of the priests sang in my mind, lulled me.

Two months later the first Plague case was diagnosed on Veden. It was a man in Kalic of weak religious background and few family ties. He did not respond to treatment.

The Plague began to spread.

3

RHANDRA, AT MY FEET—with the sweet, silent rhetoric of her deep eyes—and Majumbdahr; both regarded me quizzically.

"Ling, what you're saying is, well, interesting . . . ," she began, "but I don't see the point."

"Why?"

"Societies like this, ours—" with an arm she swept in all Veden outside our living room— "this is the way they *are*."

"And always have been?" I prompted.

"Yes," she said. "That's why we have such links to the past."

"Even though we're parsecs removed from Old India."

"I agree with her, Commandant."

"Call me Ling; this isn't working hours. But Rhandra, how do you think we got here?"

"Ramscoops," she said confidently.

"Innovation. Generally, human societies aren't responsive to new ideas. They're hierarchical and ritualistic—like Veden. But every so often the neocortex takes over and rides the horse of, well, progress."

"Progress is an illusion," Majumbdahr said quietly.

"Spiritually, maybe so," I said impatiently. "But there *are* things we know. That the oldest part of our forebrains have elements in common with the reptiles. That above the reptile portion lies a limbic system, where our emotions are primarily lodged. And spreading over all that like a capstone is the neocortex. Three brains at war in one skull."

"Why in conflict?" Rhandra murmured. She curled delicate feet under her, into the soft piles of the rug.

"Evolution proceeds by addition," Majumbdahr said to her, somewhat diffidently, I thought—because she was the Commandant's woman? Ritualistic and hierarchical, we are, yes. "Each major step in brain evolution was superimposed on the older brain, which probably didn't like the idea."

"I still don't understand what that has to do with right-and left-handedness," Rhandra said.

"Our intuition seems lodged in the right hemisphere of the brain," I said. "Verbal and mathematical ability is in the left hemisphere. But the left hemisphere controls the right hand—which is why most humans are right-handed. A lot of mental illnesses—not loss of Phase, the more drastic ones, like schizophrenia—are caused by dominance of the right hemisphere, and lack of coordination between the two. We—"

"Ling," Rhandra said softly, "forgive me, but I do not think this is the most productive way to ease into these things. They are not of the essence."

I grimaced at her. "What *is?*"

"You miss the Sabal, Ling. It is written all over your face at this moment."

I sighed, glanced up through the skylight. Veden's moon was mired in cloud, a grey ghost.

"Yes. Yes, I do." It sounded strangely like a confession of inadequacy.

"There remain spiritual avenues open to you . . . Ling," Majumbdahr murmured quietly.

I slapped my knee, stood up. "Yeah, I know. Let me be clasped to the bosom of Krishna, right?" I paced the room, whirled on them. "But we must first *understand*, damn it! These ideas aren't only mine—I got them from the research being done on the Plague victims on Earth. The Quarn seem to probe deep into those three warring brains, to reach back into that limbic system we have in common with the nonprimate mammals."

Majumbdahr spread his hands, a let's-be-reasonable gesture. "Then we must use our own wisdom to counter them. These facets—the tribrain, the left-right conflict—were resolved by Phase. That is its role."

"But it doesn't work."

"So far. Mankind is not finished."

"Ling," Rhandra said, "I believe your . . . disquiet . . . can be resolved by study of our ways here on Veden."

"They don't work, either. Read the reports."

Of late I had rummaged through Fleet retrieval codes in search of ideas about the Quarn, psychoanalytic research, anything. There were no solutions, only clues.

Quarn victims showed excesses of certain natural small brain proteins, such as endorphins. One clearly repressed atropine, and we had known for centuries that atropine induced the illusion of flying.

Did suppressing atropine, coupled with other reactions, induce fear of open places? So far the riddle was unsolved. More important, *how* was this done? The restrictions on human brain alteration which the Covenants laid down six centuries ago had blotted out our knowledge of such matters; now we needed it desperately. So I had begun to comb the files and make my own Tinker Toy models, rummaging, searching . . .

"I believe Rhandra is correct, Ling," Majumbdahr said, pulling my attention back to the conversation. "There are some savants . . . ," and he chimed in with Rhandra, both urging me gently, as friends do, to release some of the dawning anxiety I felt.

"Maybe you're right," I said to them, suddenly tired. "I'll think about it."

I looked up. The moon had ripped its shroud and now swam free.

The difference between a conviction and a prejudice is that you can explain a conviction without getting angry. This is a dead giveaway in negotiations; if your opponent flares his nostrils unconsciously before speaking, he probably isn't going to abide by any compromise settlement.

The case in point was the outer tribes, the jawarls. The people of Kalic termed them tribes because they followed a more martial Hindic tradition, practiced combat yoga, and invoked obscure, many-armed gods. The jawarls decided that Plague victims were a visitation of the evil Thingness, and this implied, as the night the day, that such people were better dead.

We first learned of these interesting opinions when three jawarl-blessed teams broke into a hospital, killed five Plague cases and a nurse, and barricaded themselves in a wing. The Kalic officials dithered. I moved up Fleet troops. The jawarls killed the remaining two Plague cases and pitched their ritually dissected bodies into the street. The Kalic officials were greatly offended and went away to meditate on a solution.

I had selected my men for their marksmanship, not their bravery; if you have enough of the former you don't need the latter.

I left Gharma in charge of the front. I took some men around the back, thinking the jawarls might sneak out that way. The jawarls were hard fighters, but I thought we could face them down.

We waited.

Firing came from the front. Small arms.

When I got there, jawarls lay around the hospital doors. Blood seeped from their blackened wounds.

"What happened?" I asked Gharma.

"They came out."

"You gave warning?"

"Some."

"Damn it, you were well concealed. You could've parleyed."

"They were armed. They ignored my first challenge."

"And the second?"

"I fired a warning bolt."

"Oh, neat. Very neat. So they panicked."

"The onus lies upon them," Gharma said stiffly.

"You should've been more careful."

"They were country men. They do not acknowledge your Fleet niceties."

"You made damned sure they wouldn't."

"I feel I was justified."

Majumbdahr approached and saw the carnage. He shook his head, his mouth a thin line.

I looked at Gharma. He knew full well that Fleet regs would uphold his decision. Behind his icy manner was a smug certainty.

I snorted wearily and turned away.

We lifted out in a twenty-copter force then, and caught the council of jawarl elders at their daily Dance of Self, their tea bowls still steaming. Such people are either at your throat or at your feet; this time the negotiations went well.

That evening it came again.

I jerked awake. Rhandra nuzzled against my shoulder, a thigh atop mine. Outside the night was still.

The dream returned.

The chaplain came to her Slot. He was a hospital employee. He administered the last rites and rubberstamped that fact on a card. The nurse closed Angela's eyes and called the orderlies. He witnessed the temporary death certificate, filled in the Release of Personal Belongings form. The body was washed, plugged, trussed, wrapped in thin sheets— we are neat here—and labeled. At the morgue the attendant loaded the body onto his rolling stretcher, waited for an empty drop tube, and then took it to the morgue icebox in the basement: last transport for unwanted goods. The autopsy was brief; the machine found nothing unusual. I sat outside while she was drained, embalmed, waxed, roughed, shaved, dressed, made ready.

Two possible ends: a quick, crisp incineration, then bones into a ceremonial urn. Or, at vast expense, a precious rectangle of earth, a machine chuffing as it lowered her in.

Then the dead children, of course. More units passing from the Slots. Through the labyrinth. No metaphysical mystery, no call from the divine. By the time people had reached the close-packed Slots you just let them go. The new ethics: Thou Shalt Not Kill, but thou may allow to die if . . .

I woke.

I rose, paced, sweated.

Rhandra stirred and then drifted back into sleep's grey peace. I moved ghostlike through the shadowed living room. Some of my familiar morning nausea howled in my head. I massaged my neck to clear my thoughts.

Rhandra or no, I was quit of Angela. Did I still love her? Impossible to say. After a while emotions are like old shoes; you forget you have them on. Do dreams of death, transposed, mean dreams of love? A question I had scribbled on my soul and could not now lightly rub out.

4

THE COPTERS BUZZED all around us, ringing the area. I lumbered away from mine. A thick acrid stench of burning buildings drifted down the broad street. It seeped in through my suit filters. Sirens wailed; they were coming this way.

"Majumbdahr!" I called. He came trotting over. "What happened to that sleeper gas?"

"Ordnance couldn't locate any more," he puffed. "They used the last of it an hour ago. It didn't stop them."

I ground my teeth. No time to have a batch made up; I wasn't even sure there was a chemist in Kalic who knew the process.

"Form up the men you have. They still carry anamorphine?"

"Yes, most of them." He nodded slowly, dazed with fatigue.

"Gharma and the Lancers were slowing down."

"I think they are," Majumbdahr said. He blinked rapidly to clear his vision. Smoke drifted across and paled Lekki's great eye. "They've been going for six hours. Our men are sagging, too."

"This should be the last of it, then, for a while," I said and saluted. Another copter decked with a whine behind me. Gharma jumped out.

"It's dying down elsewhere, sir," he reported.

"About time." I'd followed the riot from Fleet Control since morning, until I couldn't stand to be inside any longer. It was good to be out in the field and get the taste of things.

Troops formed up in a line across the street. The muted bass of the crowd deepened.

"It's hard to understand," I said, looking at the thin column moving up. "Only a month since the first Plague victim."

"How does it go in most cases?" Gharma asked.

"All I know is what I saw on Earth," I said, trying to shrug in my suit. The constant-volume joints impaired me. "It wasn't anything like this. People simply waited. Sometimes they died. They didn't turn out into the streets, burn, and loot."

"They had more Phase, on Earth?"

"I don't know. I wouldn't have guessed it. There's something peculiar about the Veden personality. They seem to be coming out from under some inhibition at last and the pressure is blowing the top off."

"The old ways are not enough," Gharma said flatly.

"Why? Why should they fail now?"

"It is a crisis point," he said. "The order we had is lost."

I looked at him closely. Behind his plastiform face shield his skin was polished walnut. "*You* say that? You, believer in formalized religion?"

"Formalized, yes. Perhaps dead as well. When something is finished, you cast it aside. We need a new social ordering here, a new dedication."

Two blocks down the mob swept around the corner and flowed into the street. Tinkling of glass. Roughedged cry of frustration.

I glanced at Gharma. What did he mean? How could he watch his world dissolve so calmly? He looked content. Almost smug.

The mob streamed toward us. I licked away a salty tang of sweat. My contact filters stung my eyelids when I blinked; I'd been wearing them too much, indoors and out.

I could feel the hollow drumming of a thousand running feet. Fifty meters in front of me the mob bore down on the line of troops. Most of the Lancers seemed young. They grinned.

When they were within a few meters of the line, my troops fired a volley of darts and some went down, drugged with anamorphine. A canister of homemade gas blossomed in our line and blew away.

Most of the crowd's rush halted, but here and there they broke through. Our line wavered. Men fell.

The mob caught the smell of victory.

I suddenly realized I was exposed. A knot of Lancers dashed by me. Gharma was cut off to the left with a squad.

I unhooked my sidearm. Majumbdahr shouted orders over suit radio that echoed in my helmet.

Three Lancers converged on me. I took ready position. One carried a chain wrapped around his wrist; no worry there. The other two had cobblestones from the old district and one flashed a knife. All relatively useless against body armor.

They came to me together in a rush.

I brought the tube of my gun down viciously, chopping the first Lancer's arm. The man dropped his knife with a gasp of pain.

I stepped to the left and took a blow on my back armor that rattled my teeth. The chain whipped around my helmet with a crash and partially obscured my field of vision.

I crouched and fired two darts. They made an angry splatting sound.

Thumb over to extra-strong anamorphine. Lancer moving in; focus on him. Fire. Miss. Fire again.

He caught it in the groin. Staggered away, collapsed.

One left now. Turn—where is he?

A bottle bounced off my arm and shattered on the sidewalk.

I heard the whistle of the chain again. *Duck.*

It missed. He felt the wind, as my instructor used to say.

This time I caught the Lancer before he could back away. I cracked the gun tube across his kneecap. He almost fell on the bottle shards but managed to roll to one side.

I blinked sweat out of my eyes. Hot. People all around me. Expand attention out, watch for an attack.

A man appeared from nowhere and threw a cobblestone. It hit my solar plexus. My armor rang.

I thrust out with the gun tube. The Lancer brought a stick around and parried neatly. He backed away, glancing to the sides for support.

I raised the muzzle of the gun. He danced to the side at just the right instant and the dart whizzed past him. The Lancer threw his pipe and ran. I ducked, fired, missed again. He dodged behind

Majumbdahr, who was coming to help me. The crowd was falling back. My troops let out a thin cheer and started to reform.

"You all right?" Majumbdahr panted.

"Sure," I grinned at him. "Those fellows can certainly be offensive, though, can't they?"

5

WE MET IN a restaurant in Old Town. Majumbdahr and Gharma had shown surprise when I told them they'd find me there, but I was bored with the stiffness of my official offices, and after the riots I needed a quietness.

Men in severe robes milled around the entrance as I went in, chattering, comparing notes, pointing at the black fingers twining through the sky from still-smouldering fires.

Majumbdahr and Gharma were already there, waiting at a cloistered table in the back.

"You've recovered from the brawl, then?" Majumbdahr said as I sat down.

"Still hurts down my back," I said. "It'll be sore tomorrow. Stupid to get caught out like that. I should've been up in a copter. How about you two?"

Gharma lifted a steaming fork of food and made a face. "Elementary violence I can usually overcome. The hot Pindang Kol in this restaurant is trying to even the score."

"Pretty bad," Majumbdahr agreed, putting down his fork. "I'm glad I wasn't very hungry." He looked up at me. "Order something for you, sir?"

"Later. I finished my report on the copter coming over here. I thought Old Town would relax me, restore some balance. I won't have the report transmitted to Fleet Central on Earth until I've a chance to go over it again."

"It must be rather difficult to compose," Majumbdahr said.

I sighed. "Rather. It's not easy to admit you're losing control of the situation."

"Couldn't you . . . in the writing . . . soften the impact?" Gharma said. "Perhaps it's not building as swiftly as we think—"

"No. Half-truths are dangerous; sooner or later you might inadvertently tell the wrong half."

"I agree," Majumbdahr said, hunching down with his elbows on the table. "Fleet has the right to hear it all, straight."

"Especially since this form of the sickness is new," I added. "There has never been violence like this before. I've asked some psychers; they don't understand it. It is out of the pattern."

Gharma nodded, his face grim.

"How is the building going?" I said to Majumbdahr.

"On schedule. The hospital space can be supplied by preform construction units, easily deployed. The only holdup was in the blueprints."

"Blueprints for hospitals? I thought they were standard."

"I checked standing orders and then asked Central on Earth. They want us to build some close-packed Slots."

I stared at him for a long moment. "I should've been told. What did you do?"

"Called in a civilian. Used ordinary hospital prints."

"Good. You're legally in the clear. Local commanders can make such changes, as long as there aren't too many of them."

Majumbdahr had sensed my mood well. I hated the cramped Slots and all the memories they brought back.

"I think it was a wise decision for several reasons," Gharma said. "The psychological impact on the people would be great."

"Yes," I said, "when you begin building that kind of Slot you've admitted it's over, you've given up."

"Well, I give up on the Pindang Kol," Gharma said, pushing his plate away. "I'll eat elsewhere."

He smiled wanly. The things we had left unspoken layered the air.

They knew as well as I that a judgment of incompetence against a fleet Director—that is, me—would not neglect the Executive Officers immediately below him. If I went, I might well take Majumbdahr and Gharma with me.

"Do you think we should stop the building of rural retreats, sir?" Majumbdahr said.

"No. Move as many as possible out of Kalic and into the retreats. You've said before—" I glanced at Gharma—"that Vedens are country folk. Maybe they'll snap out of it if we get enough out of the cities."

"Is there any correlation in the background of the rioters?" Gharma asked.

"No, none." I looked down at the table and felt a wave of defeat wash over me. "Some are from the city, others fresh of the forests. No religious similarities. Widely varying income levels and education. The only thing they have in common is that this morning they finally got fed up with it all and started burning or hitting a policeman or just running down the street."

"Berserkers." Majumbdahr rubbed his hands together, thinking.

"What?"

"Berserkers. In ancient times the natives of the Norse lands on Earth had a ritual way to break free of society. Small deviations from the conventional weren't permitted"—he smiled at Gharma—"but if the pressure got to be too much, a man could run berserk and no one bothered him. He could go mad until he felt ready to return to his life."

"You're implying that's what happened here today?" I said.

"Perhaps. I don't know. What set them off, why all at once?"

"It's not my field," I said, shaking my head. "Too much for one day."

Gharma: "Sir . . ."

"Yes?"

"There have been reports . . ."

"Of a new sect, the Lengen," Majumbdahr finished. "Gharma and I saw some mention of them in one of the surveys you ordered. We think you should see them."

"Look," I said, blinking wearily, "I've gotten blessed little help so far. There are a thousand cultists every square block in this city. I seem to have met every one of them. If there's nothing special—"

"Ah, I think there is," Gharma said seriously. "There is something strange—but you should see for yourself, sir."

"They maintain a compound on the border of the jungle, in the farm districts," Majumbdahr said.

I considered. I was tired, but underneath it I felt an odd unease, a need to act.

"I'll go." I glanced out a thin window nearby. "It will be good to escape Kalic, to get outdoors again . . . 'Outdoors'—a queer word, isn't it? Arrogant. As if the universe were defined by what lies outside the places where we live . . ." Rambling, rambling, skittering on a high wire above the abyss. I jerked myself back to the present. "Dusk is falling. Should we be going now?"

"Yes, I'll go call a copter. One can pick us up a few blocks from here," Majumbdahr said.

"Delay a bit," Gharma said. "I thought I would check in with Control first, sir. I should stay in the city. It would probably be best if one of us was on duty in case—"

"Yes," I said. "Go with Majumbdahr and get an allpoints report for me before we leave. I can review it in the copter. Majumbdahr and I will go out alone."

Majumbdahr got up, threw a few coins on the table. They rang softly in the still velvet closeness. Gharma rose, saluted a trifle formally, and followed Majumbdahr out.

This last gesture was typical of Gharma. Through ____nths the three of us had become friends, ____ch closer to Majumbdahr. His sponta-____e through the officer's crust. But in

Gharma I still detected an undercurrent of reserve and cool assessment that I did not like.

I decided to eat while I waited. The copter could wait. I would need the energy. And of course it was one way to demonstrate to my two executives officers that, friends or no, they would still wait at my leave.

I ordered the Pindang Kol and a biryani. Pindang Kol turned out to be a broth of cabbage and root vegetables, salty and thick. It was terrible.

We swooped down into a blotch of pale orange light. The Lengen compound swam in a sea of black, humid jungle. Phosphors picked out forests of tents pitched for pilgrims, cooking platform areas of rough stone, for meditation. In the center billowed a yellow tent. We banked toward it and set down in a clearing beaten clean by foot traffic.

"How can you be sure we'll be granted an audience?" I shouted to Majumbdahr as the props roared the instant before landing.

"I called ahead. They realize you have little time. I imagine there'll be no difficulty."

As we stepped off onto Veden soil still cooling from the heat of the day, a small man rushed out of the crowd gathered around our official copter.

"Director Sanjen!" he cried. "I have been sent to guide you to the master." The man was dressed in cheap robes. Most of the people standing and watching were poor, farmer class. Or else they had renounced material things to follow the Lengen. I nodded and we walked to the large tent. The crowd parted as we approached. I couldn't help comparing this with the behavior of the mobs I'
earlier in the day.

The tent was more complex th

maze of rooms kept groups of pilgrims separated
and allowed the priests, clad in deep blue robes, to
move in and out without disturbing meditations
and rituals.

We were ushered into a warm little hexagonal
room bounded by rich folds of cloth. We sat lotus
fashion before two place settings of many bowls,
plates, and tumblers. There were eating sticks from
several cultures, lacquered spatulas, and shallow
canisters. I wondered what this was all about. The
quietness stole into the center of my tenseness,
though, and I decided to wait matters out.

Presently a low woodwind tone sounded in the
still air.

A tall man walked slowly to the center of the
room. His green robes covered him entirely with
only a shadowed triangular slit for eyes and mouth.
I could see nothing of his expression.

"Finally you come here." The voice was deep
and rich with an odd inflection.

I pressed my hands together in greeting. "I—"

"Begin ritual. Silence. Attention."

He produced a bowl and began pouring a thin
liquid into the cups before Majumbdahr and me. A
priest appeared bearing foods that steamed in the
cool night air.

We began preparing the food. It was to be ladled
into the proper bowls, mixed in precise proportions,
arranged and ordered. I gave Majumbdahr a side
glance and found him watching me. He did it all
smoothly.

After a few moments I noticed a rhythm to the
procession of plates and odors. Salt of fishes. Tang
from ripe fruit. Rough feel of the broadcloth
napkins.

It was warm and soothing. I relaxed, and my

senses flowed out. I looked down on myself as I floated in a corner of the tent. Feeling all, knowing nothing.

There was a sudden glaring light. I wept.

And I was there.

Labels, you see, are meaningless.

Worse, they're distracting.

Within a breadth of time I focused on the exercises. My mind stilled. I did not think of how surprising this was, of how my present state resembled something I had known in the past, but only achieved then by months of contemplation. I didn't consider any of these things. I simply was.

. . . Let us regard the waters in their ways.

An hour passed, or perhaps a moment.

> In pursuit
> Of infinity
> Lose the way
> Thus: serenity.

"First form," the Master said. "You see." He leaned toward me from his lotus position. Bells tinkled. "First ally the mind. Cannot find its own . . . outside." He made something like a laugh. "This is done by not thinking various things, one after another."

"Unconditional nature?" I asked.

"Part. Is only part. Beginning."

I sat. The world formed, clouded, spun away. After a time of absence I returned to my place and focused once more on the eating ritual. Gradually it released its hold over me. I was coming back to the world.

But not the world I had left. Now I had a place within it.

—*let the waters, in their ways*—

We moved away from the large tent, the Ashram, the place of wisdom study. I walked slowly and felt the pleasant crunch of broken soil (glass?) beneath my feet. One thing at a time. Focus.

The Master, I noticed, is very tall. Seven feet, perhaps more. Low gravity? Focus, focus.

Majumbdahr and I lifted off and climbed swiftly. "You've made great progress, I believe, sir," he said.

I felt a comradeship with him. He had not reached this state, but he had pointed the way. He was a very good friend. There would be others, too, who were close. Community.

We slipped through the winds toward Kalic: winking lights, scattered jewels upon a rug. I thought of glass. A glass wall. A bird lying beside a glass wall.

6

RHANDRA MOVED COQUETTISHLY on me, a smiling imp. The oils on our bodies gave every caress a tingling after-memory of sensation.

Her oiled muscles rippled, coaxing me. We both knew it was no use; I was finished for that morning, energies spent.

She made a sign, a joke. Crude country humor. I laughed.

A few feet away, beyond the glass patio partition, wing-mice and a jawbird pecked at remains of breakfast. We were lying on a broad cushion, she astride. Lekki had just peeped over the afterbeam of the house. I was glad I'd put in my contact filters. I winked at her. We had so much to say—

The phone chimed.

She lifted a leg and rolled off. I got up slowly, reluctant to leave. A button on the phone glowed red, emergency pattern, so I hurried.

"Good morning, sir." Gharma's voice, tense. "I've put Fleet Control on emergency alert status. A sensor drone has just registered two blips out of Jump space, unscheduled."

"How far?"

"Just beyond the edge of the planetary system. Doppler shows they're massing into Veden orbit, fast."

"Got a mass reading yet?"

"Yes, just came in. Usual ship size. Something else, too . . . well, I'll check that later. Could be a mistake. But the two slips come in clearly."

"I'll be there," I said, and hung up.

I took my leave of Rhandra and masked my concern with irritation. Irritation at the stack of work that the sightings promised, at the delay, the stupidity of doing a job I didn't give a damn about when I wanted to be with Rhandra, to go back to the Lengen compound.

I took a copter to Fleet Control. Conversations trailed off into silence as I marched through the front offices. Everyone knew. The news was in the gossip mill by now.

It was much as Gharma had said. I watched the flickering readout from the mass detector silently.

"You have all the scoop orbits logged into our ballistic programs, don't you?" I asked Majumbdahr.

"Of course."

"Start plotting intersection orbits for them. If those two ships keep coming we can probably catch them in the backwash from the ramscoops."

"I don't think that would be wise, sir," Gharma pointed out. "The scoops won't start smoothly with merely the orbital velocities they have now. The intruders will have ample warning."

I looked steadily at him. "Okay. Use the scoop maneuvering rockets to alter their orbits and bring them in close to the bogies. Then blow them up."

"A fusion explosion?"

I nodded.

"It may work. I'll log it in."

I smiled at him wryly. "Don't worry about the expense. I'm sure Fleet will stand the cost of a few scoops."

"What are they, sir?" Majumbdahr asked.

"Quarn."

For the next few hours I watched the small dots drop steadily in toward the Lekki-Jagen system. Normal Fleet operations continued; a few colonies bought raw materials, organ replacements, sophisticated technology, or rare metals that they'd need a century from now; the appropriate ramscoops were cut out from the herd and dropped toward the Flinger. When they reached the rim of the system the scoops would flare into starbound white gems.

The computers spun silently, guilding and totaling the transactions of interstellar finance, transferring marks in one account to similar squiggles in another. I waited, watched, pondered.

In the afternoon reports came in about small incidents in Kalic and the provincial cities; arson, random destruction. The hospitals were filling with Plague victims. The only good point the Slots had was that they were easy to build; decent facilities took longer. A Fleet communique arrived questioning the holdup in Slot construction; I told my staff to throw it away.

Fleet also bothered us for more news about the intruders. Any unusual maneuvers? Spectral distribution of torch? Any transmissions, attempts at contact?

I sent answers and some questions of my own.

When were they going to send me some Jump ships? How many wings were within striking distance? What was my priority?

I got back equivocating long-winded replies. Even if they were Quarn, two ships weren't all that many, were they? Fleet had numerous responsibilities, I must remember. Ships were available, yes, but only for verified Quarn incursions. These were difficult times. Meanwhile, keep us informed.

"Gharma reporting, sir." His image appeared on a screen beside the main display in my command module. "I've been tracing down something I noticed earlier. We thought it was a mistake, but it holds up under several cross-checks of the equipment."

"Something on the mass detector?" I asked.

"Yes. It's coming in normal to the ecliptic plane. Under ordinary scanning operations it probably wouldn't be noticed."

"What is it?"

"That's the problem," he said, and looked a little uncertain. "We get a strong signal, but the object is fairly far out. Or we think it is."

"Think?"

The main screen showed crosshatching: readout from the detectors. The two intruders were clearly visible. Far above the ecliptic plane, almost off the screen, was a small fleck. It was rust-red and the computer-printed grid lines warped around it tightly.

"Appears to have high mass," I said.

"We estimate point seven solar masses," Gharma said. "But optically we can't find a thing out there. Personally, I think it's an error. The detectors are just barely able to pick it up. They could be off quite a bit on the mass."

"Doppler?"

"That's wrong, too. Very high, positive."

I shook my head. "Keep watching it. Let me know if anything changes. But don't waste time—I want to know what those other two are doing."

I didn't have long to wait. At 1700 hours they reversed torch and started slowing down. They skimmed along a path tantalizingly beyond reach of the ramscoops.

Were they taunting us, making fun of our defenses? I was sure they were Quarn. An hour later the spectral data came through. There were bright lines from fusion torches, typically Quarn. I squirted Fleet a report.

The report on yesterday's riots went with it, but I didn't wait around to get a reaction from the super-*c* channel. I had better things to do.

Rhandra met me on the balcony of my house before I'd shucked free of the Fleet boots I still wore. I had spoken to her of the Master, and now I asked her to go with me.

She looked at me shyly. "I know him."

"Huh? How?" Focus.

"I have, for over a year."

"Why didn't you tell me?"

"It was not time. The Master asked me not to speak of it to you."

"He . . . ?" I stopped, confused.

"I was a convert. Many of us are."

"Us?"

"Majumbdahr. It was he who suggested I stay on with you. He knew better than I your inner nature."

"I gathered you were here of your own free will," I said.

"I am," Rhandra said in blank-faced surprise. "Oh, I am. Now. But then I was uncertain. The Master had sent me to the city to observe, to study. When I fell in the street and you found me, I was confused. The Lancers . . ."

"And Majumbdahr told you to stay on with me?"

"Yes. He knew of the Master and recognized me as a follower."

"Ah."

"No," she said, reaching out, "you mistake things. We hid nothing from you."

"Oh?"

"We did not think you ready. We waited until your nature seemed changed, away from the grim side you showed us when you first arrived."

"What . . . what is the Master to you?"

"An answer. A partial answer, as all answers must be." She looked at me with a simple and open earnestness, so freely given I had to accept it. There was none of the coyness I saw when we played together, none of the selfless concentration when she worked at her weaving, none of the ordinary faces of Rhandra I had come to know. Any woman worth knowing has more facets to reflect the light than a gemstone, more than one can see in a lifetime.

She took my hand. "He is a man of the farms and the jungles, speaking of the times that surround us. He senses the unease in Veden now."

"Don't we all."

"You are not angry that Majumbdahr and I waited? We wanted the rightful moment to come."

"But it was Gharma, as I recall, who first mentioned the Lengen."

"He is a follower as well."

"He is?"

"Why, yes."

"He seems rather a different sort, to me."

"We are all different, Ling, but the Way is the same."

I snorted. My face tightened at her jargon of enlightenment.

"Do you remember the day we boated on the river?" she asked softly, leaning beside me against the railings. Below us a wingfox scrabbled among stones, searching for tidbits that might have fallen from the balcony.

"Vaguely. There was some incident."

"A follower of the Master rebuffed you. He knew me; that was done at my signal."

"Why?" I blurted, startled.

"The Master had told me it was not timeful for you to see him. It is his way." She paused. "I did not mean for the man to be so . . . rough."

I waved this point away. "No trouble. I had the sense to back down."

"Yes."

"Look—are many of my Fleet officers also followers of the Master?"

"Some, I believe. Not many are interested in the true roots of the spirit, Gharma says."

I sighed, suddenly tired. "Uh huh."

"You are . . . the anger has leached from you?"

What could I do? I reached out and drew her to me.

We both saw the Master that evening. We thronged the gathering grounds beside the Ashram, amid hundreds awaiting an audience. A functionary spotted me and ushered us inside. The rooms of cloth were layered with the smell of wax and incense, and a smoky murmur filled the air from the crowds outside. Shortly we were led to the hexagonal room of the Master again, and we sat, and we learned.

Rhandra knew the rituals well. The Master was gentle, coaxing the responses where I faltered. Clicking of implements, flicker of candles.

The lights quickened. I felt a tingling, a humming. The pressure of the floor matting lessened. Lights rippled, danced.

I was moving, moving, but . . . There were screens—metal? plastic?—flicking light at me.

Suddenly, no sound. No grainy pressure of floor mat on ankles. Lifting.

I dropped down the long smooth tube, a telescope. Rhandra swam with me, a warm molecular bed of cellular wisdom, receptive, and I saw that she was a shadowed inlet of rest, precisely what I needed when first we met. If there was an order in things, it was here.

And in such a harmony an *ofkaipan* could attain communion.

. . . waxy, thick air . . .

How does a man feel community and gain sense of Phase when he knows he is despised? He cannot enter into the Sabal fully. He might think so, struggle a lifetime to convince himself. But the grip would not be sure.

The Plague was designed for the Mongol empire. It spread through the Game.

I saw now that I had always kept a part of myself separate. And the Plague had brushed by me. Something did not click, and though I suffered the loss of Phase for a while, I recovered.

I escaped because I was a man distant from the center. Tonji . . . his ambition seemed to have protected him. Perhaps to him Sabal had been a mere formalism all along.

Angela and the children ... they must've believed more than I. Were they now fallen?

I felt a sudden spurt of joy. I was free. I could be
anything I wanted. My strainings to fit with the
Mongols had failed by some thin margin. A margin which saved me.

After a long and lofting time we returned, together.

The Master sat upright, the fall of his ruby robes
outlining thin legs and knobby knees. There was a
faint musty odor to him, and a cowl hid his face.
What sort of man was this, to lead me so well, to
know what I was?

Long, delicate fingers in blue gloves plucked the
implements from their stations and set them aside.
"Nature satisfied," he said, deep bass. "Are many
levels. One step, then two. Break"—he reached up
and made a quick snapping motion—"then grow."

He cocked his head over to lie on his shoulder in
the Hindic gesture of questioning. The air swarmed
with leaping motes, dust cycloning in a cool draft.
At the edge of my eyes the world shimmered, fresh.

"Let us regard the waters in their lapping, their
rising, and be swallowed by them."

7

I WAS HUMMING, skittering in a high new place, the world crackling with brimming energy.

When we left the Master, I surged forward through the crowds, alive to my own momentum. I called in to Fleet Control, using my copter phone. I saluted Majumbdahr warmly; there was no substantial news. "Sir . . . ," he said, and I saw at once he knew what had happened, and that the old Ling was shucked away. "There is an invitation . . ." From the Madi, of course.

I decided to go.

We landed a bit roughly, spitting gravel to the side. The Madi hustled out of the midevening darkness. Lights winked from the Krishna dome looming above us.

"We are most *honored* to see you again," said the Madi. She fluttered busily.

Introductions. May I present? Yes. "Professor Jampul," the Madi said. A short, emaciated man with wrinkled crisp brown skin. Rhandra bowed with courtesy. I shook hands. Pleasantries flew like birds.

Others drifted into my field of vision, murmured something, and spun away. I gathered that I was meeting people. Couldn't remember any names. I smiled, gave the right signs, and said forgettable things.

"The reception is only now beginning," the Madi said. Massive doors parted, people swirled like tidepools around us. Sandals clacked echoes beneath the domed egg ceiling far above. Jampul was at my elbow, murmuring. He was a pedant, a professor of languages; the sort of man who can see sin in syntax. "Languages?" I murmured.

"And sects. A most interesting subject," he said.

"You know the Lengen?"

"Yes, something of a mystery. Many priests and one leader, I gather."

"You haven't asked him here?"

Beside me the Madi shuffled. "We tried. He did not seem very *in*terested. In fact, we were *rebuffed*."

Things winding a little slow for me. I need air.

"We would like a place to prepare ourselves," I said. "It was a hectic journey."

"Ah, surely." Crowd parted, we went through.

Up a shadowed corridor. Thick aromas from kitchens nearby, muffled footsteps. Rhandra with me, Madi leading. "If you require servants—" No, shake head. Swish of curtain closing on departing rump of the Madi.

Whoosh, sit down. Head a little off tilt. Long day or something. Rhandra looking at me, puzzled.

Jump up, grab her. Thrash around. Eek, tip over

urn. Mad pawing. Bang into chair, laughing wildly. Sloppy kisses. Imitation of enraged ape. Shuffle around room, chasing her. She laughs. She scampers away amid the thick folds of air that fill the room, smoke-dense. We blunder into a bowl of sweetmeats. Both of us fall on them, smacking lips. Pop down four at a go. Hungry. Meditation takes a lot out of a man. Needs of the flesh follow me everywhere.

Laugh. Fall down. Lie there a few minutes. Then it's time to be getting back to the reception. Struggle up. Rhandra rises like a fog at morning.

We made our way through a rat maze and back to the avalanche of accents. Heads turned at our entrance. Formal smiles. Wonder what they think. Is my cowl on right? Lint from floor on my back?

Madi sweeps over with bow wave of lesser lights behind.

"I'm sure we all want to hear your *opin*ions on the riots, Director." She looks around for someone to second the motion, beaming. Others chime in. I didn't catch all they said. Rhandra smiles prettily.

"Well, I don't know," I said. Stalling for time. "It could mean anything, right?" Wrong note there. Try again.

"We're doing everything we can to control it." That's it. Sound statement, full of granite, means nothing. Try to look like a bank president.

"But we have all these *people* drifting into the *city*," the Madi said. Cluster of onlookers nods.

"I don't have authority to close Kalic to the countryside," I said. Even better. A little simpleminded. Act a buffoon, they never suspect you of pilfering the petty cash.

Professor Jampul shook his head sagely. "It's

simply beyond reason," he said. "There is nothing to drive those people insane. We live in a calm, stable time."

"Calm for *you*, Professor," the Madi giggled nervously. "Not for the director here. I have *heard*"—raised eyebrow at me—"of Quarn ships near Veden. That must be keeping you busy."

Think: has that information been released yet? Doesn't matter, must be rumors out by now.

"Afraid they'll rape you in your bed?"

Gasps, slight rustle. Wrong thing to say? Ride over it. "I don't think there's any danger of that. They won't be able to land unless they're much stronger than we think."

Polite murmurs. "Oh?" from Professor Jampul. "And just what is their approximate strength?" He glanced at Rhandra and back to me.

Don't want to give away classified information. Could be a spy, stab me in the men's room, press secrets out my ears.

"Why are you looking at her?" I said loudly.

White faces, nervous chatter. Cover the gaffe.

"Wondering where we went when we got here? Follow us to that back room, sneek a peep through the curtains?"

"Ling," Rhandra said, putting a hand on my arm.

"See us set upon each other lasciviously?" Cover errors with Eros.

Heavy gong.

"I believe the banquet has begun," said the Madi.

I found myself shuffling into a large canopied room filled with curved tables. Pungent vapor of soup. Waiters moving swiftly to seat the most important guests—us—first.

Rhandra next to me. Mr. Fanesh on the left, Professor Jampul across. The Madi next to him. Cozy. Meeting of old friends, kiss my forehead, initiate me into the holy rites.

I drank some water. Clear and cold. Feeling better. Focus, focus. Laughed to myself. Crowd chanting in theater. Fixed my attention on the soup. Sweet, little hint of thyme. Flavoring stone at the bottom. Don't roll it around in your mouth, not polite. Nor spit it into your palm.

Soup goes down with a sucking sound. Sit straight, grow up to be a big boy. (Why should I want to be big? Die faster.) Spine down, pointing, quivering with expectation. Perhaps some wine? Dionysus, be with me now.

Conversation swirls around. Make small talk with back part of my mind, leave motor control to another, right hemisphere idling. We only use a tenth of it at a time, they say. The rest of the cortex never clocks in. Featherbedding. Union dues in arrears.

Look around the room. As big numbers like myself eat, lowly converts are demonstrating their disciplines at the perimeter of the room. They attract some attention. People pointing, some at me. Rude, rude. Palace of peasants.

No, not at me. Something behind me.

I turn, eyes widen with surprise. A little brown Yogi is going through his exercises. Raising the coiled serpent. Kundalini. Demon eyes lance through me. Son of Veden. Evil look to him. Funny I didn't notice it before.

He shifts position. Tilts forward, does rocking exercise accompanied with rippling of stomach muscles. I feel sick. He looks like something reptilian, frog body, thing born of weathered oceans.

The frog came in on little flat feet. Will that get him to unconditional state?

Turn back to table. Soup had been replaced by mixture of vegetables. Spartan, no sauce. I crunch down on seeds, using my omnivore grinders.

"Director, you spoke earlier of the Lengen," Professor Jampul said. Madi smiled uncertainly. Afraid to start conversation again, suspects I'll pounce on her with wooden fangs, slaver over her heavy jowls. "Have you had any experience with them?"

"A little. I went out for an audience. I found the Master quite impressive." There, better. Sounded just right.

"How so?" Erudite eyebrow arches.

"His ritual. It forms a mood, a feeling I can't express." That's it. Vague.

"Oh, he uses the Hindic *rit*uals, then?" the Madi said.

"I suppose. I don't have enough experience to say where they came from." Disclaim all knowledge. Slide away from specifics.

"Well, he must be a truly mag*net*ic man," the Madi said.

Rhandra gave me a seductive wink, setting off flares in my belly. Mind darts around. Looking for way out. Getting hot in here. Look around at other tables, clogged with rheumatic and respectable bodies. All dead inside, no light flickering through pupils.

Reminds me of holy cadaver they showed me last time I was here. All sliced up for the preservatives to go in, stringy muscles. Grey look to him, an ancient saint (imported), naked teeth wobbling in the candlelight. The Madi told me to touch him, Di*rec*tor, he was a truly enlightened one. Legendary, performed miracles. I touched a knee, half expecting him to still be warm.

Main course materializes. Confection of shimmering lightness. Innocent plant with its throat cut and diced out for my inspection. Can't quite place the aroma. Spun cottony webs melt away on my teeth. Elusive flavor down into the stomach, ion processes plate it out on the sides, membranes suck it up. *Ah* it was and *ah* it did.

"Actually, you know," I said, leaning across to skewer the Madi with my eye, "the Lengen have it all over you."

Puzzled frown. Delicate tongue darts out to lick away gob of doomed vegetable from lip. "What do you mean?"

"Simplicity. Appeals to everyone. The Lengen haven't got your six-handed statues. No oil torches. Just the straight goods."

"Well, sir," Professor Jampul said, "I'm sure certain elements find that sort of thing appealing. But the nuances of one's faith, a true feeling of community—"

"Garbage. You aren't going to get it with your interreligious committees or that pitiful Yogi sitting like a frog over there."

Rhandra laughing. "Ling."

Shrug it off. Good feeling climbing up from my toes. Something they put in the main course? Feels fresh to be honest.

"What you need is a good old Hindic chant. Simple. No atonal verities. Something to give you focus."

"Really, Director," the Madi said, "the *ancient* forms are—"

"Ommmmmm," I hummed. Good. Spontaneous. Shivers down the throat. "OOOOOOmmmmm."

"I *don't* see—"

"OOOOOOOMMMMMMMMMMM!"

The anvils dropped from my feet. Up onto the table, arms spread. "OOOMMM!"

Professor Jampul peering up at me, mouth open. Wave to Rhandra, smile. Suicide perched for the jump. Crowd pointing up at him. Waiting for a nosedive down into eternity. Long way down. Yeah, lookit those eyes, give you odds he jumps.

"Alert!" I called. "Beware the frog man! He will eat your toes. Or soles. Or souls." Yogi blinks at finger lancing at him. Broken trance. See, knew it was no good.

"OOOOOOMMMM!" Over the edge. Grab Rhandra's hand. The Madi tipping over backward in her chair, clawing at the air. Levitate, lady.

Dodge around servants and down the long room, long eyes tracing us, monomaniac radar. Footsteps after us. Excuse me, sir, but the Fleet Control Director has gone mad. Would you be good enough to follow him and see that he doesn't get into trouble? There's a lad.

Out into the foyer. Robes flapping around me Rhandra sleek like a tiger as she runs. Panting. Little out of shape, office job doing me in. Your body attacks you at moments of crisis.

Someone coming. Dodge through an alcove and into another corridor. Same one we were in before. How do we get out of here? Back to foyer—no, voices coming from there now. Footsteps getting nearer.

Quick, in here. Nimble of foot, close partition. A chamber for meditation. Flickering candles, cloying incense. Empty. Little pillows for cross-legged converts, looking like a field of squashed mushrooms. A solemn little room, as earnest as Job's argument with God, and as pointless.

In the center is a small brass figure of Shiva. Rippling hands, ferocious expression. Left hand versus right, in spades. Oh thou most cerebral of cortexes, which sitteth on the right hand. Why did they name this palace after you, kid? Brahma and Vishnu get a much better press. The statue glared at me, probably getting ready for cosmic war on Rogerzee and the rest of the infidels.

Doesn't look contented. Take it? Might be useful in the afterlife. Swish, hands like birds, into my robes it goes.

Rhandra whispering something. Ignore her. Time to follow one's own divine muse. *His life was a work of art*, reads my epitaph. Attention to detail turns the trick. Voices outside moving by. Here am I, doing warmup exercises for immortality. Ah, but will I make the team?

Enigmatic sounds. Coast clear? Peek. Damn contact filters cut too much of the light, can't make out anybody. Is this world dim, or am I? Take a deep breath. Live a life of existential risk: go!

Leap into corridor, Rhandra with me. Soundless demon strikes in the night.

Nobody there.

This way. Around a corner. Voices.

Weave away from them, don't pant. Ruin and scandal await you. Through passageway, priests look up surprised. Wave, maniac grin, use the teeth.

Over to the left. Right, now down these stairs. Maybe we'll discover the secret dungeon. No, a door. Push open a crack. Fresh night air. Outside, down the path.

Stop to get bearings. Rhandra points to the right.

Yes. Landing lights are off, not expecting us. Slipped through their lines.

Into the copter, quick. Start it up. Rhandra takes the controls.

I smile, feeling weak.

She looks concerned.

Surprise, surprise: I fall asleep.

8

"IT WAS AN unusual evening," Rhandra said, smiling slightly.

"Yes," I said. I buried my face in my hands, rubbing my eyes. I felt no tension. In fact, I seemed to be perfectly ordinary. Except . . . colors danced inside my eyelids, like ghosts of dreams. "A good word. Unusual. Disastrous fits pretty well, too."

"Why?"

"A Director doesn't act like that. Fleet thinks the Empire is built on formalities. They may be right. I violated a few hundred canons regarding relations with the natives last night."

"How would Fleet ever find out?"

"Ah. Simple girl." I reached out and ruffled her hair as she sat on the floor at my feet. "Fleet has a thousand eyes. They'll know. And they might very well yank me out of this assignment."

A morning beam from Lekki slanted in to warm my feet. I was fed and comfortable. The future didn't seem to matter much. I knew the Master had touched off something inside me last night, but the underlying reason didn't concern me at the moment. That was still *me* at the Palace, not someone else. It was an identity I hadn't seen very often since the playful days of childhood, and it was welcome back. Whether it was useful to me in my present position was a different matter. I really didn't give a damn.

Rhandra must have been reading my mind. She kissed my knee and said, "Whoever it was, I liked him."

A knock at the door. When I opened it, Jamilla bowed, not glancing inside, and said in a low voice, "There is a call for you from Mr. Majumbdahr. In your office."

I pulled on a robe and went down the hall. I threw his image on the large projector, killed the camera eye at my end, and sat down. My mental Fleet harness slipped into place.

"Good morning, sir," Majumbdahr said when he saw I wasn't going to transmit an image. "Kalic has quieted down a bit. There are routine messages from Fleet Central, which I've answered. They did an analysis of the strategic situation in this sector and give us a fifteen percent probability of a Quarn thrust within ten days, falling off a little after that. Someone is a little disturbed at Central, though, because they're sending a Jump ship."

"When?"

"Fairly soon."

"Name?"

"*Farriken.*"

"Why?"

"It carries medium-range armament. We can use it to catch Quarn ships out to half a parsec."

"That's useless. The Quarn will simply decoy one lone Jump ship out until they get it clear of the system. Then they hit us fast and leave."

Majumbdahr looked uncomfortable. "Control said that's all they can spare us."

"All right." I shrugged. "I'll use the *Farriken* for reconnaissance in the immediate vicinity. It'll be a help. What else?"

"A few odds and ends. I had to listen to an hour of righteous indignation from a Vedanta sect about the gravitational radiation station on the other side of the planet."

"Huh? Whatever for?"

"They think the scientists there are drawing the energy out of the neutron star and will make it fall into Lekki. Say it's a Quarn plot. They want us to stop it."

"Good grief. Say, about that station—any chance they can pick up that anomaly Gharma mentioned coming in perpendicular to the ecliptic? It's just on the edge of detectability for our equipment."

"An interesting thought; I'll check into it. That anomaly, by the way, is getting closer. But the technicians haven't been able to straighten out yet whether it's the range finder or mass register that's malfunctioning. Gharma's been riding them but they say the instruments are fine. They can't explain the results, though."

"Keep them at it when they have time. But keep most of Fleet Control watching traces in the plane of the ecliptic. If the Quarn are going to match orbital velocity with Veden, they've got to come at us that way. Anything more?"

"Uh, yes," he said and licked his lips. "The Madi called this morning. She wanted to send a priority message to Fleet Central. She said she would pay for it herself."

"Ummm. And what did you do?"

"I think I've misplaced it somewhere."

"I see. Well, we're not here to carry letters for civilians."

"No."

"Signing off, then." As his image dwindled I thought I saw him smiling.

There is harvest of the quiet eye. I fasted for six days, and thought my thoughts, and saw the Master twice more. I learned fresh angles of my Rhandra, and saw that she was (of course) less simple than I had supposed. (Everyone is.) This was a world seen anew, scrubbed clean. I felt that I had lifted a seashell to my head and had heard finally that word they have always tried to put in my mouth, by insistently whispering it in my ear.

Fleet crept on its petty pace. There was a busyness of business, the familar wash of detail. Majumbdahr I knew better; he and Gharma and I attended the Master once, together, and it was rewarding. In Gharma I still detected a different center, a certain unease, a hidden frosty reserve. He became more bossy about Fleet matters, speaking ex cathedra. I allowed him some leash line, but not overly much; I was still Commandant, friend or no.

I puttered a bit, did some reading. For some reason I felt a sudden desire to review Jump ship tactics and hardware; interesting stuff, a kind of enhanced shoptalk. Majumbdahr and Gharma both caught my interest, borrowed texts. I unpacked my illicit firetongue Stet and placed it squarely above the fireplace, an appropriate spot. It was useless, of course—Veden didn't have Firetongue defenses, and thus I'd gotten no replacement for this outdated Stet—but it had a certain totem quality. My gaze never strayed by it without pausing for a moment.

I studied astronomy, particularly during the fast; it focused the mind. A Fleet outrider had ventured out of the plane of the galaxy for the first time, and confirmed theoretical suspicions: a thousand billion suns lurked out there, in a swarming spherical cloud. They were formed from the first great glob that made our galaxy. When those small, red stars had first shone forth, the gas and dust that would eventually make up the galactic spiral was slowly drawing inward, into the disk. The thousand billion formed a halo, were not dragged into the new galaxy's dizzy spin. They had a mass comparable to the disk itself, but until now had been seen only indirectly, because they glowed dim and distant in the great night above the spiral arms. They were *old*, M types at least—the shorter-lived stars had guttered out by now. Planets circled those embers, likewise ancient. The outrider ship had found a few, but none of interest.

I read the dispatches, three years old by now, and searched for more. None: research was chopped off when the Quarn appeared. As so much else had been.

Majumbdahr and I went on a long hike through the rumpled farming hills of Veden, and spoke of Fleet. Both of us had been consumed by it as boys, and now found ourselves fondly remembering what it had once meant. We had dreamed of being star voyagers, and ended up cynical cops, shoring up a tottering empire. I recalled the Academy, set high in the mountains near my home. The Meditation Center there shot upward from a barracks-studded plain, the ramparts soaring. Softspun aluminum, pebbled glass, tetrahedrons laced with violet organiform, all converging high above the terrazzo floor, a promise lancing toward the spaces above the sky. A standing Buddha, eyes contemplating a star. Somehow, after graduation from this vaulted pinnacle, things had gone steadily downhill for me. Fleet was for Mongols, not *ofkaipan*. Angela, part *ofkaipan* herself, had seemed to know this all along, and took her place in Fleet social gatherings, leaving the foreground to other Fleet wives. Her slimness contrasted with the fashionable ladies, who were then swallowed in their own fat. While Angela hatched me a responsibility in her stomach, and then another, I flapped my wings and failed to rise. No Prometheus, I—more like Epimetheus, the hindsighted and thickwitted brother (never mentioned in the Fleet mythology) who always learned too late, hadn't been pinned to a rock, and made a dumbbell error with Pandora. But mythology was, like history, simply aged gossip, and mulling over this easy analogy, I saw that Angela was no Pandora, however much I might like to pigeonhole her.

How to explain the incident with the Madi? I puzzled over it, found no solution. It had felt good, that's all I knew. A releasing act. I had never really understood what, to some, is obvious: the distinction between high and low acts. There are farts as enjoyable and edifying as epigrams. Indeed, they can have the same function—to relieve their author and offend their audience.

*   *   *

A pause here, then, like a summer's day that doesn't want to end. And then came another journey to the Master, suspecting nothing, and all was changed.

9

THE MASTER LOOMED above me. He filled the room, the whole universe. *Warm close feet of Rhandra beside me, sweet air of incense, sticky pull of robes on my flesh*—all fell away into nothing.

I focused on the Master. As I slid into it, I asked *What state is this?* and almost before the question had formed I felt the peace begin. Ripples of worry smoothed and vanished. A state of no definition, no thought, no method. To put aside the thousand things and, in stillness, retain yourself.

"This is done by not thinking various things, one after another," the Master said, his deep rolling voice breaking a long silence.

I laughed. Sound to the side: soft tinkling chuckle of Rhandra.

"Like—that," I said, abruptly snapping my fingers. It was very clear what he meant. Just—that. No words. Only being.

The Master nodded.

"There is more," he said. "Many things you must know. Not as they seem."

I waved a hand in question, laid my head upon my shoulder. The Master moved his body to shield his hand. I glimpsed a small sliver of metal, a box. He fingered it rhythmically. I heard a low smooth tone that died away as I concentrated. A strange prickly shock ran down my neck. I was falling. What—?

Coming back again. I expanded until I could see myself below. Deep white craters that were pores on my face. I shivered in the hurricane breath that swept down from the nostril mountain.

—You can be close. Warm. Gather once more into the lap of sunlight—

The Master said this, but with no words. I started to turn my head toward Rhandra and stopped fixed in the Master's stare. Mosaics of light swept through us. I saw Gharma and Majumbdahr standing to both sides of the Master. They must have entered from behind the folds of ruby cloth and stood quietly in place until my attention was focused on them.

You were not ready for me. It was in the place of rightness that you learned Veden first, felt what happens here, saw the signs of fresh ruin.—

Majumbdahr grinned wryly at me. I felt a sudden burst of affection for this man who had worked and planned beside me and at all times sensed my inner turmoil. I owed him much.

Gharma gazed at me calmly. His heavy lids shadowed his dark eyes, adapted for Veden and holding something forever unknowable. He was a strange, deep man moved by traditions and social conventions I would never fully grasp. His distance I respected. And he, too, had helped me.

—*Look now.*—

The Master stood in one smooth motion. He twisted two spots in his robes, and they fell away. But for a swath at his waist he was naked.

Thin, wiry. Long bones moved in his arms and legs, rippling the taut, pale white skin. His seven fingers were like sticks with large knobby joints. A barrel chest. No body hair.

His feet were dark semicircles of thick, tough fiber spanned by radial ridges of cartilage, like toes.

His eyes were deep and black. The mouth curved upward in a thin red line. There was no nose.

A translucent wedge of tissue jutted out where ears would have been. He stood, rocking slightly on the wide base of his feet.

Silence seeped among us.

He was an alien.

The body was unlike anything I knew among the races within the Mongol Empire. Even those races were seldom allowed to leave their home stars, so there was little chance that one would appear on Veden.

I looked at the Master for long moments. I could not fear him.

In a way, this was the answer I had been seeking. The two threads of my life were entwined at last.

The Master was a Quarn.

It took two days, and some of it wasn't words at all.

Like all intelligent races, they came out of nothingness, armed with their own peculiar insights and talents.

There had been another Empire, then. Far mightier than that of the Mongol, comprising many more races. It had already begun to decline when the Quarn were young.

Other races ebbed into lassitude and death. The Empire came apart from sheer lack of interest. Yet the Quarn lived on; their time was not yet come. In the dying embers of that Empire they had learned much. Through the long centuries that followed they hoarded their knowledge and studied.

Finally age caught up with even them. The spirit drained slowly away, as they had seen happen to others. The artifacts of their forefathers remained, but not the will to build more or to improve upon the old.

Then came Man. The Mongol Empire licked at the edge of the Quarn life sphere. The wisest among the Quarn, who had studied the history of the earlier Empire, recognized some of the same symptoms.

Man dominated every other race and culture he met. He suppressed minorities within his own civilization. It was easy to see why the Mongol Empire had expanded so rapidly. The history of Man was the history of cycles. A continual tension existed between Man the social animal and Man the individualist. Stress on one aspect or another oscillated slowly through the gradual upward climb toward a world culture. The Asian continent was the last local area in which the virtues of community dominated. When virtually all the human race outside of pockets on the Asian mainland was destroyed in the Riot War, this cycle was disturbed. Asia rose to dominance. Simultaneously, Man achieved the technology to reach the stars.

The Mongol Empire expanded outward on a wave of psychic energy released by the melding of the entire human race into one community.

But Man was not meant fully for community. The duality of his nature was the ultimate source of his resilience and his strength. The Mongol Empire had to fail.

When the Quarn first met it, the Empire had begun to slow down and become formalized. Given time, the formalities would chafe. Rebellion would bring harsh measures. The Empire would begin to split.

The best way to avoid revolution at home was war abroad. It was part of a classic pattern. The Quarn saw that the leaders of the Mongol Empire would find it profitable to disturb the peace of the surrounding races when they met them. The basic instability of the Empire would expend itself on other, more stable cultures.

The Quarn had studied Man for long centuries before deciding on a course of action. They would have to force Man back upon his origins, rid him of the Empire that would eventually crush him. They would use his own weaknesses against him— the only mature way to wage war between radically different cultures.

They pieced together ships that could barely survive in combat with Empire forces. It was the most they could do with the decaying technology they possessed. The ancient Quarn had left giant devices in free space which could perform enormous tasks—move a planet through Jump space, damp the bright fire of suns—but these the Quarn could not morally use in battle, for a simple clash of arms would not add a new factor to the human equation. They used what ships they could mend and make serviceable by themselves . . . plus what they knew of the human mind.

"But we erred," the Master murmured.

His voice, after so long a time without words, came as low thunder. "How?" I whispered.

"We meant only to disturb Empire"—A vision, here, of a new wind stirring human wheat—"allow time for self-study. It slips from us now." The Master's face drew down, the eyes filmed with grey.

"You did not think it could go so far?" Majumb-dahr said.

"No. Some of us have . . . walked to the darkness in payment. For us, the ultimate crime against the race. To relieve oneself of life."

"Is it too late? Can't . . ." Rhandra's quiet urgency faded as she saw the look that swept over the Master's face.

"The sickness ran deep." Dry leaves crackled inside his chest. "So many . . ."

"Can't we—can't we save you?" I said.

He pierced me with a pale glance. "Perhaps. I learn your language only now, I am . . . a measurer, not one who acts. I come to Veden in secret, as we do to all worlds. That is how the . . . cure, which became a death . . . is spread. We thought we knew you so well. It was an arrogance. When this is done I shall . . . walk."

"No!" I cried.

"I come on this journey, to earn it."

"I've seen enough of death," I said.

"You will see more."

"Why?"

"I cannot stop. I tried."

"If the Empire quit Sabal altogether . . . ?"

"The firestorm burns of itself. The ember which began it is consumed."

"Then there's nothing to do."

"There remains a task."

"What is it?" My voice was clotted, blurred.

"There are some who rebirthed. You are such."

"Survived the Plague? True, I did, but . . ."

"Because you are . . . *ofkaipan*. More than that, we know not why, but something more. A fragment of your race will survive. I did not understand this when first you came. My first sin came then."

"Sin?"

"A man, out of the sky."

"The assassin?"

"I spoke of you. A follower, too turbulent in himself . . ."

"Tried to kill me? Why?"

"I thought you carried the Plague."

"We told him of you," Gharma put in. "We thought your recovery was temporary, and you would infect Veden. The Master became concerned. But we never intended . . ."

"You see? We know you poorly. Arrogance."

"A foreboding in the Master became the deed of a follower," Majumbdahr said quietly. "I learned only later."

For a while we sat in silence.

"A wind now blows through the Quarn," the Master said distantly. "Something . . . drawing thin."

We waited. There was a calm still silence in the room. The Master's thin frame trembled.

"We . . . thought the only hope of saving many humans . . ." The words came out as though under pressure. ". . . was to isolate a world from the Plague. Veden . . . was good. Hard to reach . . . by your fast ships."

"Jump ships."

The trembling was very slight. There was a tangible layered chill in the air.

"I thought to . . . kill you . . . A thought of a moment. But it was done. It came from my hand."

"I . . ."

The tension in the Master muted. "I have moved far from my Path. The wind, the unstable wind of the mind that blows through us . . . I am in and of it, now. I . . . the Path . . . I will walk."

A time passed then and the thought came into my mind of rain, endless rain in the Philippine town I had lived in as a boy. Warm wind brought heavy drops that stripped the leaves from some of the big trees at the end of the square. They were trees from a colony world, with oily purple bark. The leaves lay heavy and sodden in the street on one side of the square where the wind had driven them and some were in brown drifts against the buildings, a brown against the wet blackness of the sidewalk. The leaves fluttered down in the wind, already heavy with wet, and they stuck where they fell. I remembered the way the leaves turned in the wind as though struggling against it, but slick with rain already and falling quickly as they crossed the square. Only the sharp quick gusts of wind were enough to carry a few of the leaves against the building, where they would stick for a while and then slide down the rough stucco and into the brown drifts. It rained like that a lot in the late fall and he had watched the rain from the upper storey of the building across the square, looking out his bedroom window with the blinds pulled up all the way. The corners of the window were misted up from the heat in the room and the cold glass breathed a chill into the room.

A long time.

. . . *regard the waters in their rising* . . .

I pressed the words out. "What is to be done?"

"I ask you all now. One . . . last thing. On Earth your Fleet now assembles the Patanen—they who laugh at Fate. Those who do not fall from the sickness. Like you."

"Cases recovered from the Plague?" I asked.

"Yes."

"How do you know?"

"Empire studies them. All have been sent from the other worlds. Assembled on Earth. We learned of it recently. We have followers there, near the Patanen."

"Lengen Masters?"

"No." He shifted uncomfortably, strained by the gravity. "We hide."

"The guru tradition doesn't exist elsewhere," Gharma broke in. "It would appear strange if the Lengen arose."

"There are Quarn everywhere, then," I said. "On all the colony planets, even Earth."

"Search for remnants," the Master said.

I nodded. Fleet would certainly pool the recovery cases for study. "Will these Patanen . . . will Fleet learn enough to matter?"

The Master shook his head regretfully. "Collapse speeds down upon them all. We cannot halt it."

"What would you have us do?"

"I reveal myself to you so you may choose. Know that: I do not command."

"I know."

"My burden is to pluck these last seeds, the Patanen."

"You want to go to Earth?" Rhandra said wonderingly. Soft as night, her eyes.

"A last duty." He breathed heavily with an aged remorse. The bony chest heaved, rattled, the ribs opening and closing like blinds. Alien. "I kenned this in a vision, once I knew you—" a flick of an eyelid at me—"and saw you whole. To Earth—it is possible?"

"I suppose," I granted, not seeing immediately how it could be done. "We'll bring them back from Earth, to Veden?"

"Here may not be safe," the Master murmured.

"I agree," Gharma said. "Veden will be free soon. The Empire cannot hold it for long, or the space around it. But the Plague proceeds here as well."

"Would destroy harmony of Veden to inject diverse cultures. Better a new world."

"Where?"

"We have an Earthlike site. I will lead you to it after Earth."

"Look . . ." I wrestled with plans in my head. "The best we can do is a Jump craft of Class Four or Five. We couldn't possibly carry a large number of people aboard."

"If they were ordinary passengers, yes," Gharma said. "But the Quarn on Earthside will cool the bodies. Lowering their metabolic rate will allow us to transport them in storage units."

I thought. The technique was standard and had been developed in the era of ramscoop exploration, before discovery of the Jump. It kept a crew alive through the decades of flight. Their true aging was only a fraction of the elapsed time. People could be stacked in a small space, fed a trickle of air and food through their veins. A ship could carry many people stored that way.

"And what of Earth itself . . . ?" I said slowly.

"The Empire has nearly shrunk down to a few systems," Gharma said. "The Quarn will withdraw, of course, but . . ."

I nodded. The Patanen were the most valuable

people in the Empire now, a last crucial healthy sample of mankind. Perhaps we could indeed make a new start with them . . . Perhaps. "Master . . ." An edge in me teetered near. "I . . . I am unsure . . ."

"True nature only now beginning to emerge."

I glanced a question.

He slapped his fists into a ball. "Locked. Your nature. Sometimes try to get out. I help it."

"Words, words . . . I don't . . ."

"Remember." Gesture to Rhandra, followed by a manic sign, a skittering dance of the seven fingers.

"The banquet," Randra supplied. "The Madi."

He nodded, smiling for the first time in the long hours we had passed together. "Nature . . . escaped."

"That was me?" I murmured to myself, not convinced, fearing something I knew I should not. To be a Fleet officer, I saw, meant you put away a piece of yourself, for good.

"You spoke clearly then." His great head bobbed.

"Ah," I said, and suddenly felt emptied. Gush, the bad air out. *Ah* it was and *ah* it did.

Rhandra gave a quick warm laugh of silk and silver.

I looked slowly at us all, four humans and a Quarn, the cloth vaulting hanging softly above us, and seemed to see it all from a vast new perspective. I saw that we were one and the same.

So did a journey end, and another begin.

Part V

1

HASTE MANAGES ALL things badly. We planned, plotted, lied—and still, it all turned on the captain of the *Farriken*, which had just emerged from Jump space near Veden. He had to believe this:

> URGENT
> STATISTICAL COINCIDENCE MEASUREMENTS OF BACKGROUND ELECTROMAGNETIC SPECTRUM IN LEKKI-JAGEN SYSTEM INDICATE PEAKED ACTIVITY ON THREE DISTINCT FREQUENCY BANDS OVER PERIOD OF LAST 37 DAYS. RESPECTFULLY SUGGEST THIS MAY INDICATE QUARN SENSORS ORBITING LEKKI-JAGEN AT UNKNOWN RADIUS. WE CANNOT ASSURE INTERCEPTION-FREE TRANSMISSION OF ORBITAL PARAMETRIC LOG AS REQUESTED BY YOU. HUMBLY REQUEST LOG BE DELIVERED BY SKIMMER CONJUNCTION 1346 HOURS 14758 ABX 409 TRANSFER. LING SANJEN, DIRECTOR

and, buying the story at face value, let our skimmer approach for boarding.

Luckily, he did. For a while.

The Orbital Parametric Log was a block of blue crystal a half-meter on a side, with delicate black ferrite stains embedded along fracture interfaces and slippage lines, carrying a thousand kilometers of magnetic memory in 3D array. A computer could read the swirl of dots at a glance. They unfolded into 3D indexing of orbital data for every ramscoop in parking orbit. To a computer eye the ships coasted in that crystal block, flecks of information that hopped from memory site to memory site. The Log was far more precise than any survey the *Farriken* could make by herself in a reasonable time. It was indispensable: the *Farriken* had to smell the sheep before it could hunt the wolves.

Our skimmer locked onto their receiving bay with a clang. We were through before they knew what was happening.

There was a vacuum interface between the skimmer airlock and the *Farriken*'s. We didn't wait for it to fill. Three Fleet men were blown across the distance by our air pressure when we opened our lock. They tripped the emergency access on the *Farriken* and wriggled through. An alarm went off. Before anybody could move on the *Farriken* bridge, two men had found the local lifesystem ducts. They shoved in stungas canisters, popped them.

The third man was Majumbdahr. He clubbed a lock officer and forced open the hatch to the ship's central tube. The *Farriken* is a Class IV Jump ship, with a big axial tube. Majumbdahr jetted down it, risking his neck. If he'd slammed into a parked shuttle craft or any temporary storage sacs, even his suit wouldn't have prevented a snapped neck.

But the *Farriken* was a tidy craft, everything secured nicely. He zipped along the tube without accident until he saw the bright orange of the lifesystem module and braked to a stop.

Majumbdahr keyed in an entry request. An attendant stuck his head out of the rear hatch. Majumbdahr kicked him back inside, pressed an injection nozzle to his throat, and was squirming into Lifesystem Core before the body stopped thrashing. (We found the man later, in the tube, snoring.) One, two, three canisters of the stunstuff, and lo— I was the captain of a starship.

The *Farriken* captain had sounded General Alert by then. Two bridge officers came swimming out into the axial tube. I was coasting inward. Training jackets us all: the one forbidden act in the tube is discharging a weapon. The rubbery walls, once pierced, quickly spurt reaction fluid into the tube, sealing off the life zones from the airlocks. So, though a flame gun dangled at my side, I didn't think to reach for it. One of the two saw us, turned, pointed—

I tumbled, switching head for feet.

Boots crunched into his chest. He spun away, rebounded off the tube wall.

The other officer shouted something, jaws gaping wide. (Suited, I heard nothing.) I snagged a hold on a wall mount. The second man braced himself against the tube legs scrambling for a hold. He pushed off.

I shoved against the mount, coming on him from behind.

A wrench in my belt found its way into my hand.

I clubbed him lightly. The wrench struck him at the back of the head and the tension went out of him.

I turned. Gharma had pounded the second man

three times in the stomach, then socked him in the jaw. He, too, seemed to lose interest in the proceedings.

Two minutes had elapsed. We found later that no May-day had gone out over ship's channel to Fleet Control. That accomplishment wasn't due to us in the tube, though, but rather to the stungas that a moment before had hissed into every chamber of the ship.

My ship.

It was good to sit once more in the Captain's couch, to see the long cylinder of the bridge encased in its swanky hush.

I let myself stretch and luxuriate for a moment, joints popping, muscles yawning to themselves, and yes, it did feel good. The *Farriken* was the best ship I'd seen, bigger than the *Sasenbo*. It had plush organiform padding everywhere, the sort which sops up debris and even human wastes (if the Captain permitted such use; after all, it went directly into the reaction mass). A fine ship to risk your life in.

"Majumbdahr reporting, sir."

"Sit. And drop the 'sir.' Perhaps the Council would consider us Fleet officers still, but I don't."

"I see your point," he said, slipping into the form-fitting couch next to me. Automatically he glanced at the screens and checked that all systems were normal; not even decades on the ground can take that out of an officer.

"Seems odd, somehow," I said. "A storm of action, and then waiting."

"Waiting is difficult."

"It would be easier if I *felt* like a Captain. The

Sabal was so much a part of the ships I commanded before . . ."

"Yes."

So I had a ship, but I didn't have a corps of faceless officers in Fleet Central giving orders. Independence brought its own fresh breath.

Majumbdahr checked a readout and turned to me.

"I just verified that all extraplanetary communications gear on Veden is silenced. They can't call Earth now."

"Ah? And how did you check that?"

"You'll remember—one of our men, a Lengen follower, sent me a signal—oh, I see what you mean."

"Small matter. I'm sure if you passed on him he can be trusted to disable the last transmitter."

"Fleet seems to have no suspicions, yet."

"When will the *Farriken* crew reach Veden?"

"Five days."

"You're sure the comm gear aboard is dead?"

"Yes. I double-checked before we cast them off."

"Good. Good. We'll be through the Flinger in another day."

He studied me. "We don't know how quickly a junior officer on Veden will react, however, if he suspects. That is a significant unknown."

"Who do you think it'll be?"

"The medical officer, Imirinichin. He's always had a itch to command. He might jump at it."

I shook my head. "He didn't strike me that way. In any case, how would he know?"

"Perhaps someone in the *Farriken* crew got off a radio burst in time. The board doesn't record ordinary local traffic, so we can't be sure."

"You know Imirinichin better than I—do you

think he'll buy the story we went on tightbeam?''

"It's not so wild, as fleet orders go these days."

I scratched my chin. "Um . . ."

"Something *might* have happened that demanded the *Farriken*'s leaving on the double. And it *would* have taken time for us to get clear of the background radiation from the reaction engines, in that ancient skimmer of ours."

I smiled wryly. "Even Fleet, failing as it is, doesn't snatch away a Director, plus staff officers."

Majumbdahr grinned, and I had a glimpse of what he must have been like when young. "Is Imirinichin an expert on cover stories?" he asked.

"He doesn't have to be. He's got the sensor network."

"All life is a gamble, Ling."

"Um." I looked around. Muffled monitoring beeps came from the hooded consoles up and down the bridge. A skeleton staff manned the stations, scarcely three dozen in all. Those, plus the Lengen priests and the Master, were all we had. "A gamble? I would prefer more chips."

There was no point in staying tight and tense while we waited to enter the Flinger. I ordered short watches and then left the bridge to Majumbdahr. I could sense the adrenalin ebbing in my crew, the excitement of the boarding fading. Now was the time to run silent and swiftly.

I made my way down—outward, really—from the bridge, through B deck to C. I passed a smashed hatchway; Gharma was looking at it, shaking his head.

"Difficult to believe," he murmured.

I raised an eyebrow in query.

"These . . . were Fleet officers. In here."

"The Plague cases?"

He nodded. "We had to blow the hatch to get them out."

"A bit messy," I said, judiciously studying the foul interior.

"They barricaded the room with furniture. Sealed off the air ducts with wadded sheets." Some of his crispness and disdain returned.

"You threw them into the skimmer with the rest of the crew?"

Gharma looked at me, his eyes intent. "This is a first-line vessel. It should carry the best crew available."

I sighed. "So it did."

"But three of them fell with the sickness before the ship could reach Veden."

"Yes."

"Imagine commanding a ship with a crew like that."

I studied him. Evidently he knew little of Regeln or the flight back to Earth from there. He probably hadn't seen my personnel file. Well, someone had: the Master had referred to it during my meditation with him yesterday.

I nodded mutely and went on. Rhandra and I had chosen a cabin out on C deck, for privacy. It felt strange to walk through a ship so quiet and still, as though it were waiting for something. I keyed into our cabin and walked in. "No news," I said. Rhandra was lying on our cushioned mat, *jonofu* style, hand over her eyes. She sat up at the sound of my voice, black hair tumbling in the weak centrifugal gravity.

"That I'm glad to hear," she said, and kissed me. "There has been too much news of late."

"Tired?"

"I shouldn't be, I know. Lighter gravity and all that. But I am."

I sat, shucked my sandals. "Things have moved too quickly for us all."

"A year ago a trip to Kalic was a big event," she said with a slight, puckering smile. "Now I'm on my way to Earth, and after that— Yes, it *is* a little quick."

"Earth is a stopover. A few days, then we leave."

"For where?"

"The Quarn region of the galaxy, the Master says. To begin a human colony on an hospitable world."

"Ling . . . ," and I saw the strain in her face.

"We don't like being conspirators."

"Yes. No whole person should have to act that way."

"If we had known the Master longer, these decisions would come freely. We would have a focus."

She nodded. I parted my robes and opened hers as well. Our bodies fit together naturally, softly, as though we had been married for decades. I buried my face in the rich crackling scent of her hair. We formed a warm, secure pocket in the austerity of the narrow crew quarters. I thought distantly of Angela.

She drew away. "It's dangerous, all of it?"

"Danger is relative."

She hit me playfully. "No need to be pompous. I don't want you to lie around like an old bear and make stuffy pronouncements. You'll begin to sound like the Lengen priests."

I faked a yawn and tugged her over on top of me. She chuckled softly in the folds of my neck. I released her hips; she pushed away to say something. Her shove tilted her back. I raised my knees.

She gave an awkward jerk that I helped along. My feet caught her just right and before she could reach out for a handhold I pushed here, pulled there—she spun in the air, a meter high. I kept her tumbling with my bare feet for another ten seconds, laughing at her startled cries of outrage, and let her drop. She thumped onto our pad. "Rrroww!"

"There'll be more if you don't allow me my proper share of dignity. Until you've spent a month in low-g you'll be at my mercy."

"So sorry. I didn't understand the gravity of the situation."

I cuffed her playfully, we wrestled, she pinned my arms. "I hope you give Fleet more trouble than this," she murmured, and then the mood between us shifted again and I found myself staring pensively into her eyes. "The . . . dreams . . . you're thinking of them, aren't you?"

I nodded mutely.

"Ling . . . I was dozing here, and I had something like the ones you describe . . ."

"Terrible, aren't they?" I said with thin humor. "For five days, now. And the headaches . . ." I stopped. I didn't mention that often Angela appeared in the dreams. Angela. Staring at me.

"Yours . . . always with the Master in them?"

"Usually, not always. Despite what I thought—or thought I thought—something in me doesn't like cooperating with the race that has done all this to humanity."

"In time . . ." she began, and then the reassuring currents lapped over me again, the chimes rang deep inside. *Let us regard the waters in their ways* . . . I reached out to Rhandra and saw at once that we were both awash in the same saving oceans, the peace that resolved all doubts.

* * *

After a while I murmured casually, "Some of the others don't seem to be bothered, though."

"Gharma."

"Right."

"The Lengen priests are keeping to themselves. These last few days they've not spoken to me."

"Or me," I said, stretching, yawning.

"They seem more rigid than the priests at Ashram."

"You haven't seen these Lengen before?"

"A few I knew, but none well. One priest from my home district was a friend of my family, and I came to know him in my time at the Ashram. He wasn't selected to come with us."

"Um. Maybe the ones here were picked for courage. Or calmness under stress. Or maybe the Master simply likes them better."

"I suppose you're right," she said, nuzzling her nose into my cheek. "I'll take some time to come to fullness with this. That's what the Master told me today."

"How was your audience?"

She chuckled softly in the folds of my neck. "I was awkward. I couldn't seem to concentrate."

"Um hum."

"I suppose I'm still reacting to his being a Quarn. I had no idea until that night."

"It bothers you still?"

"A little. He is alien. Strange. The Master knows so much about my reactions and how I feel. Even before I know myself."

I nodded and slipped off into a light, drowsy rest.

The corridors were cool and silent as I walked to my audience with the Master. Most of the violet phosphors were up by now, so I wore my Veden contacts. The *Farriken* had ordinary Sol phosphors when we took her. We had anticipated that, of course—it was one more sign of how isolated Veden was, why that planet had been granted the Hindics; adapted natives had difficulty even traveling to the more common G-type star systems. Phosphors are a monolayer that converts electrical current directly into light. We had only to paint over the Sol phosphors with a Veden monolayer and the emitted light shifted into the F-star spectrum. But we'd had little time to make up the stuff, and now ran short. Most of C deck and part of B were still using Sol light. Also, I noticed the Lengen priests, who'd been delegated the job, had slapped the stuff on in broad swabs, missing some of the Sol phosphor altogether. The result was a spectral distribution that looked like a cloudy day to a Veden and deep twilight to an Earthman. I could see complications looming up ahead. Most of the Lengen priests were Veden-adapted; they couldn't function well on Earth. But the Fleet officers used contacts, like me, and they could go to the surface. The Master had contacts, too, I'd learned. Evidently his home world had a redder sun, but it didn't matter, since he wasn't leaving the ship.

I rounded a corner and stopped, muttering a mild curse. Ahead the corridor was almost completely dark. Only Sol phosphors glowed there. The damned priests had done a spotty job. I circled around the shadowy corridors, taking an indirect route. I made a mental notation to get this situation fixed.

"Director!"

I turned. Gharma approached. "A few words." I nodded. "I am concerned about storage of the

Patanen," he went on. "We must deploy added pods from the axial tube."

I began to stroll toward the Master's quarters. Gharma walked stiffly beside me, arms held behind him and shoulders squared. He looked more like a soldier here than he ever had on Veden. "Very well. Be certain the storage units are put into the pods correctly. The bodies must be arranged so their feet point outward from the axis."

"Space requirements probably will not allow that. I—"

"*Make* them allow it."

"I'm afraid—"

"Look, these are people we'll be stacking in, not cordwood. How would you like to lie on your side—or upside down—for a body-time of a week? When cooled bodies lie in a static gravity field they undergo corpuscular damage and muscle deterioration, because a few layers of tissue are supporting the rest of the body."

"The effective gravity in the pods is low."

"We have no idea how long we'll be in transit. Even low acceleration can cause damage, given time."

"I see."

We approached the Master's quarters. "Well, here we are," I said lamely. Something in Gharma's stiff manner made conversation with him difficult. I kept feeling as if I had to think of something to say next.

"This is your regular audience time?" he said.

"No, I called down when I had time."

"I hope you appreciate the honor of being so close to the Master. Most must wait for their audience."

"You've had yours today?"

"No. No, I am later. I saw the Master a short while, and now I go to deliver a message from him to Majumbdahr."

"About what?"

"Lengen priest matters. Selection of ship's tasks."

"Why doesn't the Master tell Majumbdahr himself?"

"He has elected to relay instructions through you and me. He tires easily, as you know. The Master is living under conditions that differ considerably from his home world."

"What do you know about his planet?"

"Nothing more," he said quickly.

I tilted my head. "How long have you known the Master was a Quarn?"

He hesitated a moment, blinked. "A while longer than you. He went among the high castes first and was rejected by all but me. I am the only one from the very beginning."

"Well," I said uncomfortably, "very good. I think I'll go in now."

I passed through the antechamber, where four Lengen priests sat in zazen pose. We exchanged ritual greetings. I brushed aside a beaded curtain that tinkled. In the inner vestibule the Master welcomed me.

My meditation was as before, a deepening and yielding to inner nature. After, we talked.

The approach to Earth occupied our thoughts. I was uneasy about our passage through the Flinger and whether any moves could be made against us from Veden, but the Master swept these aside. Earth was the focus, he said, and I should bend my thoughts to it. Our task was made easier by Fleet's caution: they'd assembled the Patanen at one location, for study. There were thousands.

I shook my head in amazement. "How can you get all this done under Fleet's nose?"

"Same as Plague. Reach into centers of being."

"How?"

"We studied. We have knowledge from your past. When you evolved. Accidents of form in each species. Scent centers. Pressure areas. Neural matrix. All define and constrain."

"I learned . . . ," I began, and then stopped, wondering *why* I'd read all that about left hemisphere and right, the limbic brain . . .

"I ken. That was my doing."

"Why?"

"So you see the path. I ken you are . . . seeker. Must know. Humans have—tension." He made a steeple out of his hands and pressed the bony fingers together, smiling with thin lips. "Early primates hunted in packs. Tribes. Sense of community."

"Our natural state?"

"Then, yes. Not now." The steeple crumbled. "Mind whispers, says you are alone."

He peered deeply into me and the lights rippled, the waters lapped, and I saw it: Half-men cowering in caves at night, the sweaty scent of tribe around you, pressing close, safe and sure, a mate of your own and a place of your own, and yet . . . always, the voice in the back of the mind, speaking, thinking, turning the world this way and that to catch the sunlight a different way. If you did *this*, the prey did *that*, and you had to imagine these things, act by yourself in the hunt, the tribe together, running, calling, yet apart . . .

You, and others. The balance lay somewhere in between.

"A balance you destroyed," I said, a sudden angry flame within me. But the room sang, the waters rose, and I felt the peace descend.

"Restored. You have natural fear—repressed terror—of crowding. Is individual voice crying. Sabal submerges it. We"—a snap of the fingers, clouds dispersing from his hands—"release. Fear comes out."

"You use direct sensory input?"

He nodded. Bells chimed.

"Fear of humanity . . . Why doesn't it go away when your . . . treatment . . . stops?"

"Sabal resumes then. Amplifies fear again, so soon after."

"You have killed billions."

"We mourn." His face froze into a mask. "*Arrogance*. I help to correct. Restore natural order. The way it was long ago. Then I walk."

"No!" But as I said it, the anxiety eased away upon the waters.

"It will be. I earn it now. To take the Patanen to the Firmament. To bring all things to rest."

"The Firmament?"

"Outside the galaxy."

I saw it all suddenly. "The halo stars. The ancient ones."

"True. We fill them."

"You are *that* old?"

His eyes gleamed in the shadows of his cowl. He made a weary sign of assent.

We fill them.

I tried to think of what it meant to span the great swarming sphere, a thousand billion stars, and peer down at the bright disk, knowing it was an astrophysical stepchild. Halo stars are on the average more isolated than disk stars and poorer in heavy elements. Civilization must have arisen more slowly there, had to claw its way up without rich lodes of metals. Their night skies would be dim. Red embers smoldered there, not our gaudy O, B, and A stars that burned bright and flared into early deaths. And in the distance the disk would burn, a gumbo of blues and yellows, dust lanes and misty nebulae, the hub an incandescent blob where the aged black hole spun and sucked, spun and sucked. What did it feel like, to live in the gutted halo worlds, your race ancient beyond reckoning . . . ?

I shook my head. The vision left my head as quickly as it had come. "We . . . I am to navigate above the galactic disk?"

"In time. When the Patanen are in place."

"You had me study it, back then, didn't you?"

"Yes. You would need it."

"The expedition reports . . ." I pondered. "I'll have to recalibrate the Jump programming . . ."

I became lost in thought, and then lost in the rhythm of the ceremonies, and drifting, drifting with the tides and times, seeing all from a rocking swell in the great ocean, at peace.

2

JAGEN CLUTCHED AT US. It pulled me back into my acceleration couch, trying to drag me down the bridge into the tail of the *Farriken*. We were skimming closer to that ball of neutronium than I'd been in my pod, so long ago. The tidal stresses plucked at us. I knew the *Farriken* could take stronger strains than this . . .

The mind reassures, but the body is ignorant. My muscles tensed to fight the pull, even though I knew I was safe. *Ping* and *crack*, the ship flexed. A stylus rolled on my console and fetched up against a toggle switch.

I eyed the screen. Lekki boiled below, streamers coiling like snakes along the magnetic field lines. Ion winds whipped in a violent, violet dance. I wiped my brow, though I was cool.

"Something coming in from the satellites," Majumbdahr broke the strained silence of the bridge. "It looks like a torch spectrum they're picking up."

I swiveled about to watch the screens face-on, bracing against the tug. "Course data holding firm?"

"Yes sir. Point zero zero five c." He thumbed to a new index. "Several sensor satellites have the signal now, sir."

"How far away?" I said.

"Eight six point three million kilometers."

"Sure it's a fusion flame?"

"Yes."

Sometime in the last few minutes, while we were close to Lekki and our ship sensors blinded, the white torch of a reaction engine had flared on. It lay ahead of us. The satellite eyes had whispered warning now, but they had to be minutes late.

"A ramscoop."

"I expect so," Majumbdahr said.

I pressed *Emergency Stations*. Wailing sounded down the bridge. Heads raised to look at me, then ducked back to their cocoon consoles.

"Imirinichin," Majumbdahr said.

Gharma, sitting beyond in Engine and Fuel Systems Command, nodded grim assent.

"It appears as though our esteemed medical officer has plucked up the fallen standard," I said. "Give me an intercept."

"Computing," Majumbdahr muttered.

"We're going into rebound, sir," Gharma said over intercom. I glanced screenward. Jagen grew into a sullen red ball bathed in a radial spray of blue lines: images of the stars beyond, their light warped by the deep gravitational potential around the Black Dwarf.

"Max stress," Gharma called. I thumbed in a satellite view of us. A gleaming blue ball was arcing in a tight circle around a black nothingness. The *Farriken*'s organiform had filmed over with a metal-like polish hours ago, to reflect away all but a millionth of Lekki's light; a chrome starship.

"That ramscoop is nearly dead on our course," Majumbdahr said quickly. "Intercept in fourteen minutes, twenty-one seconds."

The *Farriken* groaned. Our instruments began to unfog. Plasma roiled, red and wispy, sucked free of Lekki by Jagen's grip. I felt pressure begin to ease. We were zipping outward now, our velocity matched to Earth-Sol.

"Compute a dodge pattern."

"Done, sir. Wait . . . our mass detector is coming online again. I'll try for some new data with it. The readings should be more accurate than these correlation measurements I've been using from the satellites." Majumbdahr punched in commands.

My intercom buzzed, but it was a low-priority call. I chopped it off. I noticed I was biting my lower lip.

"How does it appear to you, sir?" Gharma asked.

"Imirinichin is smarter than I guessed. He waited until we were so near Jagen our mass detectors went blind. Then he moved. He must have guessed we're headed for Earth; that would tell him our exiting trajectory."

I studied readouts, and then: "We can't clear the blast, sir," Majumbdahr reported. "It looks like Imirinichin has a big fat window for detonation. The scoop itself can't get close, but . . . he'll blow the ramscoop fusion plant."

"And let the ball of debris expand at relativistic speeds, snagging us."

"I can cut down the radiation with some maneuvering."

"Do so," I said. "And check back with the mass detector. You've narrowed its range down to get a good reading on that scoop, haven't you? Now scan for anything further out, too."

He and Gharma began working feverishly. I listened to the whine of the air circulators, trying to think. The main screen showed us a fat blue dot surging up from Jagen. Goodbye, Dwarf.

I glanced down the bridge. In each console cluster many couches yawned empty. Here it was easy to remember we were pinned to the wall of a cylinder: the floor stretched away two hundred meters to right and left, but curved up and away into the ceiling, in front and behind me. Far to the left, a Lengen priest on standby duty made ritual hand passes, perhaps to calm himself.

"You're right, sir," Majumbdahr's words were clipped. "Three more scoops are moving, further out from the first."

"It's a blind," I said. "Even if we dodge the first fusion blast, it'll jam our sensors. Then the later scoops hit us before we can recover."

"We have attained max rebound velocity, sir, as computed," Gharma broke in. "Vector sigma not exceeding point zero zero zero four."

"Give me a new course, Mr. Majumbdahr. Maximize the square of the distance we can get between us and all four of the plasma clouds, if those scoops detonate. Include the shock wave effects."

"Computing."

I glanced at visual display. Ahead, an orange cone burned: ramscoop exhaust. Our projected trajectory was a dashed line. The cone pointed toward a red-tagged dot along the line, the place where we would intersect the blast wave. As I watched, we crawled visibly toward the dot.

"Log new course," I ordered. "Automatic firing sequence—nose about."

Immediately I felt the rumble and tug of our own motors. Gyros brought us around, pushing aside the fingers of Jagen's tidal grip. Somewhere a servo whined.

"Get an estimate of probable radiation damage," I called to Majumbdahr. He thumbed in orders, and downbridge a technician responded: numbers flashed on my screen.

"High," I said between narrowed lips. "Too damned high. We can't take that."

"I can't give you anything better, sir," Majumbdahr said. "He has us boxed in a narrow channel."

I nodded. "Prepare for Jump space."

There was silence. No one moved.

"It is a risk we must take," I said.

"Yes *sir*," Majumbdahr said with a note of glee. He slapped a switch. A hooting wail sounded along the bridge. Lights dimmed to conserve power.

"Metric Computing!" I called. "How large are the Riemann-Christoffel elements in the region just in front of the first scoop?"

An under-officer somewhere answered me. "Within four percent of critical, Captain."

"And how many ships have been lost going into Jump under those conditions?" I murmured, thinking to myself.

"Several. The probabilities are difficult to calculate in a highly warped field such as this, sir, and—"

"I know." The *Farriken* had come out of Jump space well clear of the entire Lekki-Jagen planetary system where the tensor elements were well known, and then coasted in to near Veden. Taking her into Jump on Jagen's doorstep was—

"Jump computation finished, sir," Majumbdahr called.

"To what order?"

"Third order in local coordinates."

I grimaced. What good was a calculation good to five decimal places, when we couldn't measure the input data to better than three places?

"Power reserves adequate," Gharma said calmly.

"Wait—I'm getting something more," Majumbdahr said. "Mass detector is back on full scan and—oh, I see."

"See what?" "It's that anomaly again, sir. High above the plane of the ecliptic."

"That again? I thought it was a sensor malfunction."

"So did I. But it's still there."

"It cannot be a ramscoop," Gharma put in. "We never orbited any that—"

"Of course not," I said irritably. "It registers as a large mass. How far out is it?"

"More than a billion klicks," Majumbdahr said presently. "Perhaps further. That's a lower bound."

"Oh, no trouble after all," Gharma said.

"The range of scan on this Class IV detection system is greater than I'm used to," Majumbdahr said slowly. "Sorry."

"No matter," I said.

"Still, I wonder what it is," Majumbdahr murmured. "Mass reads larger than any ship. Could be a large asteroid."

"How accurate is that mass data?" I asked.

"I would have to do an autocorrelation analysis—"

"No time," I said with sudden energy. "Majumbdahr, put an automatic scan-and-file on that thing and forget it."

I peered at the screens. While the talk had gone on, I had made my decision.

"Sir, are we going into Jump count?" Gharma reminded me.

I sighed. There was no way out. "Yes. Commence sequence."

I noticed my hands were white on the arms of my couch. I breathed, and the air seemed cool. The orange torch crawled toward us.

Then it was an expanding scarlet ball, a firework.

"The ramscoop just blew, sir," Majumbdahr said intently, his face hooded by his console.

"So I gather. That's the plasma cloud we're seeing. Oxygen lines, I'd judge. High-energy paricles should be along in a moment."

Rad detectors in the *Farriken*'s skin gave a confirming buzz. Our sheath of reaction fluids would screen out this first flux, but the heavier stuff lagging behind . . .

"Imirinichin is willing to sacrifice several scoops to stop us," Gharma observed. "That represents a substantial financial loss to the Empire. He must be very sure something is wrong."

"A good officer," I murmured. "Willing to play on a hunch. If Fleet had had more like him . . ." I broke off with a faint smile. The past is prologue.

"Mr. Majumbdahr," I said formally. "What speed do we need to skim by the surface of the expanding debris cloud?"

"Let's see . . ." Calculating. "Using our present computed Jump point, we need one seven eight four two times *c*, Captain."

"Punch it in."

"That's right at maximum boost, sir."

"So it is. Bridge! Metric Computing."

"Sir."

"How does the failure probability increase if we go to maximum boost?"

"Ah . . . rises by one point eight four, sir."

"Interesting. Not that it matters, gentlemen." I looked around me at tightened faces and kept my voice conspicuously calm. "We're fresh out of alternatives."

The red ball clawed out to meet us. Plasma billowed in great banks, lit by hydrogen lines. In such a sleet of protons we would fry in twenty seconds.

Far away hung Veden, a creamy dot. Star of India.

"Time," I called.

A rush, a swirl of light.

The falling—

Metal groaned. Someone screamed.

The world outside the *Farriken* smeared. We shot by the fireball, through the Jump. With a Pythagorean power, Number held sway above the Flux.

3

<small>THROUGH THE STARLESS, NAKED NIGHT—</small>

Our run to Earth took nine days. The blank bare silence outside made the Lengen priests uneasy; a disquiet seeped into the ship. I noticed it and began their training early. We needed teams to bring back the Patanen from Naga, where they were assembled. The exercises and weapons training raised everyone's spirits, including mine.

I spent days reprogramming the *Farriken* so we could make one long Jump to get free of the galactic plane. The Empire was vast, but its kiloparsec diameter was a fleck in the turning sea of the galaxy. Earth lay a third of the way out from the galactic hub, near a spiral arm. The galaxy was ten kiloparsecs thick in Sol's neighborhood. Clearing that vast chasm in one Jump would burn two-thirds of our fuel. There was no coming back from the halo stars.

I designed override subsystems to stop the *Farriken* from dumping us out of Jump space too early, when its safety monitors panicked. Gharma and Majumbdahr labored on backup systems.

Activity lifted my spirits. I had always detested intrigue; thus my failure at the low-order palace politics of Fleet. The week before we occupied, the *Farriken* ran thick with deception and the stench of the half-lie. I became depressed almost without realizing the cause. But when Imirinichin showed his hand—I was sure he was cursing himself now for playing it a moment too soon—I had felt an old exhilaration, one I thought long dead. It came from being involved again.

I had come to think of myself over the last few years as a man of contemplation. As a young scholastic, I had decided that men of action—the only kind worth admiring, I thought then—seldom heeded or needed men of contemplation. Oh, perhaps for an occasional practical reason, yes, but not as a habit of mind. So, much later, when I sought solace from the world, what in boyhood was a conviction had become an unconscious axiom, and it placed me firmly in the role of an introvert among men who did-things.

These recent days brought my youth swimming back in a way different from the rekindling Rhandra caused. I liked action and movement, the singing zest of conflict, but it had to be to some purpose: something better than patching up the Empire. I needed momentum, a vector, not the constricted sense of human possibility—of which Sabal was a subtle but integral part—of the Mongol.

My work in Fleet had a touch of that energy, once. It ebbed away as I rose in the ranks. Finally I did not even know it was gone.

There are many ways to shorten a man. Cynicism is the easiest. That, too, I affected for a while, in my middle years with Fleet. Then I had turned to Sabal for what refuge it could give. And now in a curious cycle I had returned to the consuming concentration of work. I spoke of it to Rhandra, and she quoted a Veden song-thinker: *Doing's the one reward a man dare ask.*

While we worked, Earth drew nearer. We were running scared. I had captained mining shuttles, hop transports, suborbital cyclers, cargo barges— everything but prime Jump vessels. Running the *Farriken* with a skeleton crew meant I was on the bridge fourteen hours a day, minimum. I prepared routine-sounding reports and sent them under my signature as Veden Fleet Commander. I also wrote humdrum *Farriken* reports and transmitted telemetry. I threw in some complaints from each Commander about the other, just to keep things plausible.

Plans win through or fail not because of great ideas but by small details.

Numbed by a fretwork of small items to remember and deal with, I lost my way on the route to the Master's quarters. I blundered into the dreary twilight of a Sol phosphor corridor, tried to work my way through it anyway, and failed. The Lengen priests were the only free hands we could spare to prepare extra Veden phosphor mix, and Majumbdahr reported them blithely uninterested in work. As a commander, I was irked by their bland unconcern, but I said nothing of it to the Master when I reached his quarters, late, and my audience began.

I was only fractionally immersed in the lilting rituals when the Master nodded abruptly and spread his hands, palms down and flexed, to signal the end.

"State is not right," he said rapidly. "Attempting focus while mind—" He twirled a bony finger by his head.

"I—I do not *feel* so—"

"Ah," he said, nodding vigorously. "*Are*. Look—position. Not resting weight through body center."

I glanced down. As far as I could tell I was in proper sitting form, a slight variation in the stylized Buddha pose. Alignment of spine felt correct. Odd; surely I wasn't fooling myself that well. There had always been some telltale signs before to show how I was throwing off my own concentration. Today my mind was fuzzed a bit, yes, but I felt properly placid.

"See now?" the Master said quickly, breaking the pause.

"No . . ."

"Ah." His eyes darted to the side. I noticed that he was unconsciously tapping the *majatin* mat with a webbed foot. "Can ken. Important moment approaches. Perhaps—perhaps is bad time."

"Master," I said, "I can learn as much in these moments as in any other. My inner place is undisturbed by the days to come, I feel that securely."

In truth I felt slighted by his assumption that I was getting nervous about the mission. Enlightenment opens to one the eternal moment and seals the future until its time has come. While I had not attained the Buddha state, the evidence of my own mind told me I was not now deflected from the right path. Or was this presumptuous?

"No." Once more a side glance. A slap on his knee. "You do not ken. I judge your mood not right for study. There are many things you must learn."

"Master—"

"Wrong time," he said abruptly.

With a start I realized it was not I who was distracted, but the Master. He carried no aura of serenity about him now; he appeared as simply another mortal, worried about something. He had misjudged my own state and not been sensitive enough to catch the error.

I frowned and made ready to go. Rhythmic motions, the old encasing rituals. And even as I passed outward through the *kandimaji* shrine I began to question my own responses, to wonder if I had seen correctly or if this was simply another layer of confusion I had to pass through, a cloud of illusion my own resisting habits threw up to shield a part of me that I would, in truth, be better off without.

"Sir?" Majumbdahr caught me on the downramp from the bridge.

"Tomorrow," I said. I rubbed a sandy eye.

"Very well." I waved him to walk and we went "down" onto B deck.

"You remember the anomalous mass we saw on the detectors back at Lekki-Jagen?"

"Yes. What of it?"

"I . . . I've taken the scan-and-store readout."

"Why?"

"Something bothered me about it."

He said this straightforwardly, as though daring me to criticize him for wasting time. But I knew he had been working very hard, and a good fleet officer cannot be as meek as a file clerk. "And?"

"Its velocity is high and rather remarkable."

"How so?"

"It will pass quite close to Lekki."

"Couldn't it be interstellar matter drifting in?"

"Not likely. Velocity is far too high."

"So? It could still be an odd fragment."

"Suppose it's something more? Our readings give a mass of about a tenth Sol mass. Suppose it's a Colossus?"

That stopped me. In the twenty-second century some factions had abandoned Earth for political reasons and cast off into deepspace. They didn't have Jump ships or even ramscoops in those days. Instead they built crude reaction engines into asteroids, socked most of their party into coldsleep, and set out. Most never reappeared. Those who did were often turned into weapons.

"I see. No Colossus has been seen for centuries."

"Another possibility is that it is a simple rogue rock, on freefall into Lekkispace, but . . ."

"Improbable, I agree."

"So, sir . . ."

"What?"

"I would like computer time for a full recorrelation of the mass detector data. Our velocity fix on this thing is poor. I can improve it by a high-accuracy resifting of the data."

"Um." I frowned. "We need read-and-register space badly in the ferrites. I—"

"This could be important for Veden."

I sighed. The Empire was nothing to me, but Veden . . . "All right. Rig it to run after we're in Earth orbit, though. While we're on the surface, in fact. There's no time now."

"Very good, sir."

I picked our exit Jump locus carefully. We filed the official *Farriken* reports a few hours before Jump. I'd suggested days earlier that we return to

Earth, and Fleet had rubber-stamped the request. They directed me to remember when speaking to the Veden Commandant that he was inordinately sensitive about his defensible volume, like all regional Directors, and therefore to stress the scarcity of Fleet ships.

I confirmed their first commanded Jump exit. It was far from where I wanted, but if we ignored them and emerged elsewhere there would be red-ruby hell to pay. Earth could pick up any Jump transit within half a parsec; the super-c radiation burst was like waving a flag.

Just before we Jumped I sent a request for a new Jump locus, explaining that we had too high a matching velocity and didn't want to waste time cutting it down. A Jump time was already computed and anyway the Farriken could decelerate enough if Fleet Central would simply shift our exit point further from Earth. They grumbled and gave us—as I'd guessed—some last-minute choice about the precise spot. That meant they wouldn't have a precise fix.

Rhandra stood beside me at the bridge as the Jump came. A flicker, the prickling tension—

We popped into being half a million klicks from Earth, with Luna hanging directly between us and man's home.

"Fleet's squawking about our choice, Captain," Gharma called, listening with one hand to the running telemetry.

"They don't want to bother getting a fix on our M and delta-V through Luna Control," I said.

We glided around Luna at high relative velocity. There were unavoidable lags in telemetry between Luna and Earth, I knew, that shaved a hairline of accuracy off our known location.

"Incoming orders," Majumbdahr called. The screens rippled. Fleet was evidently pulling most craft not immediately needed into a dense screen around Earth. We were stationed a bit in from Luna orbit as part of a shifting defense grid.

"Umm," I said. "As far as I know, no Quarn ship has violated Earthspace. These precautions seem rather heavy."

"Perhaps they're frightened," Rhandra volunteered.

"The Empire may be weaker than I thought," I said.

Luna swept below, her ancient craters seeded with yellow gems. The atmosphere shimmered grey-green. I popped my contact filters into my palm; yes, now it was a natural blue-white. Rhandra had to get along with a dimmer, achromatic image. I wondered again how easy it might be to find a suitable F star among the halo swarm.

We left the bridge for a while, since it was time for my audience with the Master. He saw each of us daily. When I emerged this time, feeling rested and my mind drifting peacefully, Gharma was waiting at the *kandimaji* shrine that framed the Master's portal. "He tires?" Gharma asked.

"The Master? A little."

Gharma fretted. "He should not keep to so difficult a schedule. This is a great and tragic mission. He is passing through what is, for the Quarn, the last journey. He is filled with an anguish such as we cannot sense."

"How do you know?" I asked, not because I doubted him, but because his solemn air I found wearing.

"I have been with him the longest. I sense his essence.'

"I see."

"I left my family to follow his path."

"And Majumbdahr?"

"He, too."

These men had given up much to follow the Master. "Such power . . ."

"Yes. The Quarn works are many."

"Yes, vast," I conceded. "Though not perfect, you'll grant."

"The Master senses doubts in you, Ling."

"He does?" I thought of my audience days before, and the Master's odd, edgy quality. Perhaps I had been wrong, though.

"Your center resists."

"Ah." My eye was caught by Rhandra, approaching for her audience. She gave us greetings.

"I should think increased meditation would benefit both of you in these last hours," Gharma said.

"If there is time," Rhandra began. "Surely—"

"Proper equilibrium is essential."

"My hours are not so easily arranged," I said.

"I believe before you leave the ship you should ask for added time with the Master. His hand should guide you."

"Perhaps," I said grudgingly.

"Ling needs rest," Rhandra said.

"I speak for the Master himself."

"Oh?" I murmured.

"There are levels of knowledge among the Lengen," Gharma said, "just as there are grades of priests."

"We are not priests," Rhandra said.

"In these hours of this final task I should think—"

"The Master himself is pinched by the forces around us," I said. "I feel we should all give mutual aid."

"The Master tires, perhaps, but he is still the Master," Gharma said stiffly.

"Can't you talk to him? Convince him to rest a bit, if you're concerned?"

"No, he must see us all each day."

"Why?"

"It is the Way."

I shrugged. Argument accomplished nothing in this odd mystical navy I'd joined; I returned to the bridge.

When I tried to think about the Master, as in the talk with Gharma, ideas kept slipping away from me. There were things the Master had done, vast damage to people and cultures, that vexed me . . . yet the rising of the waters washed all care from me, and I saw these cares as yet another false way to pin me to the past or prevent my own realization. The past, after all, was dead. The future loomed.

I had designed the fusion warheads myself. Gharma knew a little about fusion jacketing, and he helped me seal them with barium and potassium casings, all layered in shells to make the brightest possible ionization cloud around the fireball.

The Earth Defense Screen was a piece of history, a spiderweb of microelectronics that, the press agentry gushed, could pick up a sneeze on Venus. A gossamer net, sensitive, delicate—and stupid.

I had always thought the EDS was badly designed. It began as a simple tracking system. As Fleet grew, they patched in more sensitive satellites with greater ranging. With the Quarn war they added many more sensors until they could nail a ship down to half a klick absolute. The grid even registered lifeboats running without comm gear.

All this came from multiplying the number of units, but never changing their sensitivity. The sensors could weather a solar storm, given warning. Otherwise they peered naked into the void; that was their weakness.

The torpedoes went out with hollow thumps. I watched them sprint away. Clumsy weapons, never used successfully against Quarn. Our eleven torpedoes twisted, fanned out—

Ahead, aft, at all sides: the sky splintered.

"Send the emergency distress signal," I called down the bridge.

"Done!"

A boiling wave of electromagnetic energy obliterated the nearest sensors. Further out, high-energy ions and electron-positron clouds seared away microelectronics. Nothing between Luna and Central could pick up our silhouette through that.

We boosted inward. We buttoned up tight, antennas tucked in like a frightened dog's tail to escape the scorching barium clouds. I listened to Fleet's Emergency Response trigger. Bells clanged, our screens flared with confused images. Earth's magnetic dipole field smeared the cloud into a wedge as it expanded. Soon Eskimos, had there been any left, would have noticed a brightening of the aurora borealis as high-energy electrons sleeted down.

We flew blind, sniffing our way in with occasional radarlike pulses from our mass detectors. But the *Farriken*'s permanent log knew Earthspace the way my tongue knows my teeth; we kept to course, bead on a *konchu* wire.

When the *Farriken* burst free of the snarling plasma, we hung over a herd of ramscoops, glinting metal-grey. They were awaiting loading for the

Empire worlds, unmanned. They rode a standard parking orbit that had not deviated in centuries; I could've given the orbital coordinates to two places from memory. The scoops were the sheep we wolves would hide among. They drifted, several hundred strong, webbed on repulsion lines to prevent slight perturbations from causing collisions. Some were damaged, fire-pitted, probably useless. Others gaped wide in their guts, mouths being loaded by automatic shuttles. Every few days a scoop was nudged out by low-impulse reaction motors and cast off on a long hydrogen-gobbling course. Sol system had no Flinger to make the first acceleration cheap, so Earth usually had an excess of scoops waiting for reflight; more came to Rome than returned to the colonies.

This ever-changing flock of metal and organiform was a nuisance to Fleet Ships Catalog, I knew; they hadn't the resolution to pick out every scoop. This close in to Earth—a nose-rubbing three hundred klicks up—Fleet might overlook us.

Might.

4

MAKING LOVE WITH Rhandra was by now a lesson
well learned, a refined process. We had each
stamped the other with a style fresh and adapted.
I no longer felt (when I did *this*, say, or *that*) a pale
shadow of times spent with Angela. I had unmemo-
rized the past. We coiled together in these last
moments, finding new geometries for our well-
rehearsed arms and legs in the low gravity: Galactic Man at the old slap and tickle.

I lay awake for a while staring into the blank
darkness. Outside, Earth waited. Outside was
everything, and inside here was my mind. Consciousness was an analogue map, a point-by-point
tracing of the world, and it was generated by words.
The left side of the brain, painting reality over
with a lacquer of language. Yet something inside
resisted the steady rain of words. Our time sense,
for one. Something stretched and compressed time
according to the intensity of experience, following

the ticking of its own ancient clock. What part of us did that? The Quarn knew, I was sure. Had there been a time when the right brain ruled? Did the Quarn know us then? Did the Master himself? The right brain spoke to us now with a thick tongue, muttering below the bright clarity of pressing sentences from the left, raising lids of boxes we could not pry up with language. Was there buried down in there the link between animal shame and human guilt? The swelling hunters' fear that became human anxiety? Perhaps the Quarn knew all that. But the Master's worrisome anxiety, during that one audience, pricked at me. Did he know us entirely? We were not the creatures of millennia ago. Now we could summon up our past for revision, sweeten our afternoons with daydreams, rehearse the future—my mind flooded with gaudy images of the Earthward blooding to come—and forge many futures, events branching like a fragile tree. The ability to aim and fire is not a verbal one; the old cleverness ruled there. So I would need left and right brain. And the Master knew better than I what this fresh-scrubbed Ling could do.

After sleep, with Rhandra still dozing, I rose and went down to the armory. I had on my field Fleet uniform. It was clean-cut, dark, excellent for concealment. The team we were sending down carried all the usual Fleet personal weapons; I found them rather unimaginative. I had worked in the backwaters most of my career, and there are places where a flame gun is just so much gaudy hardware. I needed a few touches of subtlety.

I'd made up a few items on the voyage. A pencil-sized tube went into my pocket. Throw it ten meters away and a small powder charge disperses a paralyzing irritant, neatly taking out a five-meter volume, but no more. Below my belt I tucked a silent air pistol. It fired shells stuffed with poisoned flechettes, fine needles that followed ballistic paths once the shell exploded. Some shells I'd packed with white phosphorus, too, to shed a little light on problems. Inside my shirt I wedged a particular nasty: a plastic-jacketed pancake, green when wet. Slip it from its jacket and the wetting agent escapes in twenty seconds or so. Slide the wet cake under a rug or into some grass. Once dry, any impact will explode it. Tear off a piece and stick it like an old wad of gum to a door jamb; when the door closes, presto. I'd picked up that one on Laganat, from some terrorists we'd captured. They used it because it was cheap and easy; they preferred flame weapons if they could get them.

To this I added the usual: a strangling-wire that reeled out of a wrist band, night specs, gas grenades. All the comforts of the modern world.

We used drift-craft for the descent. The *Farriken* carried pods of them. They were gossamer ships, metal-free to avoid EM detection, with fall-away jets for suborbital work and then sails, chutes, ailerons, stabilizers, swoop-rudders, and the rest for skating through the atmosphere. Most were four-man jobs. There were a few one-man gliders, though, and I snagged one. They were programmed, so all but the last fifty klicks down were ordained. I reviewed the troops as launch time approached, said a few words of encouragement, slapped a few shoulders. They were nearly all Fleet men, most with their Sol-adapted vision intact, and a few Lengen priests who'd never been off Veden. They'd be nearly useless except in dealing with the Quarn on the surface.

We dealt with a thousand last details. We sang our final *gonjii* chant. We climbed into the stiff-winged gliders. We coasted out to the lock. Farriken's launch rachet seized us each in turn. I relaxed utterly, saving energy.

The hatchway slid open before my bubble. Stars burned.

God kicked me in the tail.

I shot out, across a harvest field of ramscoops, and plunged down toward our grazing impact with Earth's film of air.

It was a dreamy time.

A *thump* as the low-luminosity burn came on (invisible from below, we hoped). A hissing as winds plucked at me. Below, blue—a stark titanium blue that would swallow all other colors. Earth spread out below me with its tangle of small lives and deaths that from a distance appears a lawn but up close is wrenchingly confused and cruel, a mad jungle.

Drifting. Chutes popping dutifully open. Sails slanting me down. South America, yawning in summer's heat.

Then we were drifting over New Guinea. Tumbled ridges of green-brown jungle, sliced by muddy grey rivers. Men lived there now, but still not many. I had ventured there once, been bitten and pricked to distraction, and sworn I'd never go back. Now it was absolutely certain I would keep the promise.

To the east lay the Solomons, now an *ofkaipan* slum. My slightly pinked skin would not raise an eyebrow there. Lumps of brown strewn to the horizon by a careless Creator, now bathed in Pacific sunlight that swathed it in ruddy splendor, a light like the crystallized air of the centuries. I had holidayed on one of those specks, sleeping on a pallet with relatives who sweated in the fields each day, eaten a fierce vegetable curry, washed it down with a dark, solemn stout. A soft and quiet time, before fleet and Angela.

Leaves falling on a still day: slipping down the winds, a covey of stupid birds too lazy to flap. Leyte and Samar we skirted around as dawn broke on their urban sprawls. Panay sulked on the horizon. We slipped lower. Quezon gleamed with street lights.

North now: Cataduanes. Luzon. Mountain ridges clutched up at us. We dipped, skimmed. Then Naga.

No sign of detection. No *scree* of intercept jets.

Outside Naga we found a soccer field. It lay in dark, though mountain peaks nearby glowed with dawning. I banked and surveyed the surrounding land. Nothing stirred.

I ordered them down. My little convoy peeled off one by one and swooped in for a bouncy landing. Waiting, I studied Naga's shadowed profile. No movement, not even air cars.

A long column of smoke traced a finger from far beyond the city, smudging the air nearby. Above, the stars swam in shroud.

My flock was down. I swooped, glided, wind sang in the struts. *Thump* and I was back in Rome.

Military history is the story of the terrible murder of beautiful plans by ugly facts.

I'd selected a second-rate farm road for our approach to Naga. I'd hauled vegetables over it a hundred times as a boy, working for summer wages in the fields. A sleepy road, nothing more.

There was no reason whatever to put a Fleet recreational facility seven klicks from Naga along that road. None.

But there it was, complete with three gate guards. I got out of the car we'd stolen and tried to talk them around. Seems the soccer field was in a Fleet enclosure, and they were curious about how a team of officers and men had spent the night in a days-only facility.

One of them wanted to call in about it. Once he got this idea, he refused to let go of it. Maybe he just didn't like taking an *ofkaipan*'s word. And he never took his hand off his sidearm.

His arm moved—

So I shot him.

Then the others.

The air pistol coughed three times. The flechettes bored deep. It was messy.

We cleaned up quickly.

We swiped some Fleet cars.

Naga was stirring as the east cracked open with dawn. Trash drifted in the gutters everywhere. Shop windows were often boarded up. Pedestrians eyed us, then moved on, scurrying.

I felt exposed as hell. Every tenth block in Naga had a Fleet box on the corner. A sentry lounged in it, squinting at us as we rumbled by, an arm casually draped over a BFX autoweapon on a tripod. Occasionally its snub snout followed us in a lazy arc.

We went by Fleet offices, a rotunda and marble colonnades basking in the rising sun. They needed a washing; streaks of black and brown wrote an old story on their faces.

Away from Naga center there were no more signs of Fleet. Official buildings gave way to long, gracefully arched residences, prickly with brick pilasters, fragile colonnada, *ostraku* arcades. But here, too, few people walked the streets gold-rimmed by day.

Here the plan went well: I found the warehouses easily, in fact remembered them from times I had worked nearby as a boy. There were no Fleet police in this district. They seemed drawn up around Fleet buildings, letting the civilians fend for themselves.

Someone spotted us and *clunk* a warehouse door slid aside. An arm beckoned. Our party of eighteen covered the vacant street, then slipped inside one at a time. I went in first.

"Sanjen?" He was a short, stocky Fleet Lieutenant, plainly edgy and worried. "I'm Cantalus."

We shook hands. Cantalus was orderly, efficient. He had the Panaten already in coldsleep vaults. His working crew was mostly civilians. I counted vaults. "We can squeeze this many in," I said. "But it'll be close."

"This isn't all."

"Why not?"

"You must understand . . . I have been taking a few dozen Panaten at a time from the Fleet quarters. We infiltrated the staff there. There were hundreds left."

"We're not finished, then."

"Sir, I—we've been discovered."

"What? How?"

"Or I *think* we have. Last night a high officer came to the Panaten quarters. He wanted three of them, so we did not have to open the wards. Still, I think he was suspicious. He took the three away, but I believe he may be back."

"Why? Why do you think so?"

"The three Panaten were . . . related to you."

"What?"

"Your wife. And two children."

"Impossible."

"No. I verified it myself."

My mind spun in a high and airless place. I had thought little of Angela, had given up Chark and Romana as lost. My opposition to their lobe-tapping must have given them some added advantage. But to have recovered—

"Sir," Majumbdahr said at my elbow, "they've got the trucks. We can start moving."

"Yes . . . Start." I looked at Cantalus. I knew the next answer. "Who took them away?"

"General Tonji."

I had arranged a pretext through Air Control, to allow us access to the automatic surface-to-orbit shuttles. It was no great trick: we stripped encoding ferrites from the ramscoops parked near the *Farriken*, and used those to order automatic shuttles, using ordinary comm lines in the ramscoops.

The problem was getting the vaults to the shuttles. Cantalus had trucks. Could we get them through the streets? "That what we'll *have* to do," Cantalus said. He looked appealingly at two figures seated in the shadows that cloaked the huge warehouse. They were heavily robed and sat very tall and erect. Quarn. But they did not speak, and their hooded eyes stared out at us impassively. Cantalus turned back to me. "We have no other way."

"No access to copters?"

"Not now. There is great demand. I could not—"

"All right, the trucks. You have permits?"

"A few." He produced some ferrite stickers.

"Enough to get all these through?"

"I don't know."

"Let's pack them in. Then we'll see."

The morning heat rose thick and cloying from the street outside. I stood watch at the entrance bay of the storage warehouse. There was surprisingly little activity in the business district. As a boy, I'd been jostled and awed in these streets, had flowed in the rivers of men and women and goods, swam in air freighted with price calls and bitter bargains, grunts of labor and cackles of glee. All gone now.

"We're ready for the first detachment to shove off. Captain," Cantalus reported.

I eyed the narrow docking lanes. The hover trucks purred beside the loading cranes, riding low beneath the vaults. In the murky distance Mayon spit orange into the tropical blue, ringed in grey haze.

"Go."

The Lengen priests conferred with the Quarn, who still sat stiff and somber. Around them the men who were their followers sweated in the damp air. The Quarn looked exhausted. They had accomplished much in so short a time.

A priest approached me. "A moment?" I nodded.

"The Masters wish to be . . . to go in the vaults."

"Why?"

"They wish to awaken amid their home worlds. They have no heart for the voyage."

"Well . . . all right."

I listened to Fleet comm traffic over Cantalus's unit. It was spotty and oddly incoherent. Our fusion explosions had raked great holes in EDS.

Then came a coded blip from our first detachment. They had gotten through and loaded an automatic shuttle. They were riding up with it.

I sent Gharma with the second group. I helped load vaults myself to work off the tension that hung in the air like smoke. We wrapped the Quarn. Their suety skin gleamed in the noonday light. I marveled at their bone structure: humanoid, unlike the other aliens we had encountered, yet different in pelvis, joints, spine. They lay silently, their eyes filmed. The coolant fluids bubbled up to cover them.

I clicked off the comm. "Gharma is lifting," I said.

"We are nearly ready to leave ourselves," Cantalus said eagerly.

"Mr. Cantalus."

"Yes?"

"Where did Tonji take the others?"

"The base at Mindoro."

"How do you know?"

"He said so."

"Why do you suppose he did that?"

"What?" Cantalus waved to the men to finish the loading.

"Why leave word of his destination? Unless he wanted to be followed."

Cantalus looked at me.

"Here's the entrance," Majumbdahar called back to us. We crouched in the rear of the hover truck. Dusty lanes zipped by as we sped down the last highway. Mahataqua trees nodded in the midafternoon heat. Behind us in Naga a black finger curled up into a clotted cloud: a fire. A Slot? Eventually there would be no one healthy enough to tend the victims. Then a fire would rage beyond control.

A massive organiform cube reared beside the road. I wrinkled my nose. The stench reminded me of the Slots. Around the cube nothing moved.

We hummed, slowed, stopped. The whine died, and we lowered to earth. I swung down from my perch.

"Where's your passes?" a guard was asking Majumbdahr. I joined them. Majumbdahr handed him a clip of ferrites and yawned. He leaned against the truck.

The guard inserted the ferrites in his casette. It beeped. "Looks okay." He turned to me. "We had a call through from Central, sir. Can't firm up this departure time until we recheck. Some kind of hold on movements, don't know why."

"More chickenshit." Majumbdahr growled.

"Yeah." The guard eyed Majumbdahr, squinting at his Hindic features. He waved us through.

"Double-time it!" I called to the men below. I swung the autocrane around for another flat of vaults. I was loading them into the gaping shuttle bay in triple lots, exceeding the max on weight.

Majumbdahr climbed up into the cage beside me. Sweat glistened on his face; a bead of moisture dropped from his chin and spattered on my flashing console. "How long do you think we've got?"

"An hour at the outside."

"Right." He nodded, weary. "We can load by then. But how about takeoff?"

"When're we programmed?"

"I just phoned it in. One hour, forty-two minutes. But there's a hold on it."

"What's the tower say?" The crane screamed, bucked. "Take one off!" I shouted down at the fork lifts. "Too much." They moved in, the insect arms grappling.

"They're not letting anybody out until that hold is lifted."

"Shit."

"Maybe they found those guards."

I grimaced. I felt a twinge of guilt about it, even in the midst of this. Those three men were going to be with me a long time. Heat shimmered the air. I tried to think.

"No, I don't think so. Anybody could've done that."

"Then what?"

"General Tonji. He knows it was the *Farriken* that touched off that fusion blind. Fleet may accept the most logical explanation—that we blew our core and are now just dust. But Tonji . . ."

I squinted at the sun. A light winked on. I swung the crane around, cables ringing, and set the load down inside the shuttle's hatchbay.

"No, it's too much of a coincidence for him to shrug it off. That's why he took Angela, my wife."

"Sir?"

"For bait."

The shuttle's bay doors clanged shut. Cantalus and I dogged and sealed them. Sweat darkened our suits.

"This craft won't move a centimeter without tower approval. They've frozen the magnetic servos." Cantalus gazed at me steadily, plainly asking for an answer. I was in charge, wasn't I?

"Quite so." I studied the bare, vast field. The

tower was a blockhouse with a tall spire, a full klick away.

The men stood around the loading bay. I waved the Lengen priests aboard. There were cramped but adequate personnel racks inside. Enough for us all.

I climbed up onto a catwalk, boots clanging on the metal, and made a megaphone of my hands. "We're going to take the tower. I want three volunteers."

Majumbdahr raised his hand. Five others followed. I picked Majumbdahr and two others. "The rest—inside." They filed toward the shuttle, most of them dragging their feet with fatigue.

Cantalus approached. "We had not planned to leave with you."

"I think you should."

He looked uncomfortable. "As I said, we had not so planned. However . . . I called through on comm band to my duty station. The wards where we kept the Panaten are surrounded."

I frowned. "By who?"

"Fleet infantry."

"More of Tonji's work."

"Perhaps."

"Board the shuttle then. No point in your staying here."

"Will there be room for us all?"

"Just barely. When Majumbdahr gets back from the tower, button up and lift immediately."

Majumbdahr was at my elbow. "Why me? What about you, Captain?"

I pulled out my air pistol and rearmed it. The magazine made a loud *clack* in the bay. "I'm not coming back with you."

"You must," Majumbdahr said.

"This is a personal matter."

The men stood around me, silent. I obliviously went on checking my weapons. "Sir . . ."

"No discussion, Mr. Majumbdahr," I said sharply.

"I will go with you."

"No you won't."

"You know the Jump programming. You've altered our inflight subsystems."

I could feel my face tighten. "So what?"

"The *Farriken* can Jump without you, certainly. But it will be more dangerous."

"Not much."

"But some. If I go with you, the chances of your returning are better."

I sighed. "I don't ask for your help."

"I didn't say you did. I am offering it. And you cannot very well stop me."

I waited. Majumbdahr gazed at me, impassive. Then he smiled very slightly.

I began to wonder who was the hero here, and who the fool.

"All right," I said. "All right."

We got most of the way without trouble. The admin offices were nearly deserted. Ho-hum. Business as usual. Few heads lifted to study us as we went by.

We skipped the elevators and went for the emergency stairs. At the base of the spire I unshouldered my equipment bag and fished around for a lock decipherer. The *Farriken* carried a few for emergency purposes, and Gharma had thought to bring one along. I fumbled through my encoder sigs, stets, and assorted gadgetry a Captain acquires by rights, and found it.

The emergency stairway popped open without

activating its alarm. I resealed it from the inside. We went up the stairs single file, pausing at each floor.

Through a side portal I could peer down at our ground car. Nobody went near it.

At the top floor I sigged the double lock, then popped the alarm before it could blow. We waited for signs of interest from the other side of the fire door. Nothing.

"Fast and easy," I whispered.

One of the men kicked the door open.

We charged through.

I pitched a gas grenade. It went off in Forward Control. Brown smoke poured out. Two Fleet officers turned toward us. They opened their mouths but no sound came out. One pointed. Then they both fell.

A Lieutenant rose up from his console and scrabbled at his side. The man next to me launched himself forward.

He hit the Lieutenant just as a pistol appeared in the space between them. They crashed into readout casement. The pistol didn't go off. Majumbdahr was there by then. He clubbed the Lieutenant with a flame pistol.

The gas hissed away, dissolving into harmlessness. I swung my air pistol around to cover the rest of the Control pits.

They were empty. The tower was run by a skeleton crew.

We held the tower top for over fifteen minutes.

I dropped grenades through a rollout window, directly on the first squad that came to check out a call from below. By that time Majumbdahr and I had figured out enough of the launch procedure to lift the hold on our shuttle. Majumbdahr programmed and called through on comm to clear our passage. I covered the stairs. The other two bracketed the elevators.

That's where two underofficers appeared. The elevator zipped open and there they were.

One step, two—flame guns brought them both down.

Majumbdahr called out that we were cleared. I swung around from covering the stairs. Only then did I notice that one of our men was lying with his side blown away. One of the elevator men had got off one shot; I hadn't even heard it.

I peered down from the tower. A chunk of concrete blistered and crumbled above my head. They were firing from below. Three men, as near as I could see.

"We're trapped," Majumbdahr said.

"Unless we can draw them inside." I leaned toward the open window and dropped another two grenades. The firing from below stopped.

"Down the stairs," I said.

We clumped down as fast as we could. The man ahead of me stopped at the ground floor, where we had come in. I motioned him on.

We ran down the last flight to the basement. It was dimly lit. We wandered down two corridors before finding the surface exit.

I could hear muffled firing: flame weapons. Time ticked on.

"You think they haven't got this covered?" the man with us asked me.

"These are ordinary Fleetfield police. No guarantees, but maybe they're thinking of saving the equipment upstairs more than getting us.

"I hope you're right," Majumbdahr murmured.

I wasn't.

Two steps out the doorway the man crumpled. Blood sprayed from his chest. I was right behind him. A flame bolt seared the air by my ear.

I dropped behind an abutment. They had left one gunner by our car. I could see him crouching behind it.

Two crisp frying sounds passed over my head from Majumbdahr. Both missed. I aimed my pistol at the man's feet, which were still visible. One, two, three shots—all kicked up concrete near him.

"Don't use a grenade," Majumbdahr called. "We need the car."

I nodded. Aimed.

One cough, two—a foot jerked to the side. The man fell into view. I fired three more times. He went still.

"Come on!" Up and running with a blind, furious energy.

I reached the car. Its side window evaporated.

I jerked open the door and Majumbdahr lunged through it. I slumped halfway into the car and thumbed on the pilot.

Whoosh—we shot up fifty meters.

I slipped out of the seat. I clutched at the side rail. The car tilted, ready to boost to cruising speed. I screamed something. A hand appeared. I snatched at it.

Air ripped beside me. A hot tongue licked at my leg. I wrenched myself up and got a thigh over the seat railing.

A giant slapped the car.

I lost one handhold. Into the cradle, endlessly rocking—Majumbdahr grabbed the other hand and tugged at me. I felt something tear in my biceps.

The car was still accelerating. I looked down. The grey field flashed by below, blurred.

All reality, I remembered, was a mere illusion. Really.

Majumbdahr tugged on my hand. I got a purchase on the seat mounts and heaved upward. Wriggled partway into the seat.

Wind buffeted me, howled. I rolled in. The car door hissed shut.

"You all right?"

"Call the shuttle. Tell them to launch."

Majumbdahr fumbled at the comm and barked a few words.

Squawksquawk.

He nodded. "They're off. Nothing will stop them now. Hey, you all right?"

"Just glad I didn't have time to think about that." I panted.

"You're all right?"

"I'm all right."

5

JUST BREATHING, FOR A WHILE.

It was absolutely fine to simply suck in the air. Feel it fill up the lungs. Then push it out. Sweet wind.

Breathing had been something else back then—an hour ago? Thirty minutes? An ordinary thing.

After a while I began to notice jungle rippling by below us. Green sea. Spatterings of blue, yellow, colors clear and bright. Slowly the trembling in me started to ease off.

I summoned up an old joke: It's not that I'm too young to die, it's that I'm too *me* to die.

I grimaced. Some jokes don't get old. Maybe that's because they aren't jokes.

I started to think and then, shakily, to plan, and here's how it went:

Land at a civilian lot. Short-curcuit the lock on a cheap skimmer. Send the Fleet craft off like a bat out of the proverbial, north. Lift the skimmer, heading west.

Ditch the skimmer at Batangas. Swipe a cruiser. Hop it to Lucban and leave it parked near the main street. Take a bus for two klicks. Get off. Buy five matanaglos from a street vendor. Speak to each other casually, walk easy, two officers taking a lazy day off. Stroll into the Toshogu Shrine and out the other side, to the House of the Ascending Dragons. Find a cloistered garden and eat the matanaglos. Drink from a nearby fountain. Catch a belt to the commercial district.

There we had to move more carefully. I made a business 3D call to the orbital trade center in Yomeimon. Then I had them route me through their net to offplanet comm. Then into Earthspace Licensing. By that time I was patched through enough channels to cover the origin of the call. I punched through the encoding I'd set up before leaving the *Farriken*.

Gharma answered. Then our backup scrambler cut in. I had to recode. The screen cleared. I told him—not in so many words—to look for a Fleet booster coming up on the ramscoop fleet, maybe toward morning. That would be us. Anything else was trouble. If there was any doubt, Jump immediately. Never mind the backwash—ramscoops be damned. Oh yes, and incidentally—forget us, too.

"The Master orders you back *now*," Gharma broke in.

"Why?"

"This is unnecessary."

"I can't leave without them."

"You *must*."

"Uh huh. Watch for me by morning's light, friend." And signed off.

6

DARK BEHIND, DARK AHEAD. A drop traced itself down my brow, hung on my nose. I puffed and blew it off. Insects pricked at my neck. Every moment or two something rustled nearby.

Let them go. Some of those beasties were big enough to set off trip sigs, which meant Mindoro Base couldn't use sigs this far out. Area Denial Theory, Course 213B.

Clouds boiled in from the South China Sea, blotting the stars. The lights of Mindoro danced in the warm air. A bird warbled to itself. My night specs clipped on silently. I kept my eyes fixed ahead and turned my head slowly, using peripheral vision. Nothing. A raw field ahead. Low, shiny-leafed bushes. A hooting call, fading.

All this because Angela and the children refused to stay pinned in the past, in that Paradise where choice had fled.

"I'll move up to the Stet key," I whispered to Majumbdahr. He nodded.

I wriggled forward, mud's liquid fingers tugging. Ten meters, then twenty. The stubby box winked an orange indicator when I inserted the signet. I fumbled with the Firetongue Stet and *snicked* it into the receiver. Rigid geometry among a sea of mud.

Orange winked to red. Rejection.

Not the winking red that sprang an alarm, though. The key mechanism knew this was a legitimate Fleet Stet. But not the correct one.

Majumbdahr crawled up behind me. He saw the red dot. "That's the current Stet," he whispered, unbelieving. "It was on the *Farriken*."

"Right."

"Tonji must've known we'd have it."

"Right."

"So he's changed the Firetongue over to some other scheme."

I nodded. Recoding the Stet entry-point by entry-point was a huge job. Tonji hadn't had time for that yet. So he must have used some fallback Stet. That way the change took only hours.

Majumbdahr had followed the same chain of reasoning. "That's that," he said. "Let's get out of here."

"No. Wait." I rummaged through the equipment bag. If Gharma had loaded everything in my quarters—

"Here." I fished out the Stet I had kept from my earlier commission.

"Where did you get *that*?"

"A keepsake. Now if Tonji did the easiest thing—" The change in Stets had been made a year or two before. There were undoubtedly some older Stets around. But a man in a hurry . . .

Snick. Orange. Orange. Wink: green.

"Damn!" Majumbdahr grinned.

We walked and crawled the klick, slow and easy. No fire flashed out of apparent nothingness to lash us down.

Most of Mindoro was dark. We slipped from shadow to shadow.

Nothing moved. Where were the patrols? Had Fleet cut back so far they no longer had troops for their bases? I remembered the ancient quotation in script above the Toshogu Shrine: *All the flowers of all the tomorrows are in the seeds of today*. But the script was streaked and weathered, one letter hanging by a single tab. There was no one to keep the ancient shrines. And for this tarnished Empire, no seeds of tomorrow.

I peered around us, uneasy.

Majumbdahr had no warning. There came the scrabbling of nails on earth. A shadow oozed forward, coming fast, and a dark form struck him. He pitched backward, flame gun coming up.

The thing slashed at his gun hand. I heard something rip. Majumbdahr rolled. The thing snarled and bit.

I threw myself on it. Musty damp fur. Nails raked my side. The thing turned. "Kill," it said quite distinctly. "Quarn."

My strangling-wire reeled out. Majumbdahr moaned as jaws closed on his arm, legs kicked at him.

I slipped the wire around its throat and jerked back. Breath strangled out. I jerked again, lifting its throat.

Once more—the head toppled away.

It was a German Shepherd. Fifty kilograms of muscle and teeth and black hair, and all of it quite dead. A smart dog, genetically altered to know the best moment to hit us.

I felt sick. We had learned a hard lesson centuries ago about tinkering with human genetic material. Fleet had no such qualms about turning man's best friend into fanatic, smart killers.

Three buildings away a flashlight bobbed. We melted into the shadows and worked our way toward it. The small Fleet field glowed in the distance. Stubby noses pointed toward the scum of sky.

I sniffed. An acrid tinge in the moist air.

"Ton! Here old fella! Ton boy!"

But Ton boy wasn't in the watchdog business any more. We waited for him.

Majumbdahr was tired and angry. I could sense it in his ragged breathing. The dog had gnawed into him. It took five minutes to seal-and-freeze the gashes. He had to stay alert, so there was nothing to do about the pain.

The man—a Corporal—passed nearby. Majumbdahr stepped from shelter and clubbed him solidly.

I had to use a stim tab to get the Corporal awake. Majumbdahr meant business.

Pharmaceuticals are bad for the character. Within ten minutes Ton boy's master was babbling quite happily about matters he'd rather have died than give away, normally. Luckily, he wouldn't remember any of it later.

We searched him thoroughly and got his encodings for the Mindoro locks. Insects clicked and sang. Clouds rolled over. A booster burst orange on the field and arced away. Troops passed in the distance.

The Corporal called in his dogs. They were quite docile. One of them even carried on a passable conversation about the funny smells around the base tonight. We put them all out for the evening.

The Corporal marched his rounds with us beside him.

Like all security people, he knew a lot more than he was supposed to, most of it by simple deduction.

Mindoro was on stand-down. Most of its troops were offworld. But its area defense systems were second to none, and that was undoubtedly why Tonji had brought Angela here.

The Corporal was quite bleary-eyed, pale, and drawn by the time we reached Central's main building. He took us through most of the checkpoints. Then he collapsed in a side corridor. Pharmaceuticals have their limits; so do human beings.

Majumbdahr stayed behind. I approached the next checkpoint. Nobody even glanced up. I dropped the pencil-sized tube. It hit my boot soundlessly and rolled under the guard's desk. A Lieutenant looked at me, at my uniform, frowned.

"Ah!" I snapped my fingers, grinning. "Forgot something."

I turned and walked away. The tube went *skreee-ebam*. I turned around. The Lieutenant was choking, stiff-limbed, eyes bulging. He fell.

Then we walked some more.

After a series of unlabeled doors I motioned Majumbdahr back. I slapped a boring charge on a door's lock. I set the tiny timer and stepped a few meters away, *Chuung* it flared orange. I eased the door open.

A foul reek seeped out. A hoarse voice pleaded from inside. Someone jibbered.

Regeln swam back to mind. I thrust it aside and slammed the door.

We walked on quickly.

Tonji wasn't hard to find. His name was on the door.

He looked up from a console when I went in. A hand convulsed, froze.

He said something obscene. My air pistol looked at him. He didn't move.

"Get them here." Mujumbdahr closed the door behind us.

"What?"

"You knew I'd come."

"How did you do it?"

"You've been reading your own press releases. This isn't a Fleet base any more. We never would've made a hundred meters across a well-organized base."

Tonji stared at me, eyes jittery. And I suddenly saw that he was older. Lines around the mouth. Crow's feet webbing by the eyes.

"We're arranging a last-ditch attack," he said with a thin voice. "Most of the good troops are seeking the Quarn home worlds."

"That won't work."

"Not with bastards like *you* sucking up to them."

"You don't understand."

"What could they possibly offer you, Sanjen?"

Something in his face made me look away. The waters, the waters lapping, washing all . . . cleansing . . . renewing . . . lapping . . .

"Get them."

He called to another room in Central. He wanted to visit the woman and the children. Wake them up, yes.

We took a route without crossing a checkpoint; it was only two corridors away. In the enameled light Tonji shuffled along, the usual bounce missing from his step.

"You've been trying to keep all this together?"

He nodded. He didn't seem to want to talk.

The guard was muzzy with a just-awakened look when we got there. He unkeyed the door and we went in. Majumbdahr stayed outside to keep the guard company. I had been using my equipment satchel to conceal my air pistol. When I put it down Angela came into the room. Then the children.

"You're all right?" I said.

She stared, eyes wide. I asked again. She murmured, "My God. My God." Chark said, *"Daddy."* Romana just looked.

I turned to Tonji. "We're leaving."

He looked at me stolidly. He was an exhausted man, and he knew he was going to die.

"The roof. You've got a copter there?"

"Ye . . . yes."

Somehow I felt as though I wanted to talk to this man, shake him into conversation. I had thought of smashing in that poker face a thousand times. My skin was dancing. I felt a jittery joy. I was radiating energy. I wanted him to protest, to rage, to curse me. Something to *push* against.

After a moment I said, "Let's go."

We landed at the field's tower, a squat three stories of rough-cut rock. Chark was twitching with excitement; he wanted to hold one of the guns. Romana is younger, but she seemed to know better what was going on. She kept glancing at Angela. They exchanged looks of numb terror. "What'll we do, Dad?" Chark said.

"Stay right here." I turned to him so the women were at my back. "Now look," I said in a low whisper. "I'm leaving you to take care of your mother and Romana. Keep them in the copter. Don't let them even open the hatch unless I'm outside."

"Hey, give me a gun."

"We can't spare one. We've got to take the tower."

"Are you going to shoot that guy?" His forefinger jabbed at Tonji.

"Never mind. I'm leaving you in charge here, right?"

"Right."

"We'll be back as soon as we can."

"Where're we going, Dad?"

I didn't know what to say. To the halo stars?

"Hey, let me have a gun?" Chark asked.

"See you in a few minutes," I said.

Majumbdahr was coming out of the shock from the dog business. His arm was closing up from the seal-and-freeze. The blue swelling had gone down. He jumped onto the tarmac and watched Tonji get out. I noticed that Majumbdahr's uniform was mud-streaked and torn, and then that mine was, too. Finessing that by the officers in the tower wasn't going to be easy.

I turned to Angela. "Stay put."

"Ling—"

"We're going into the tower for a while."

"What will we *do*?"

"When?"

"After we leave here? The city is so terrible now, we—"

"Look, Chark is going to keep his eyes open and see that nobody gets into this copter. Right, son?"

"Gee, I sure would like to have a gun, Dad."

"I'm sure you would."

I jumped down. The three of us walked the hundred meters to the tower. Majumbdahr shouldered his flame gun. They could see us clearly from the plastiform top floor of the tower, and we wanted to look like an ordinary patrol.

"Do you think I will keep quiet?" Tonji said between compressed lips. "That I will ask them to let you have a ship?"

"That's exactly what I think."

He looked at me. I gave him a very thin smile.

"I knew you had come ... that was a Quarn maneuver, destroying the EDS net."

"A by-product, that's all."

"So you think."

"I know rather more than you do about it."

"You didn't simply come back for your family."

"Quite so. But you tried to use them against me."

"I had to."

"Did you have to send me to Veden without mentioning that I'd have to go through the Flinger?"

"We couldn't find an on-line officer who would."

"Uh huh." We had reached the entrance. "Key us in."

Tonji hesitated and I stood there, letting him think about it. Then he fished something from his pocket and the entrance slid open.

Skeleton staff again. We nodded to the desk officer and went up the slideway to the tower. Tonji was the biggest frog in this pond, and nobody got in his way.

There were three officers in the Operations pit. One looked up. I smiled. "Need a POX for a survey flight."

Tonji was stiff, robotlike. They saw him and nodded. One punched in a spec and handed us an encoding. "Ready, sir."

I nodded and we left. Outside by the slideway. Majumbdahr said, "Somebody's going to find that Lieutenant we left back there."

"I know."

"Even if we lift, they'll track us as soon as they hear."

"Any ideas?"

"Kill the power in here. We're cleared, we can lift. They can't track us then."

"Right." I looked at Tonji. "Where's the inload?"

"I don't know."

"We don't have time to look for it." Majumbdahr said, the words clipped.

"We could just shoot them," I said. I didn't want to, but I said it.

"We could."

I thought. Shit, what was I doing here? I was on the goddamn ragged edge, rubbed raw, nerves skittering like a caged rat. If I hadn't taken an hour of meditation in the jungle this afternoon, I'd be wilted away by now. And now I was supposed to decide life and death for three Fleet officers who didn't know my name. This was the nub, the end.

"Wait. You go in and divert them. Ask a question. Tonji, you hold the door open when he does."

Majumbdahr gave me a questioning look. I waved him toward the doorway to the tower center. He opened the door and went in. Tonji held it ajar. I took the plastic-jacketed pancake from inside my shirt and ripped the sleeve. I wadded it along the top of the door, pressing the stuff around the edges. Majumbdahr's murmur came from inside. I finished. Tonji started to let go of the door. I sprang at him, snatching at the handle. I caught it. I looked at him, lips drawn. He backed away. I was sure he knew what he was doing. But it could have been a simple error, yes. I shook my head. It was hard to decide.

Majumbdahr came out. I slipped the door closed. The plastic goo jammed into place. It fit snugly, sticking.

If they came out before we were clear, that was it. If not, we could tell them on the comm lines to stay put. It was the best I could do.

Out, onto the tarmac. Soft air caressing. Insect buzz.

We took the hundred meters at quick-step but my back burned all the same. Chark slid open the hatch. "Nobody came, Dad."

"Good." Into the cabin.

We shot skyward, banked, coasted. I set down beside the PQX the tower had assigned us. I got Angela and the kids into the PQX entry and sent Majumbdahr up to activate ship systems. Tonji stood at the entry portal, silent, watching.

"When we lift, you'll alert them."

"I doubt it."

"Why not?"

"I won't be alive."

"Why are you so sure?"

"I can see your face."

"You always were a good judge of character, Tonji."

"Sarcasm from scum is—"

I raised my pistol. I thumbed it over to phosphorus shells.

Tonji backed away. I sighted at his drawn, pale face.

Time ticked by.

I remembered the three guards.

"It would be easy, all right," I sighed. "Come on."

He stumbled away toward the copter, following my gesture. He moved like a drugged man. Once he was inside, I would give him a satisfying tap on the head, and we would lift.

We reached the copter. Tonji looked a me for directions, then climbed in.

From the tower came a *crump*.

"Goddamn," I whispered.

In the tower one viewport was smashed to a blind star. Behind the plastiform windows on the top floor flames leaped like children wanting to see out.

I jumped into the copter and clipped Tonji at the base of the skull. He pitched over.

I landed running. Something whizzed by me. I fired three phosphorus rounds in the direction of the tower without looking, more to cause night blindness than to dissuade anyone.

Thirty meters, twenty—I stopped at the ramp to free the securing bolts. The air sizzled. A round ricocheted *spang* harmlessly off the ship.

I turned to the ramp. Something hit my arm and spun me around. A shattering pain leaped into my shoulder. I lifted my arm—lifted my arm—

Something was lying on the ground. A hand.

I staggered. Lifted my arm—

Halfway between elbow and wrist was a black stump.

Very carefully I bent over and picked up the hand.

Blood spattered the tarmac.

I took one step up the ramp. Two. So dark.
Shouts, a hammering.
Purple speckling in my eyes.
So dark.

Part VI

1

A RUMBLING, GUT-DEEP. Metal smooth, so smooth I glided down it ice palace skating taste of winter slick slick so white God why's the snow smell so . . . So. Mouth gravel-dry. *Skreeee-hummmm*.

An eye worked open.

Golden.

Biting.

I closed it.

But no—my throat worked, rasping. Force open the eye.

Gold needles sticking in it. Look to the side. Viewport rim. Squint. Oiled light. Blink. The sun. Sol burning, rose-red, twice as old as time.

"Ling?" Angela's soft voice.

"Ling? Try to sleep. We'll be there in a few minutes."

I was swinging a rock. So heavy. Swinging it toward the flame flower outside, shut it out.

"Ling! Don't move your arm! You'll jar the healant unit loose." Gentle pressure. I relaxed.

"Your officer is hiding us somehow, that's what he said. So the radar below won't find us."

"Ah."

"Sleep."

So I did.

2

TIME.

I floated up. Saw the ceiling. Knew I was aboard again. Flashed through dead pictures: the *Farriken* hanging among the war stars, giant creamy ball. Zero-torque cranes and grapples. Clutching at our ship. I plunged down the *Farriken's* axis tube, stretcher-strapped.

Rumble. Mumble. Drifting . . .

Lancing pain. My *hand*. Gone. I felt a hollow space somewhere. A lifting new freedom. Struggling damp feelings, moist, warm, a tree like a cloud of leaves, breathing—swift and darting images—sleek animals running sweating in the cloak of rising dust—throw—dancing dancing mad—the curve of spear in flight—soft warm moist—left *gone*—the voices—low slithering—peering eyes—dancing laughing—foam curls at the lips —voices—muttering without sense—hoarse breathing—blunt, gummy—without words—something pinned—enpowered—commands—cannot speak—

dancing dancing mad and running—sweet slide of arms, legs—swollen leper moon—loose thunders—something wrenching deep—deep—inside, vast—rolling whispers *ah*—no words *ah* it was—shooting pain—opening—the voices, *ah*—fresh channels—I plunged through—seeping—now—moist—the fluid filling me—warm lapping—certainty—lefthand-righthand—voicesvoices—the hand gone—something slips free, *ah*—rises—rises—*ah . . . ah . . .* drifting . . .

And in the endless light and airy drifting I saw anew the halo stars oozing red across the sky. Rust and diamonds. A shooting pain. *Ah.* I raged. I stamped down, crushing stars. I shouted, voice all hollow . . .

Diamonds and rust.

After a while they went away.

Sheets, so cool. A slight finger's press of gravity. *Ah* it was.

Angela's cool brow crinkling. Fingernails plucking at my sleeve . . . Sprinkle of yellow pain. I shoved a breath up through clotted lungs. Wheezed: "Got . . ."

Majumbdahr's voice: "I've got new data. When he's better . . ."

I twisted. "Got . . ."

"Quiet, now. Chemotherapy is cycling."

Time . . .

Angela. Then a long time later, Rhandra. Hair billowing as she leaned over me. Prickly bright things running through me. Soft sibilants. Ah, women. All rest and refuge do they contain.

Time. The tinkling of currents. Drifting.

Two eyes. Shadowed, lurking beneath a cowl. The figure was a dark galactic arm, dust-shrouded,

hanging in space before the stars. Those shrouded
eyes . . . Eyes? Or—two stars? Red-bright.

The Master. Lofting among the star rifts.

From his eyes streamed blood.

He loomed above me. I wrestled with the thoughts:

He had flicked a finger and *tick* I danced, strings
invisible.

Met Rhandra.

Studied the halo stars, dutiful.

His master's voice.

Run amok at the Madi's. Careening through it
all.

He had turned me inside out like an old pocket.

Morning's humming nausea: his treatments, I
knew.

I felt a surging in my head. No helpful waters
came to calm the thoughts. No restful lazy lapping,
dissolving all.

The vapor haze blew away.

I remembered it all now. All the kneeling and
bowing and washing in the great liquid song.

Rage forked lightning-bright, yellow. We were
men, Goddamn it, not . . . not . . .

I blinked. I sat up.

My left arm was a blue sheath. A bioadapt unit.
Inside, I knew my arm swam in womblike fluid,
healing. The hand was stored elsewhere, probably,
awaiting a regrafting.

"Rhandra!"

She appeared from around the corner of our
quarters. "Ling, you're not supposed to be awake."

"Something woke me up."

"Well, I've tried to be quiet but—"

"No, something I was thinking . . ." I frowned.
Dreaming? But the tightness in my muscles remained. Anger was boiling up from my unconscious.

I felt myself caught in it, in the swirl of a blind tide.

I shook my head. "What . . . how are the others?"

"Fine. I met your family. Ling, I think we ought to, to talk—"

"Later. Later. I don't . . . Majumbdąhr, how's he?"

"All right. He's working on something. Angela said he came to see you about some readouts."

"When was that?"

"Yesterday."

"Yesterday! Why haven't we Jumped?"

"We have."

"How far?"

"A short distance. A . . . parsec, isn't that the word?"

"Yes. Yes, it is. Fleet can still pick us up at this range, if we're unlucky."

"Well, Gharma said he didn't want to risk going further."

"Why not?"

"He doesn't understand all the changes you made in the Jump subsystems, he said. I think that was the right phrase." She looked at me, concern tightening her features. "Ling, I think you should rest."

"No."

"You almost *died*. If Majumbdahr hadn't gotten that freeze capsule on you—"

"I know. I know." I waved the subject away with a weak right hand. "My hand will live?"

"They say."

"How sure are they?"

She cupped a palm to my face. "They said the chances are good. Don't worry, Ling."

"Who's this 'they,' anyway?"

"A doctor. They unsealed a vault to extract him.

We didn't have anyone who could deal with your case."

I lay back. "I see."

"That's right, Ling. Rest. Sleep."

I blinked drowsily. "Sure ... oh, would you do something? Go and ask Gharma for a readout of our Jump sequence. I'll need that to compute the long Jump."

"Rest, first."

"No, get it now. That way I'll be able to work on it when I wake up again."

She nodded and helped me lie back. I tried not to wince. Sheets of pain shot up my arm. That meant the locals were wearing off. But it also meant my head was clearing.

She arranged my pillows and dimmed the phosphors. Veden phosphors, I noticed—I was wearing my contacts again.

She stepped softly. I heard her click the latch on her way out.

For a long moment I thought of just lying there. It was clean and flat and the sheets smelled sweet as the wind. The Paradise Milton had scribbled about and never gotten.

Heaven. Stars.

Diamonds.

Diamonds and rust.

The rage seized me again. The blazing star-eyes. I sat up. Pulled the covers away. No pajamas. Good; they would've stuck out under my robe, anyway.

I braced myself with my right arm. My legs swung over the side. My arm buckled. I toppled backward on the bed. My left arm shrieked at me.

I rolled over onto my right side. Painfully I worked myself upright by pressing upward with my hand and rocking my legs in synchronization.

Then I stood up. And sat down, knees buckling.

The second time I lurched sidewise and caught a deck chair for support. I breathed a little and tried not to think too much. Then I took a step. The mists inside lifted a bit. I stepped again and nearly lost my balance. I waited some more. Another step, wobbly but workable.

I reached the closet in slow motion. Fishing out my robes took time. By then I was concerned that Rhandra would return. So I hurried, and very nearly fell. I caught myself against the wall and just sucked in the soft, soft air for a while. Finally I found my Captain's belt and wrapped it around the quilted robes.

Time for a walk.

I made my way to B deck without seeing anyone. I began to feel stronger, steadier. Majumbdahr lived in a small staff officer's cabin. I wanted to see him where we wouldn't be disturbed, even by Rhandra. I hoped he would be in quarters. If not, I'd locate him on the in-board comm line and have him meet me there.

There was no response to my knock. I listened to the sighing of the *Farriken's* air circulators. No movement inside. I used my Captain's key.

I was wrong. He was there.

He swayed gently in the air currents. Blood dripped steadily from him and spattered red the deck.

Mahesh Majumbdahr had been trussed expertly. Knees bent. Ankes bound. Wrists wired and oozing blood behind his back. He hung face down. Bright scarlet threads laced him. Flexible tubing linked knots at wrists and ankles. Ship's cord bisected the tubing. The cord looped through the air duct overhead.

Blood now filming over to a muddy brown made an X in his chest. It sliced his coverall and cut deep into the abdomen. His face—I looked away.

I recognized this vaguely from my reading of Veden history. A ritual Bengali execution. Usually performed with a shortsword. In ancient times it symbolized a necessary death, a sad but unavoidable passage.

I stood and looked at him a while. Then I began a search. There was no sign of a sword. An empty fax folder yawned open on the floor; a few books were disarrayed. I found a small wire cutter and cut the ship's cord. I caught the body as it fell free. Pain lanced my left arm. The body slipped away from me and sprawled. I covered the face.

From the blood clotting I judged he had been dead at least half an hour. With head wounds the brain damage from oxygen loss would be extensive already. No chance to save him.

I punched on the comm. Rhandra answered on the second buzz. "Ling! Where *are* you? When I—"

"Are you alone?"

"Yes." I gave her the cabin number and asked her to come. Alone.

I sank down on the bed. I waited. I watched the lake of scarlet around him scum over with a ruddy, used brown. This was no longer Majumbdahr, only a butchered side of meat.

A part of me skittered away from this room thick with sullen air, and I remembered the walks we'd taken together, an impossibly long time ago now. We walked through slippery mulch of packed leaves, along chattering streams. Ferns. Soft stands of scented weeds. Rasping briars. Our boots thumped in the hush of woods. We talked. We worked up the dry, cottony taste in the mouth which chilled water cuts as a knife. The valleys of Veden's great plateau cupped us beneath a spitting blue sun. Time hung still and silent in the fragile air. And as this memory hazed my mind, I lay back on the bed and knew at once that I hated this artificial place now. It was a warren of cushioned sounds inside a metal box, an artifact I had memorized into a profound disgust, a craft whose prime purpose was an Empire where both the police and the poor were polite. Yet on the other side was, inexplicably, the thing lying in its own muddy pool . . .

Rhandra's rap startled me. I creaked up and opened the door.

She said and did the things I'd expected. It all went by in a curious milky green light. Words slid into more words. There was sand in my eyes. Gritty bags were pulling down on my eyelids and blurring into a drone Rhandra's sentences. A hand shook me. I sucked in air. The light cleared a little.

"Look . . . for . . . stim."

"What?" she said. "Oh."—and went into the small bathroom. Time slid along. A prickling feeling in my face "Ling!" Another slap. "Here—" Hiss. Cool spot on my wrist. She took the stimulant injection tube away. I blinked. A faint tingling seeped back into my body. In a moment I felt somewhat bright and clear again.

"God, I'm weak."

"Of course. And to find *this* . . ."

We sat for a moment. "I'll call," she said. "We'll get some help."

"No."

"Well, whoever did this must be—"

"No!"

She sat silently. I struggled to think clearly. I noticed something new on the bed. "Where'd those come from?"

"What? Oh, those must be the readouts he wanted to talk to you about. Plus the other things in your Captain's input slot on the bridge."

"The fax folder." I gestured. She handed it to me. It was identical to the empty folder lying on the floor. I opened it.

"Ling, I don't see how you can sit there calmly opening your *mail*, for God's sakes, with—"

"Quiet." I flipped through the faxes inside. "I wonder if . . ."

"What?"

"This is the same type of fax folder as that one. Maybe Majumbdahr had two copies of something, and left one in my slot so I'd get it when I was able."

"Oh. And the other copy . . ."

"Somebody took it."

Rhandra's face was compressed and rigid. She kept looking back over her shoulder at the body.

"These are faxes of a correlation analysis. Majumbdahr wanted to do a better study of the Veden mass detector data. He left it as an available-time job for the *Farriken's* computers."

Rhandra looked at me apprehensively. "Ling, I really do think you're too tired to . . ."

"Come on." I got up.

"What . . . ?"

"The Quarn."

I locked the door behind us. I walked as quickly as I could through the curved corridors, watching for anyone else. Most of the crew was probably stowing the coldsleep vaults; securing them adequately in the axial pods would probably take a full day. We stopped at an officer's cabin I chose at random, and I clicked it open.

Inside, I spread the faxes on a narrow bunk. Majumbdahr had used the satellite data to get a refined parallax fix on mass and velocity. I pointed at a display fax. "It's big, all right. About a tenth Jupiter mass. Now the velocity . . ."

I checked it.

Checked it again.

"What's wrong, Ling? Why are you looking that way?"

"This thing—whatever it is—will hit Jagen. Not Lekki. Jagen."

"I see," she said, not seeing.

"He integrated the trajectory out. Look." The dashed line of the projected path swerved neatly around Lekki and arrowed precisely into Jagen.

"Why is that so important?"

"It's just about impossible. Lekki has more than twice Jagen's mass. Its gravitational potential well is much broader. Any random fragment zooming out of interstellar space would have one chance in a million of hitting anything. Even if it did, Lekki is much more probable a target. But Jagen!—a little dot whirling around at near-light speeds? Impossible."

"But it *has* happened."

"Yes." Suddenly I remembered the Master's voice long ago: *The ancient Quarn left giant devices . . . they could move a planet through Jump space . . .*

"When it impacts, Jagen will shred that mass with its tidal forces. Rip it to atoms. Then heat it up. X-rays. Gammas."

I didn't need to check Majumbdahr's faxes to know that Veden would be within the cone of emission.

The planet would fry. And the ramscoops, irradiated beyond use. The storehouse of the Empire, burned away.

"What will it do?"

"Ever watch a time-lapsed 3D of a supernova? This is like a pocket edition. The radiation will fry Veden. Probably kill all higher life forms."

"But *Ling*—"

"I know," I said bleakly, watching the horror crinkle her eyes. "And I know who caused it."

"What . . . ?"

"The Quarn."

"I don't believe that. Neither do you."

"Ah, but I do. Rhandra, the Master didn't want Majumbdahr and me to stay down on the surface, to be out of touch. He wanted us around for our regular session with him. Balm for the mind. Those wonderful washing waters. That's how he has managed us like a Punch and Judy farce from the beginning."

Her face became stony. "*No, I . . . I . . .*"

I watched her struggle with it. "Rhandra. I know you're confused by this. I know something of what you feel. I felt it, too."

"But Ling . . ."

"I want you to help me. I'm going to see the Master. Perhaps I'm wrong," I said, knowing damned well I wasn't. "We can only find out what is behind all this by speaking to the Master."

"Yes . . ."

"But we must be careful. Whoever killed Majumbdahr can do the same to us. So I want you to help me. Will you?"

"Of course. But . . . the Master . . ." Her face twisted.

"I know. We—"

The comm speaker sounded a soft, persistent beep: an all-stations message.

"Officer Gharma respectfully requests the Captain's presence in the Master's rooms. Officer Gharma respectfully . . .'

I listened to it repeat five times. A slow, wan smile spread across my face.

"So it's Gharma."

"Why are you so sure?" Rhandra murmured, her voice reedy.

"He wouldn't call if he hadn't already checked our quarters. And if there's ship business, why not summon me to the bridge?"

"Well, he might—"

"No. No, it's Gharma. He has a taste for the ancient Veden practices. And there is something in him I have always sensed."

"Well . . . what shall we do, Ling?"

"Do? We go see Mr. Gharma, just as he asks."

3

WE WENT TWO corridors laterally, along the gentle curve of the ship, before I caught a flicker of motion out of the corner of my eye. A head jerked back around a turn in the hallway.

"Run," I said. Rhandra's shortbreech gave her ample room for her long legs; she easily outdistanced me. I puffed along, thoughts racing. "Left," I called. We turned and there ahead was the dim grey light I sought. The priests had left a third of the B deck phosphors untreated; they gleamed with Sol light. Vedens with adapted eyes could make their way here, but they could see no further than fifty meters. I popped my contact filters into my palm.

Rhandra slowed. "Where should we go?"

"Not back to our quarters, that's certain. This way."

I soon found it. The emergency arms locker went *ting* and eased open beneath my Captain's encoder. I fetched out stun guns and laser pistols, hitched them in my belt. I gave Rhandra a stun weapon. I showed her how it worked. "Don't even aim it at anyone unless you're going to use it."

"What setting shall I use?" She fingered the dial in its butt.

"Here. Stun. It won't kill."

"But if we need—"

"Come on."

The cushioned floors of B deck were the thickest in the ship. They muffled our running. I cut over three corridors and peered around. There—a bulging green color-coded hemisphere, down a short passageway.

It clicked open, revealing a tangle of power lines, connector boards, microswitches, alternate circuit elements, and inloading sequences. I studied them.

The routine shipboard elements disconnected easily. The manual override net took more time. I took a cutter from the tool wall inside and slashed crude gashes in the plastiboard.

The lights around us faded, pulsed once, and died. A rattling alarm spoke nearby. I cut some more, and it stopped.

"Ling, I can't see."

"That's the idea. I haven't lived this long by walking into situations with long odds against me."

"What does it matter if we're all in the dark?"

"Those small round splotches—no, sorry, you can't make them out, can you?"

She squinted. "No."

"Those are emergency phosphors. They're running lights that go on when central power fails. The *Farriken* has a separate power source for each deck."

"The priests didn't paint them with Veden phosphors?"

"They didn't know what they were. The emergency system is just bright enough for an Earth native to see by. But to you they're emitting in the wrong part of the spectrum—too red."

"All the Veden natives are blind now," she murmured slowly.

"On B deck, yes. That's all we need."

But how long did we have it?

The bridge officer was busy supervising storage of the vaults, I was pretty sure. He was probably frowning at his readout panel right now, trying to figure why the B phosphors should fail. Did he have an extra man who could come down and troubleshoot, carrying a hand flash?

I started along the corridor, leading Rhandra.

"Where are we going?"

"Tramping into the vineyard where the grapes of wrath are stored," I said. My head had lifted lightly from my shoulders and floated a meter high.

"What?"

"A snippet of ancient culture. Non-Mongol."

Through the curved lattice, all padded and restful: officer's country. Near the Master's suite the warren was more complex, for an added sense of isolation from the rigid pattern of shipboard. This made it easier to approach, since no one could hope to hear us.

I saw the first priest two intersections away from the Master's area.

He stood with his back turned, arms raised as though talking into a wall ship's comm. As I watched, he slammed the receiver down, felt his way a few meters along the wall, and stopped. He had just found that the comm ran on the same power source as the phosphors and wouldn't work, either. And, being untrained, he didn't know that an emergency comm station was recessed in the wall scarcely forty meters away.

"Ling, I . . ."

I tugged her back around the corner. *"What?"*

"I've got to ask something. How long will it be before that . . . thing . . . collides with Jagen?"

"About ten days."

"Then there's no hope of stopping it? Or saving people?"

"No. Or . . . wait . . . We can send a signal. Maybe they can get deep enough underground." I thought. "Yes, that's right. Ten meters of dirt would shield them."

"But there's no hope otherwise?"

"No."

"Then let me go to the bridge. I can tell them. Before we . . . see Gharma."

I grimaced. "I know how you feel, Rhandra," I whispered, "but you won't be safe on the bridge. Gharma wouldn't leave it uncovered. If you appear there, they'll stop you. Kill you, probably. They don't seem much interested in discussions, not when there's a shortsword handy."

She looked very solemn, and nodded. Things were moving too quickly for her. *Hell*, I though woozily, *they're moving too damned fast for me, too.*

We cut to the right and circled around the priest. I spotted three others, each at an intersection. They had taken up positions roughly equidistant from the Master's suite. They blocked all paths to it.

But they'd made a simple tactical error. They were too far apart. The intersections were all over fifty meters from each other. In B deck's hushed corridors that was more than enough to isolate them. They'd formed their net in virtual darkness; given time, they would probably correct it.

"You're going to follow me at a few paces behind. Here—" I reeled ship's cord from around my waist. I'd taken it from the emergency locker. "You can hold this as a guide. If the Veden phosphors suddenly go back on you'll have to drag me out of sight. I'll be blinded even worse than you and the priests."

I paused. Gharma might have sent a man to the bridge, letting him feel his way out of B deck, with word to bring flares or anything else that emitted the Veden spectrum. In that case aid might come any second; there had been enough time.

But if Gharma was cautious, he might well keep all his priests with him for protection. He could wait me out that way with less risk.

Which had he done? Flip a coin, Sanjen.

"Damn," I fretted. "Look, I've got another idea. I'll lead you to almost within sight of one of the priests. These stun weapons are too noisy; the others will hear. So I'll double around and come at him from another direction. Wait about a minute, then make a small noise. I'll rush him."

"What sort of noise?"

She looked suddenly frightened. Well, so what? I was, too. But I was more angry than scared or else I wouldn't be here.

"Just a few words. A question. Ask him why the lights are out. He'll probably think you're just wandering around in the dark."

"I am."

"Quiet." We edged along the passageway for a moment until I could just make out a priest around the next corner. "Here I go. Count the seconds in your head."

I raced around to the other corridor. To me these halls were pooled with wan reddish light, dim but enough. I crept forward until I had a clear view of the priest's flowing *maquanan* robes, and stopped. He was shifting uneasily from foot to foot. Unnerving, to stand within easy laser shot of an armed man and still have to force yourself closer. Several times he looked directly at me.

I froze. His gaze drifted on without pause. Precisely how dim was this light to him?

Step, wait. Step, wait.

My left arm spoke with a low, pulsing ache. I inched forward, handgun covering the priest. A thousand years ago I had sat in a restaurant with Mahesh Majumbdahr and talked of reverence for life, respect for living creatures. Now I was preparing myself to kill a man simply because he blocked my way.

Faintly: "Why are—"

I ducked low. Lunged forward. The priest turned, robes swirling, his pistol coming up, eyes shifting uneasily as he tried to locate Rhandra's voice.

"—the lights—"

At the last moment he did. The pistol leveled. He squinted down the V-and-blade sight. Finger squeezing—

"—all out?"

I hit him with a boot heel in the shoulder. It was a high kick I hadn't tried in years. It caught; he staggered sidewise. His finger slipped from the trigger.

Right foot back to the deck. I followed the weight shift through with a short chop to his neck. Breathe out, focus down, turn—

I twisted, caught his solar plexus with my left elbow. A biting pain shot up into my shoulder.

Wind whooshed out of him. I moved in, butted him aside—winced—and snatched at the pistol.

Fumble, fumble—I suddenly thought that a laser beam could be seen quite easily by Veden eyes, alerting the priests—I got it.

I clubbed him with the butt. He sagged to the deck.

I froze. No sound but the hollow sigh of air circulators.

I dragged the priest into a cabin and locked him in. When I went back for Rhandra, she was jittery, but she listened carefully to what I told her.

The Master's suite. I cracked the door ajar. Silence. We slipped into near-darkness. A dim emergency phosphor glowed red beyond the antechamber.

Suddenly a chant rang out. Voices joined it. A singsong wail echoed over us. Tapping drum, chiming cymbals.

The beaded curtain before us swayed and rattled in currents that bore the sweet tang of incense.

We slipped through.

Four Lengen priests sat in zazen position before the Master. None were armed. The wavering music spun on. On. On.

And stopped, as though sliced by a sword.

"Leave us now." The Master turned his cowled head toward us.

"I believe we have some business."

"It awaits you. Outside."

"You'll get no help from them."

He paused. "Leave us now."

Of all receptions I had imagined, being brushed

off wasn't one of them. I sat, and gestured Rhandra to do the same.

"Gharma has erred again." His voice rolled out, deep and somber.

"Because those priests didn't get us?"

"I knew it was you when the illumination failed."

"I expected Gharma here."

"He is dispatched elsewhere. To complete the circle."

The priests began to murmur a slow rhythmic chant. We talked over it. "More murder?"

The Master clasped his hands and said nothing.

"Why did Gharma kill Majumbdahr?"

"We only hastened him by an hour."

"To stop him from warning Veden?" Rhandra said abruptly.

"In part. My hand rests only lightly on such matters."

"Looks like a dead weight to me," I said bitterly. But something restrained me from approaching him. I sat. "Why kill the Vedens? An entire *planet?*"

"A point of . . . there is no word. Let this suffice: millions of your years ago we caused the neutron star to wind inward. We did this in the last phase of . . . matter shaping. Then we retreated to the nest of the . . ."

"The halo stars."

"You would call them so. They are the true center. The sum."

"Then why don't you damned well *stay* there?" I spat out.

"A star does not ask the galaxy why it spins."

"*I* am asking."

"So." He joined in the murmuring warm chant for a moment. His great head bowed. Incense sweetened the air.

"We returned this last time to the disk. We looked upon our works. The neutron star was infested. The ancients timed that star for *our* use. You had begun to spread. To have festered so, to take our works and turn them to a purpose we had planned for ourselves . . . We knew then that the legacy we had planned was rotted. Spoiled. You—our children—were now rivals."

"How?"

"You violate the Precepts."

"*Piss* on your Precepts. Why should they apply to us?"

"One always knows one's children better than they know themselves."

"What . . . ?" Rhandra asked.

"We made you," his voice boomed. "Made hunters, learners, from eaters of fruit. Hormones. Mating ritual. Family grouping. All bear our imprint."

"No . . ."

He shook his head wearily. His voice floated across to us. "We do not know why the great old ones did this. A last groping. For a vision. I do not *kenne* . . . it lies to us to right the errors."

"By tinkering with us?" I almost shouted. "Your damnable Plague? The men you've killed—or made me kill?"

"To complete the circle."

"How? Was it that business I studied about left hemisphere versus right? You had me read that, didn't you?"

"I erred. It vexed you, to direct your knowledge in these paths. I see now I erred often with you. My first decision was correct."

"The winged man?"

"Yes. I saw you would be a threat. My charge was to bring the sickness to Veden."

"*You* caused the violence. The riots."

"A facet of the design. You might have interfered."

"So you ordered me killed. What made you stop trying?"

"The craft that brought you to Veden sent a message packet."

"That's customary."

"Gharma read it that evening. Too late for me to stop the winged follower. It told of the Patanen. They were to assemble on Earth. I saw we would need you to take us there when the time came."

"So you gave me a stay of execution."

"Remember, when you think these harsh things, my aim?" Hand passes. A misty low voice.

The priests. Their cadences swelled in the dry light. A sea's green sameness washed the room. Metallic flutterings veined the air.

Regeln swam in my memory. Tunnels. Mud and squeezing terror. The clutching fear, now gone, washed from me . . .

A distant twinge from my left hand. I willed it to silence.

"I . . ."

"To seek the rightful stations for us all. Bring the essence in us to rest."

"But we . . ."

"We share a destiny."

Swaying, I pondered. "What paths lie open . . . ?"

"There remains only the Path of Last Things."

"The Patanen?"

"They were the remaining part of you who would survive. It is a measure of our fall that only with difficulty can we snuff out our ancestors' dark legacy."

Chiming. Swimming in the waves of the chant.

"That is our station?" The Master's hand moved over a small black metal object.

A sadness welled from him. His great eyes transfixed me. "I speak to the tension in you. It is the impurity. Without it you would have been a fitting testament to us. We know you in the core. Where the animal mind gropes for exit."

"I . . ." Drifting.

Arm aching.

I struggled to hold on to . . . something.

"It is the final act. To earn my Walking."

"No . . ."

"I am charged to this task. Others of us labor on your distant worlds to bring about this consummation."

"Ah . . . I . . ."

"We erase the errors made by our passing. We leave no blemish smudged upon the galaxy."

The waters, they encased me. Their soft lapping swept clean the abiding tension I felt. Tapping of drum. Flickering ghost images. I struggled against the current. They were warm, so warm . . .

Humming. Humming, the wailing singing waters washed over me—

My left arm. Sheets of pain lanced up. Clouds thinned.

Left hand. Right hand. Voicesvoices—hand—swelling tension—

Something within me clenched my fist. My hand—

Orange carved the night.

The Master toppled. He fell stiffly, surprise frozen in his depthless eyes. A red splotch stained his barrel chest.

Left hand spoke. Right hand answered. We would not go meekly into their vast night.

The being who had brought me such comfort as I had never known sprawled, eyes open to a final blindness.

The rasping sound was my own crying.

The room bulged and melted and ran down my face.

I lurched away, out.

4

ON THE BRIDGE.

I fought the deep trough of sleep. The bridge swelled, paused and then collapsed, like the lungs of a great animal.

"Stim," I croaked to Rhandra. She pressed the hissing serpent to my arm.

"Gharma. Where's Gharma?"

"He is suited up, working the tube, sir." The bridge officer, Hassat, blinked at me.

"How long?"

"Nearly an hour."

"With a team?"

"He took some priests."

"Ah." I thought. The bridge went *peep* and *click*.

"Are all the priests armed, Captain?" Hassat said. He was worried. When the power returned to B deck, he had gotten a call from me to send a squad. There had been shooting. Two wounded, one dead. All this, and he didn't understand what it was about.

"I expect so."

"Sir, if you want me to go after him . . ."

"I do. And I'm going with you."

We were in the suiting room when the fist of Shiva shook the ship. It slammed me into a bulkhead. A loose tool cracked into my helmet. I staggered, fell.

The viewpoint into the axial tube spanned ten meters in the ceiling of the suiting room. I peered up at it.

Silently, a waterfall swept by.

"They've blown the tube wall," I croaked over suit mike.

"Bridge here, Captain!" a metallic voice rattled. "We monitor a seven meter diameter incursion in the tube. It's filling fast."

The greenish fluid gushed by the port, churning. Bubbles danced.

"Where?"

"Fifty-two meters above the retainer, Captain. Aft."

My team was coasting up toward the viewport, gaping, apparently uninjured. I let myself go slack, ignored the sleeting ache as my left hand tried to talk to me, and thought. A picture of the *Farriken* hung in my mind's eye: a spinning ball. The axial tube lanced through it. All turned, making centrifugal gravity and stirring the reaction fuel that filled the ball. The axis was a thin tube where it broke the ball's surface, but at the ship's center the tube bulged: decks A through K. I was in the innermost part of the bridge. Where the bulge tapered down was the retaining sheath. It supported the *Farriken's* center against the pressure of the reaction fluids. Further out, beyond the retainer, sacks of cargo hung from the tube, immersed in the fluids.

Where was Gharma?

Near the hole he'd blown, probably. He was not in the tube—as the watery colloids rushed in, the currents would've smashed him to ketchup. No, flooding the tube was a diversion. It gave him time. We would have trouble making our way along the tube. The delay might be vital. So . . .

There was no place else to go. He had to be outside the tube, in the reaction fluid.

I sighed and found I had closed my eyes. It was restful here at nearly zero g. If I could sleep a bit, everything would become clear . . .

I slammed my left arm into the deck.

Agony.

The voices. They woke me.

Why flood the tube? It wouldn't disable the *Farriken*.

No, Gharma was on his feverish way to something else.

"Hassat! Into the lock."

The Veden phosphors gave the rushing waters a greenish cast. The rippling currents had become sluggish.

"Tube is filled, Captain," the metal voice rang.

I hitched on a tool belt and snagged a laser sidearm into it. "Cycle us in," I called.

Hassat and the men listened to my conjectures as the air pumped out. The greenish fluid frothed in and stilled. I waved us out. We swam like the first fish, awkward and bulky. *Ping*, pressure balancing.

Aft, along the tube. Machines, pod equipment, grapples—they bobbed in the currents set up by rotation of the tube walls. The men swam faster than I could. They were earnest and devoted followers of the Master, unaware of how the alien had used their own evolution against them. I had sent Rhandra to search the Master's suite, remembering the black device in his hand, to find polytonal inducers, subliminal flicker screens, a host of devices. Probes into the depths of our competing three brains. Paths to enlightenment, surely; I knew that. Paths to a prison, just as certainly.

These men would follow my orders despite their confusion. And in time, as the tinkering wore off, as it had for Majumbdahr and me on Earth, they would return to whatever it meant to be human. Merely human.

We thrashed on. The section numbers coasted by. 16 H. The tube necked down here. Collars of steel yoked the spot: the retaining wall. Here the storage sacks began. Their access ports punctuated the tube walls at regular intervals, receding into the murky distance. Swimming here was not much different from negotiating in air, since there was no gravity. But normally one could see from one end of the tube to the other. Now all faded into green depths. I felt sluggish. The waters plucked at each motion with liquid fingers.

"Slow down," I called. Foxhounds to the hunt.

Docking equipment swung lazily ahead of us. I peered, squinting. There: a ragged tear in the thick organiform. An explosion had ripped through from outside.

Something tugged at my attention. I turned, studying the tube. The others surged ahead toward the tear.

It was small, innocuous. A grey patch clinging to the tube wall.

I swerved and kicked toward a grappling module. "Cover!"

I snagged the edge of the module.

Crump. A muffled jolt. Frags spun past me. I hugged the module like a lost love.

Crump. The module bucked, began to drift.

I hung on.

A corporal coasted into view. His back was smashed.

I swam toward him. His suit life indicators read zero.

Two others floated nearby. Dead, all. Bubbles oozed from their suits, filmed in red.

The limpet mines had sprayed the area with shrapnel. Neatly timed. Gharma must've been able to see our approach. How?

I rotated, fanning the waters. The viewports. They looked out on the cargo sacks, to aid in loading.

"Captain." Hassat appeared from behind a quantat casing. "They're all . . ."

"Right." I thrashed over to a viewport.

Lamps glowed blue in the murk.

They were inside a sack. It hung down, a teardrop ballooning away from the tube. Dim figures moved inside. It was the sack nearest the retainer.

I watched, thinking. The figures seemed to be sitting on top of some coldsleep vaults. They were performing a ceremony much like the Master's. The Hour of Last Things.

"If there are more mines in here," Hassat began, "we should—"

"Right. Out—through the hole."

I pushed away and kicked awkwardly. Cold seeped into my bones; the reaction fluid was a colloid to prevent its freezing at the low temperatures it reached in flight. My suit therms cut in.

We reached the ripped wall and I gingerly pulled

myself through it. I backed out, groping with my feet. My magnetos purred, seized. Boots clamped down to grip the ferrous strip running along the outside of the tube. I swiveled out and stood upright.

I took a step. *Click*: magnetos clutched the metal. Hassat followed.

The sack flared mushroomlike forty meters away. I could make out Gharma now. He made ritual hand passes. Their lips moved. Chanting. Their rocking rhythm cast shadows in the blades of light that cut shafts down into the cloudy fluid. Beyond, along the axis, the milky bulk of the retaining wall.

We stepped carefully forward. It was like walking along the top of a vast cannon barrel toward a bag of blue light.

"Look for the power plug," I called.

Step. Step.

"There." Hassat knelt on the curved organiform. The color-coded cap swung out. I unreeled the cord for my suit power. He plugged it in.

I snapped it into the butt of the fan laser in my tool belt. It was intended for broad area heating, operating in air. I had no idea what it would do in a liquid.

"Try your handgun," I said.

Hassat fired. A ten-centimeter bolt leaped out. Steam burst white in its path.

"Not much range," he panted.

I cradled the fan laser. "This one may—"

A dull thunderclap.

I jerked my head up. Beyond the sack a yellow ball glowed for an instant. It guttered out.

"Shit," I said. "They've blown a hole in the retainer."

A tide brushed at me. Growing stronger.

We both stood shock still. Debris from the explosion caught the blue light and then swooped back toward its center, sucked in.

"Captain!" the tinny voice rang. "Massive incursion in the retaining wall. Bridge is flooding."

Gharma was going to drown the whole ship.

"Try to deflect the stuff," I said numbly. "Stack furniture. Run it down the nearest ramp."

"Sir, at this rate—"

"I know. Look, send some more men after us. We can't do much by ourselves."

But I knew that by the time help arrived the fluid would have caused vast damage inside the *Farriken*. We were far from any star. Immobilized, we would never reach a port.

Something bumped against me. It was a ribbed drum, probably unmoored by the first explosion. I watched it accelerate toward the gaping hole in the silvery retaining wall.

"Sir, we've got to—I can't—"

I shook myself into alertness. Hassat was wobbling, one foot free. I suddenly realized that the current was pushing me forward.

"Don't try to walk," I called.

"But we have to—"

"Duck!"

Another drum swooped toward us. It slammed into the tube wall, sending muffled vibrations up through my boots. When I looked up, it was vanishing into the jagged hole in the retainer.

I braced against the surging currents. My arm stung and throbbed. I hunched down to present less drag against the stream. My boot broke free. I slapped it down again, rocking, pulling on the power line for support.

Wan light. Murky motions.

What had been the Master's plan? To kill us all? Gharma's sword lifted high, coming down with ritual grace on the necks of the Lengen priests. Chopping. But how were the rest of us to die? Or . . .

Floating. Warm and lazy.

The waxy light . . .

The voices murmured. Tongues speaking without form, of days before we became encased in words . . . cutting across the filmy bonds the Master had laced around my bicameral mind, lefthand-rightbrain, ancient . . .

But the voices faded . . .

My head buzzed. A fine weakness washed over me. It would be so fine to fly in this swift breeze, to spread wings and loft through it. To skim by good Gharma and his madman chant, *consider the waters in their ways*, yes, give a last wave and zoom past, singing my own private song. Then a last gyre, banking and swooping. The tinkling rapids would laugh with me. Sing the war galactic, Ling. Strut a time on this final stage. Comes the high dive. White foam. Zip, and you're through. Back on the bridge, Captain of a Starship all spattered with gold. Epaulettes for all.

Let me go.

Let—

A boot slipped.

I twisted to bring it back.

The other *click* broke free.

I reeled out the power line. Gauze clouded my helmet. Air rasped raw in my throat.

Battering, battering, the current swept me down.

All these years riding the high vacuum . . . never thought . . . it would come by drowning . . .

My right hand twitched. The fan laser blazed. A beam orange-hot shot out in front of me. Steam jacketed it. Cotton streamers belched back toward me. I felt it punch me in the gut.

Turning—

Flying—

I rolled my eyes up, searching for the blue mushroom. Heels looping over—

I arced the laser beam around, letting the steam jet play against me. It buzzed in the cold, watery hand that clasped me. I was using the hot steam jet to steer myself. I fired. The gas deflected me sideways.

Punched me.

Again.

The sack loomed. I thrashed uselessly. Fire the orange plume. Wait. Fire again. Fire—

I thudded against the fat blue balloon. I released the laser; it was still clipped to my belt. I snatched at the folds of the sacking.

Got a grip. Swung down.

Boots clapped to metal. I leaned against the billowing sack, taking shelter from the current.

I peered in. A blue lagoon.

Gharma's head jerked around. Eyes widened. He started scrambling over toward me, calling the others, mouth awry.

The idea hung before me, glimmering.

I thumbed the fan laser up to peak power.

Gharma saw my hand move. He snatched at his robes, trying to drag a pistol out.

I braced myself and pointed the fan laser at the bottom of the sack. Inside, priests scrambled over the vaults. One knocked over a blue arc lamp. It smashed into a vault and winked out.

The orange line leaped out. I fanned it across the

base of the sack. The organiform crinkled, turned brown, then black. I felt a flash of hot pain in my left arm. I looked up. Gharma's laser was cutting away at my suit. Metal beaded and sputtered away into the waters.

But—

Directly in front of Gharma, where his beam lanced, the sack blackened. Broke. The fluid smashed into him, driving him against the far side of the sack.

I chopped at the base. It gave. The sack lifted under the fractional tug of centrifugal gravity. It rippled. Inside, priests tumbled in panic. The Hour of Last Things was coming a bit early.

The sack wilted. The current caught it. Bubbles belched out, rose.

It began to drift. The sucking hole in the retaining wall dragged it down. Inside, faces: mouths stretched open, hands clenched, eyes frantic.

It struck. The vaults jammed in the hole.

Soundless, the sacking folded over them. Air dribbled away.

The sacking clogged the hole. Flow ebbed and stopped. The plug settled into place.

So many. Majumbdahr, the Master, now Gharma. And so many more. Sleep's dark and silent gate . . .

5

THE BRIDGE WAS a foul mess. The colloidal fluid reeked of oil. It slopped at our ankles. Hassat—who had hung on to a strut the whole time, and lived—organized a team to flush out the ship.

K, J and I decks were submerged. Multiple subsystem failure. Two crewmen dead. My console half red and winking. Everywhere, equipment dripped.

I thumbed my readout screen to activity. Where would we go?

A home away from Rome, that's what we needed. Far from Fleet. A comfortable G-star with room to let. Amid *Farriken*'s dry catalog of facts and numbers there was surely a clue. The galaxy was open. We had fuel, reaction mass. We would explore.

The message to Veden had gone out moments before. Now my energy seeped away and amid the lapping waters I lounged, watching the cleanup crew with sandy eyes.

Time for another message. Yes.

I switched through Comm. "Fleet Central, urgent." I blinked, squinted, rummaged for words.

"This is Ling Sanjen, late of Fleet. I'm serving notice on you, and on your damned Empire. Do what you can about the Quarn. Then forget this war. The Quarn will vanish anyway. They're busy cutting their throats right now." ·

A crewman splashed by. *Lapping waters* . . . The sound no longer had power over me. Music, I remembered, reached into both the limbic brain and the neocortex. It triggered the emotions in one, the analytic appreciation of order in the other. Mathematics could do that, too . . . delicately touch the limbic . . . music sliding into number . . .

I shook my head. We were no simple assembly of "the seat of reason," "the seat of emotion," Tinkertoy parts. A man was more than a mere man could know.

I grimaced, feeling things shifting inside my mind. Whatever fine-grained work the Master had done on me, done on us all, was coming apart, leftbrain-rightbrain all unscrambled now, returning to our own human equilibrium.

The Quarn had sensed us as a lattice, each human a point in an array. A crystal. Only from outside could one see the overall structure. They sensed what we could not, some unspoken symmetry. A craftsman, striking along the planes of cleavage, can shatter a diamond into a jumble of shards. If only one knows how to strike . . .

I shivered.

"Look," I said, "What we never understand about the Quarn was that this war was a last task for them. They had to wipe us from the slate because we were their worst failure. A symbol of their decline. If you go out to the halo stars, I think

you'll find their works. Their art, their libraries,
all carefully preserved. All the things they wanted
to be remembered by. Libraries—not us. They
never understood us. And they were so sure they
did ..."

I coughed. My throat rasped. "Listen, Fleet.
If you're smart, some of you will survive. And
if you do, my grandchildren may run into you
sometime. Watch out if they do though—you
won't understand them. They're going to be like
me."

I clicked off. I chuckled, imaging what Tonji
would think when he heard that. Ling the madman,
yes. Maybe someday I'd be rheumatic and respectable, but not now.

I'd gotten married to Fleet and Angela about the
same time. Now I was divorced from one, but the
easy analogy told a lie; Angela was a person, not
an idea.

Rhandra splashed over to my couch. "I'll help
you back to our room." Her face, lined with care,
seemed much older now. Yet the light still glim-
mered in those eyes. And there were rich years
ahead for both of us. For all of us.

"You *must* rest. Your arm—"

"No. I've got one more thing to do."

Things happen, that's all.

I made my way down alone. Oily puddles glim-
mered in the dim light.

She answered the second knock.

I went in and sank down into a deck chair. From
the next cabin came the scuffle and chatter of
Chark and Romana.

I put my face in my hand and pulled the snagging flesh down, up, rubbing the eyes.

I raised my head.

She looked at me expectantly.

"Angela," I said, "let's try to talk again."

AUTHOR'S NOTE

THE LAST ACTS of pushing a book out into the world—typing the title page, boxing the manuscript, weighing it in at the post office like a prize fighter—remind me of a parent bidding a reluctant child forward to entertain houseguests at the family piano. For all concerned it's probably best simply to let the music begin and see who listens.

But with a book which stumbled into view in vastly different form eight years before, I feel some toe-scuffing explanation is necessary. The first version of this novel was hastily written because of other pressing matters. Even so, I thought well of it. The paperback went out of print. When an editor suggested reissuing it. I assented. Rereading it, I found it dreadful. So I had to rethink what I had imagined was in the text and why none of those fragile images made their way to the printed page.

Hemingway described novels as "getting into the ring with Mister Tolstoy." Science fiction writers have been conditioned to have no such dreams and that's probably for the best. But it's true that you often write your first book while looking over your shoulder at your ancestors. In science fiction that more often than not means a memory of teenage excitements, of vast sweeping imagination, of pill-sized ideas, easily digested. This book was originally designed to lay that ghost to rest in me.

Rewriting it, I found that time-worn path of gaudy space operas slippery and well-nigh impossible. It bothered me that the central eye (and "I") of these fondly remembered adventures was so certain, so cocksure. I kept asking, where did they come from? Who were their parents, to have such impossible children?

I'm not saying heroes don't exist. I'm just wondering whether, once they've come home from their galactic romps, they have any small talk. (And if so, what does it sound like? Should it be just like ours? Whether you answer yes or no, each choice has interesting implications.)

I suspect these puzzles don't bother readers nearly so much. Those occasions when a writer meets his readers—often by chance, in my case—seem to bear this out.

The reader comes bearing a fresh, colored, outside impression of a tale the writer recalls from the inside. We have to live through these worlds of ours, over a period of months or years. The reader gobbles them up in hours. To us a grey fog has settled over the work. We remember a blurred intention, some grand designs which now appear as ruined battlements of a distant castle. We recall moments of zest and—more often—troughs of uncertain drudgery, when the fingers fumbled for the thread we once thought was a firm rope, capable of carrying limitless freight. After our long march through the manuscript, there's that weighing in (with the post office, not with Mr. Tolstoy), the quick note from the publisher followed by a blank silence, then the sudden eruption of a flock of galleys. Then a curious rectangle of paper and ink arrives, a box of words with some remnant of you inside it. You lived through the events described in there, making finally—as for this book you hold— about 75,000 words concerning what you saw. Once the box arrives you spy 75,000 decisions that need rethinking.

The reader has had the same outside experience of the jacket copy—a peculiar brand of literature seemingly always written by dwarves—and the inevitable reviews, but his sense of these things is different. For me, science fiction has a vast attic of machinery that once worked. It can spin and clack again, too, but only with fresh oil and repairs. To set that machinery of old ideas and dusty conventions in motion again, without tinkering and rubbing the rust away, is virtually a form of automatic writing. The machinery clanks awkwardly and may jam up entirely.

When I looked at the first form this novel took, I saw that it was a stamp-press job from the attic. To revise it at all required new cogs and rachets. I've tried to retain something of the old version, though, out of some shadowy sense that I can't chuck aside the entire past.

Some readers will prefer the earlier work. That's part of the inside/outside mirror, and that's fine. The author's vision of a work isn't better or deeper than a reader's, it's just different. Writers play the God game with their books. Weary, they will see a plastic epiphany where other, fresher eyes sense a true revelation. That's the business.

I've spent a summer trying to set old flywheels in motion here. It's been, in sum, enjoyable. After the eight years I took to write *In the Ocean of Night*, delving back into this star-spanning opus has been fun. But I think now I'm done with the habit sf has of making the universe familiar and, essentially, of human scale. A cozy cosmos is a deception.

I'll grant it takes a certain audacity to parallel the collapse of a galactic empire with a faltering marriage. But, then, one tissue of metaphors is probably as good as any other. What matters most, reader, is that we still have the faith to set out on paths together. And if science fiction means anything, we should prefer the unmarked trails.

—GREGORY BENFORD